BUFFALO WOMAN

Other Books by Dorothy M. Johnson

BEULAH BUNNY TELLS ALL
THE HANGING TREE
A MAN CALLED HORSE (original title INDIAN COUNTRY)
THE BLOODY BOZEMAN
THE BEDSIDE BOOK OF BASTARDS (with R. T. Turner)

For Young Readers

FAMOUS LAWMEN OF THE OLD WEST
GREECE: WONDERLAND OF THE PAST AND PRESENT
FAREWELL TO TROY
SOME WENT WEST
FLAME ON THE FRONTIER
WARRIOR FOR A LOST NATION
WESTERN BADMEN
WITCH PRINCESS
MONTANA

BUFFALO WOMAN

Dorothy M. Johnson

DODD, MEAD & COMPANY · NEW YORK

To Rosemary Casey
Creative editor, understanding, endlessly patient

ACKNOWLEDGMENTS

Thanks are due to my Muse—at her worst, skittish, frivolous, disloyal, exasperating, but at her best, inspiring and indispensable and (present or absent) wiser than I am unaided; to James E. Gouaux, M.D., modern "medicine man" who is no more startled when consulted about the ailments of fictional people than he is about my own; to David Maclay and Suzann Stickney and her son Michael for some fine points about grizzly bears; to Professor Carling Malouf for advice about Indian customs; to Professor D. O. Magnussen and Lorretta Breslin for Indian names; to Dorothy Paxson, who owns some beaded burial moccasins; to Professor Joseph Epes Brown, whose heart beats with the Sioux; to Brigadier General W. M. Johnson and his wife, Virginia, and Lillian Hornick for sympathetic listening to my problems with my Muse and research; and to the unidentified truck driver behind my car who wasn't cross when I delayed him at a stoplight one day while thinking.

1 2 3 4 5 6 7 8 9 10

Library of Congress Cataloging in Publication Data

Johnson, Dorothy M
  Buffalo woman.
  1. Oglala Indians—Fiction. I. Title.
PZ3.J63115Bu [PS3519.0233]   813'.5'4   76-53436
ISBN 0-396-07423-5

Foreword

The word *lodge* is used in this book instead of the more common *tepee* because *lodge* has a broader meaning. A tepee (Sioux word) is a conical, movable, pole-and-hide dwelling used by many Plains tribes, while a lodge (English word) may be either this structure or the family group living in it or both.

The Indians now commonly called Sioux (*soo*) did not call themselves by that name. *Sioux* derives, through French, from a Chippewa word meaning "snakes" or "enemies." They called themselves by a name that means "friends" or "allies," and pronounced it Nakota, Dakota, or Lakota, depending on what dialect they spoke of their own language. The Sioux Nation was made up traditionally of seven "council fires," consisting of three groups. All the people in the western group were Tetons, who spoke the Lakota dialect. They included seven subtribes: Oglalas (the largest), Brulés (Burnt Thighs), Black Feet (not related to the Blackfeet tribe, which lived farther west), Miniconjous, Sans Arcs (No Bows), Two Kettles, and Hunkpapas.

There are several ways to spell some of these names. The Indians didn't spell them at all.

Contents

Part I

1820

"This Is Our Child and We Love Her"

Living in the Lodge:

Eagle Walks, 36, head of the family
Many Bones Woman, 25, his wife
Grey Bull, 16, half brother of Eagle Walks
Antelope Woman, 25, widowed sister of Eagle Walks
Running Wolf, 10, nephew of Many Bones Woman
Earth Medicine Woman, aged mother of Eagle Walks

Chapter 1

On a bitter cold night in a village of Oglala Sioux Indians a girl baby was born to a mother named Many Bones Woman and a father named Eagle Walks. They lived in a conical lodge, covered with buffalo hides, snugly furnished with many furs and buffalo robes and heated with a fire in the center.

Many Bones Woman remarked in a low voice, "It is time," and her mother-in-law suddenly became very active and

1

bossy. "You men go away," she ordered. "We don't need you. Antelope, you can stay to tend the fire, and anyway you can learn something. You will marry again and have children." She waved her fist at the men and shouted, "Out! Out!" Her status in the lodge was the old-woman-who-sits-by-the-door, and sometimes she had a right to give orders.

The men hurried to put on their heaviest moccasins and high leggings and warm buffalo robes, because the night was cold and the snow was deep. Running Wolf, dodging a blow from the old woman, grinned and ducked out to go to his parents' lodge. Grey Bull followed with more dignity, because at sixteen he already had some war honors and was not to be chivvied around by women. Eagle Walks knelt beside his wife, who crouched on her bed of warm fur robes, and put his arm around her.

"This time it will be all right," he promised. "This time it will be a fine, healthy baby."

There were tears in her eyes as she answered, "Yes," and watched him swing back the lodge door and go out into the night. They had mourned the deaths of three babies, two boys and a girl, who had not lived even long enough to creep about on the hide-carpeted floor of the lodge.

Outside, Eagle Walks told his half brother, "We will go to the lodge of the Kit Foxes and wait." The Kit Foxes were a warrior society with a big lodge of their own for meetings, sometimes social, sometimes secret. Eagle Walks was a long-time member and an officer in the society. He knew, but did not say, that his half brother would soon be invited to join.

Many Bones Woman walked around inside the lodge until she knew the baby was coming soon. Grandmother Earth Medicine had everything ready, things she had kept packed in painted rawhide parfleches, like boxes, and in little bags and bundles. Antelope kept the fire going and encouraged

2

her sister-in-law: "This time the baby will be fine and healthy, a real Lakota, active and strong."

Earth Medicine announced, "It is time. Now kneel down by the post." This was for the mother to grasp during childbirth; the grandmother had planted it in a hole she dug at the back of the crowded lodge, and it had been in the way, but she believed in being ready, and because she had a touchy temper nobody argued about it. Eagle Walks and all the people who lived in his lodge were much concerned about the coming baby, and they all agreed that Grandmother Earth Medicine knew more about midwifery than any other woman in the camp.

When the infant was born, she caught it on a square of very soft tanned deerskin and announced triumphantly, "There, it's a fine girl." She cared for it with the skill of long experience.

Earth Medicine cleaned the squalling infant with a bunch of sweetgrass soaked in warm water and wiped her all over gently with warmed buffalo grease. She dusted the skin with the powder from a big dried puffball and then tied a strip of soft buckskin around the baby's tiny middle over the navel.

Meanwhile, Antelope Woman made the mother comfortable by washing her and wrapping a broad band of buckskin, not too tightly, over her abdomen. Many Bones kept pleading, "I want to see the baby!" and the other women kept promising, "Soon, soon." When the mother was comfortable on her bed of furs and the baby was cozy in a little blanket of rabbit skin with the fur left on, Earth Medicine laid the small bundle on the mother's arm.

"Now," the grandmother said, "Antelope, help me straighten up around here, and then you can go get my son from the Kit Fox lodge."

He was not at his club any more. He spoke from right outside the lodge, with happiness in his voice: "Antelope will not need to go far to find me. Just tell me when I can come in."

Even his mother was startled: a distinguished warrior with many honors asking permission to enter his own home, and it was very cold out there! But she took her time and let him remain outside until the lodge was all neat again. Then she called triumphantly, "Come in now and see your daughter!"

He knelt and looked long at the baby. He stroked his wife's forehead and said, "She is strong and beautiful, our daughter."

But it was not true. She was a puny baby, and her cry was no louder than a rabbit makes when a coyote kills it.

Many Bones Woman had been stubborn for five years now; she had opposed the idea of Eagle Walks' taking a second wife. He did not even discuss it with her, but his mother had nagged her. "We need another woman in this lodge. There is too much work and I am old. When you are pregnant, you must not lift heavy loads or reach to put up the lodge cover. He can find a good strong girl who will get along well with us. There are lots of them! It's too bad you have no younger sister."

But Many Bones always answered, "I want the first child of my man to be mine, not a second wife's."

Earth Medicine argued, "You will always be his chief wife, the sits-beside-him wife."

Female relatives had helped with the hard work, and for a year now Eagle Walks' sister Antelope, a young widow, had lived with them. She helped with tanning hides and butchering meat and moving the lodge and packing the family belongings on pony drags when the village went to some other place for a while.

4

Now Many Bones realized that she could not be stubborn any longer. A good man wanted Antelope, had asked for her, and needed her to keep his lodge, but everyone had been waiting out of kindness to Many Bones. There *had* to be another strong woman in the lodge of Eagle Walks.

Admiring his weak, newborn daughter, Eagle Walks said, "I have made a vow. If she is well at the end of seven days, I will announce it."

His wife shivered, guessing what the vow was. "I have made one, too," she said. "Now I will sleep."

As soon as the child's young uncle, Grey Bull, and her cousin, Running Wolf, paid their respects, they took their weapons—bows, quivers and arrows, knives—and, well wrapped against the cold, set forth to hunt small game so the new mother could have tender meat and nourishing broth. (There was plenty of buffalo meat and venison, both dried and frozen, stored just outside the lodge in a tree so dogs couldn't reach it, but they wanted to bring special delicacies to celebrate—and to prove what skilled hunters they were.)

Kills-at-Night came, an outstanding warrior, with his wife, Many Bones' older sister. Running Wolf was one of their sons. The relationship between Kills-at-Night and Eagle Walks was common among the Lakotas. They were *kolas*, closer than brothers, the truest of friends. Each of them had sworn to help and protect the other. Kills-at-Night came armed and, after congratulating the new parents, departed to hunt for delicacies. His wife brought gifts of dried wild root vegetables that she had prepared the summer before and saved for winter treats.

But most of the people did not come to visit yet.

All over the camp they were saying sympathetically, "They are not going to have the naming feast on the fourth day, according to custom, because the child is so feeble."

The baby kept spitting up her milk, and her crying was weaker. Grandmother Earth Medicine tried giving her warm broth from a container made of an animal's bladder, ingeniously stoppered with a bit of soft buckskin that she could suck, but she needed milk. The mother asked on the fourth day—when the naming feast should have been held— "Can the medicine priest help her?"

Earth Medicine replied firmly, "How many babies has he had? He knows prayers and chants and many medicines, but I know more about babies. We can pray, too, but now I will try some tea from a root I have saved."

She gave the weak tea of her medicine root to the baby, and a few hours later the little one nursed and was not sick. When seven days had passed, she still lived. There was hope.

Eagle Walks spoke quietly to his wife that night as they lay under their warm robes and the firelight glimmered. Grey Bull and Running Wolf were staying in another lodge to be out of the way, and only the child's parents, grandmother, and aunt were there these days.

"We can have the naming on the tenth day," he said. "A very quiet feast."

"I feel well," his wife assured him. It was customary for a new mother to spend most of her time in bed for the first ten days. There were always relatives and friends to help.

Eagle Walks added, "Tomorrow I will announce my vow to Wakan Tanka, the Great Mystery. In the spring, I will dance the Sun-gazing Dance. Tomorrow the camp crier will tell the people."

Many Bones Woman caught her breath at the thought of the sacrifice of pain that he was promising. She could almost feel his pain now, the payment of his vow.

"It is good," she whispered, and cried a little with his arm protectingly around her.

6

In the morning Eagle Walks hunted up his half brother, Grey Bull, and his *kola's* son, Running Wolf, and told them, "We are going to look at my pony herd and choose a good one to give away." Neither boy asked any questions. When Eagle Walks was ready to tell his reason, he would tell it.

The camp was in a place sheltered by a cliff on one side, where there were plenty of cottonwood trees. When the snow was too deep for the horses to paw it away down to the nutritious dried grass, the people fed them cottonwood bark. The three walked among the winter-shaggy horses. Eagle Walks and Grey Bull patted their favorite fine war horses and talked to them a little. They patted and praised their best buffalo-hunting horses. Running Wolf, still too young for war or for really dangerous hunting, trudged along with them through the snow and longed to be grown up.

"That's the one," Eagle Walks announced at last. "The buckskin, that's the one I will give away." To Running Wolf he said casually, "You can bring him back to camp. I hope you remembered a rope."

Of course he had—a lead rope made of braided rawhide, in which he hastily made a loop to go around the buckskin's lower jaw. The boy would have liked to leap onto the horse and ride him, but to ride while his elders walked would have been rude. He walked with them.

With the two boys and the horse, Eagle Walks strode along the snowy street of the camp to the lodge of the old-man crier, who was the official announcer of important events. Eagle Walks scratched on the entrance of the lodge until the crier's wife opened the swinging door a little. He announced, "I want to give the crier a horse. I want him to do something for me."

The crier called, "Let him in to talk." Leaving young Running Wolf shivering outside with the horse, the two men entered and stood politely by the entrance until the crier, from his lodge-master's place beyond the fire, invited them to sit down beside him. They smoked a long pipe ceremonially, and by accepting it when Eagle Walks offered it, the crier promised to do what he asked.

"I have made a vow to Wakan Tanka," Eagle Walks told him. "I want you to announce it to all the people. I have brought you a gift, a buckskin horse. It is outside. It is yours."

"Tell me about the vow," the crier said, "so I can explain it properly. I am grateful for the gift."

"I vowed that if my little girl lived for seven days, I would suffer at the Sun-gazing Dance when the grass is green in the spring. She is still alive, but very weak. Tell the people of my promise, and Wakan Tanka will hear and remember."

"Ah, that is a good thing, a great thing!" exclaimed the crier. "I am glad to proclaim the vow and the gift. A good thing," he repeated with sincere admiration. "I did that when I was young. You can see the scars on my chest. You yourself have done it before, I remember. But the scars are on your shoulders."

"That is true. May I help you dress, Crier, to ride through the camp and tell the people?"

"It is an honor," the crier agreed. His wife had been unpacking the parfleches in which his ceremonial clothes were stored—folding boxes made of tough, stiff, painted rawhide. She brought out his buckskin clothes, fringed and heavily embroidered with dyed porcupine quills and a few bright beads. The people did not have very many beads for embroidery, because these came from the white men's trading posts, far away. She brought his face paints and a small expensive mirror that had been bought with beaver furs from a trading post. Eagle Walks held the mirror while the crier put

8

on his face paint and topped his head with his eagle-feather war bonnet. The crier had been a great fighter when he was young.

His wife scolded lovingly and coaxed until he put on a blanket—too bad to cover his fine clothes that way, but he was too old to ride out in winter weather without it. Then he went out and Grey Bull and Running Wolf helped him onto the buckskin horse. But he did not go anywhere until Eagle Walks had returned to his own lodge.

Then the old man rode through the camp, shouting: "Eagle Walks is a generous man! Eagle Walks gave me this fine horse!"

The words could be heard through the buffalo-hide walls of the lodges; many of the people peered out to make sure they didn't miss anything.

"Eagle Walks is generous! Eagle Walks is brave! He wears a feather marked with red, because he has been wounded in battle. He has gone out against our enemies many times. His medicine is good in battle. Now Eagle Walks has made a vow."

The people held their breath, waiting to learn of the vow, the sacred promise.

"This he vows to the Great Mystery. He beseeches Wakan Tanka to let his little girl live and grow and be healthy. Already she has lived seven days, and his vow was that if Wakan Tanka let her live that long, he will dance the Gazing-at-the-sun Dance. This he promises. This he will pay!"

All the listening people said "Ah!" in admiration. Eagle Walks would give his pain and his blood, staring at the sun, which represented the Great Mystery, to pay for the life and health of his little girl.

There was much talk and excitement in the camp, much

remembering of other sun-gazing gatherings and brave men who had voluntarily suffered in them for the good of their relatives or close friends or the whole tribe.

That night the brutal cold of winter eased, and the new baby could retain a little milk. When the child cried it was a good cry. Grandmother Earth Medicine said proudly, "She says, 'I came to stay.'"

But there was much doubt. Many winter-born babies died.

If the naming feast had been in warm weather, and if the baby had been normally healthy, there would have been a great deal of noise and jollity with everyone gathered at once. But because of the cold, the ceremony was quiet, only a few people came at a time, the talk and the laughter were quiet, as if death's shadowy wings still hovered. Relatives of both parents brought food as well as gifts, and the women bustled about serving the visitors, who did not stay long. There was plenty to eat.

The only guest who stayed the whole time was the old camp crier. If the baby-naming feast had been in summer, he would have shouted the child's name at the end of the celebration, but the circumstances being as they were, he announced it in a quiet voice as each group finished eating:

"This little one will be known as Whirlwind, in honor of her mother's father, who was a great warrior."

Many Bones Woman, proudly holding the baby and gladly showing her, had a private pet name of her own for the child. It was They Love Her.

There was so much coming and going that the snow was tramped down on the path to the lodge where the new baby was. Five women had brought fine gifts of cradleboards, made of soft buckskin and embroidered with dyed porcupine quills, even when there was doubt that the sickly baby would live long enough to need a cradle in which she could ride on her mother's back or coo when it swung from a tree branch in the warmth of summer.

Other aunts and cousins brought soft buckskin to wrap the baby. Grandmother Earth Medicine Woman gave the feather-light, feather-soft little rug of squirrel skins that she liked to sit on when her bones ached. But Many Bones burst into tears at this sacrifice. She accepted the gift but returned it, saying, "Your grandchild gives it to you. She wants you to have it, because she loves you."

That was a busy place, the lodge of Eagle Walks, with so many people coming and going. Earth Medicine Woman clucked about the snow they brought in on their clothing. She brushed it off with a wolf tail. Women were in and out all day, carrying firewood and water and delicacies for the young mother and helping keep the place tidy. She thanked them and, turning aside a corner of the baby's wrappings, let them peep at her face and exclaim about what a fine child she was.

Men brought gifts, too. Eagle Walks was a man of standing in the camp. He was a good hunter, a brave fighter, he spoke wisely in meetings, and he was generous to the poor. He thanked them with dignity for presents of meat, and sometimes invited one or two of them to sit with him for a while. He sat in the lodge-master's place at the back of the tepee, opposite the entrance. His guests spoke little but let him know they shared his concern for the sickly baby and felt his grief for the three that had died before she was born.

They were good men and women, the relatives and friends of the worried parents. The women were virtuous and industrious, faithful wives and loving mothers. The men were of proved courage in battle and wise in counsel. The baby's father was rich in honor; he owned many horses and had given away even more. But all these attributes and all their

11

worthiness could not keep dark death out of the lodge if it chose to enter. There was nothing more they could do but pray to the Great Mystery.

The child was still feeble, but she lived.

Chapter 2

Many Bones Woman was by nature gentle and quiet, and the years of heartbreak in which her earlier babies died had made her seem timid and even apologetic. Now she changed. She felt secure and complete. When the baby was two moons old and growing fat, and the two boys had moved back to the lodge, Many Bones astonished everyone in it by saying rather crossly to her husband, "It is time you brought another wife to the lodge. There is too much work to do, and your sister wants to marry again and set up her own lodge with her own man."

Eagle Walks stared at her as if he thought she had lost her wits. Then he burst out in a roar of happy laughter, understanding that all was well with her, and what she said was true. All of them in the lodge laughed so hard that the neighbors several lodges away heard and wondered. (A couple of the women put on their blankets to come over and find out. There was very little privacy in any Indian camp.)

Eagle Walks said with mock humility, "Yes, that is right. I will see about it soon." He added, "It is too bad that you have no unmarried sister. I would like a second wife just like you."

He looked fondly at Many Bones and saw tears in her eyes—tears of happiness.

The two most inquisitive neighbor women scratched on the tepee door and Grandmother Earth Medicine let them in. That was part of her duty and her privilege, as the old-woman-who-sits-by-the-door. She told them of the funny things that had just been said, and they laughed and sat down on the floor to admire the baby.

Young Grey Bull threw his warmest fur robe over his shoulders and slipped out to go on a pleasant errand. He visited a tepee at the far end of the camp, where a young man named Looks Ahead lived with his parents and some other relatives. This was simply a social call, apparently, but Looks Ahead saw the smile that kept flickering on Grey Bull's lips and finally said, "Let's go and see how the ponies are doing. I am tired of doing nothing."

As they waded through the snow, Looks Ahead demanded, "Why are you smiling that way? Did you come to tell me something?"

"Yes, but keep still about it for a few days. I thought you would like to know that my brother Eagle Walks said today that he is going to take another wife. Many Bones told him he should, because sometime my older sister will want to marry again and set up her own home with her own man."

Looks Ahead said with delight, "Ah, that is good! That is very good! And how soon will this be? When can I tie some horses out in front of your lodge as a gift offering to Eagle Walks for his sister? When my brother spoke to him about it last summer, he refused because she was needed in his own lodge. But I have courted her for a long time, and I want my own home."

Teasing a little, Grey Bull told him, "How can I answer? I am only the younger brother. And nobody has thanked me for bringing good news to a man who has courted a good-looking young widow for a long time—a girl who would like to marry again."

"I thank you, I do thank you," Looks Ahead assured him. "I'd give you the fur robe off my back but I'd freeze out here without it. Your good-looking sister would not want a frozen man for her husband."

"All right, I can tell you this much, and you can give me that robe some other day. My brother Eagle Walks already has another wife in mind, but he would not take her without his first wife's consent. Yes, I know he spoils Many Bones, but he loves her and wants her to be happy. He has in mind the young woman who was captured when we fought the Crows last summer. He has talked to the man who owns her. I was there when they talked. She will not cost very much, because her owner has two wives and two sisters to provide for, and she is timid and not like our own women. She doesn't know our language very well yet, either."

Looks Ahead nodded thoughtfully. "I wouldn't care for a scared woman myself. The good-looking young widow I want isn't afraid of anybody. When we are married, I may have to beat her."

Both men chuckled at that, and Grey Bull warned, "When you try that, she will throw you out. Now remember to be surprised about all this next time you hear it. When it is time for you to make an offer for my sister, Eagle Walks will send word to you properly so that everything will be done according to custom."

"I'll send one of my sisters over with something for the baby," Looks Ahead decided.

Grey Bull laughed. "Your sisters have already brought presents. They must be anxious to get you married off."

"They can take more presents," Looks Ahead said, smiling. "Now do we really have to go and look at the pony herd?"

"We have already looked," his brother-in-law-to-be assured him. "The pony herd is getting along just fine. Let's go back."

The sun shone warmly one morning, and Many Bones Woman told the others in the lodge, "The baby and I are going somewhere." She put on her heaviest moccasins and warm leggings up to her knees and wore a warm fur robe. The baby, snug in her cradle bundle, was warm enough, although she cried at the bright sunlight.

Many Bones climbed the hill behind the camp, following a path through the snow that the men used when they went out to care for the horse herd.

The mother took the cradleboard off her shoulders and held it in her arms, telling her child, "This is the earth and this is the sky. Behold them, because they are holy."

Then she held the child up and sang a little song that she had made up. To the Great Mystery she sang, "You who are above, this is our child. Behold her! This is our child. We give thanks."

She held the child up again for all the spirits, the mysterious ones, to see. She sang first to the Woman God, daughter of the Sky and the Star People, protector of chastity and little children:

"Gracious One, Beautiful One, this is our child. Behold her! This is our child. We give thanks."

To the sky spirits she sang, "You who are above, this is our child. Behold her! This is our child. We give thanks."

She sang to the earth spirits: "You who are in the earth, this is our child. Behold her! This is our child. We give thanks."

She sang the same song to each of the six directions: to the spirits who live where the sun goes down, those where the cold comes from, those where the sun comes back, those where summer comes from, those above the earth and those below.

Then she put the cradleboard on her back again and returned to the lodge, feeling happy, feeling well, because she had prayed. She had hope and faith, and it was only right that Eagle Walks should take a second wife. Many Bones would always be first, always the sits-beside-him wife.

Chapter 3

It was decided: Eagle Walks would buy the captive Crow woman right away, to give her time to become accustomed to his lodge and his family while it was still winter and there was not so much heavy work for the women to do as there would be later when they would move camp often.

Many Bones Woman was content. Her husband would need a wife, because she herself should not become pregnant again as long as the baby needed nursing. She would not be very jealous. This was custom, that a man who was a good hunter should have two wives or more.

His sister—always cheerful now that she knew she would soon be the wife of Looks Ahead—took a greater interest in his plans for installing another woman in the lodge than his wife did. Like most Lakota women, she tended to speak her mind. She asked him, "Shall we take her gifts so that she comes to you with honor? She has no relatives to make her a proper outfit for a bride."

Eagle Walks looked surprised. "I am paying a horse for her. She will simply come with me to this lodge after I pay it.

She is not one of The People—she is only an enemy captive with no right to expect any ceremony."

Antelope Woman knew how to coax and flatter her brother. "If she has a new dress, a Lakota dress, and a horse to ride, that will do *you* honor, Brother. You don't want a mere slave in the lodge. You can afford something better. I will take her a new dress and go with you."

He frowned, but she had touched his pride. Her argument made good sense. "All right. That will get things off to a good start."

"And," his sister added, "she should have the gift of a horse to ride to her new home, so everyone can see how generous is the family of Eagle Walks."

He scowled. "That is going too far. She is not a sought-after maiden of The People, to be treated so well. She's a captive and a widow—at least I think her husband was killed in that battle."

"Oh, *I* will give the horse," his sister assured him. "Remember, I own several good horses myself."

Eagle Walks began to chuckle. "I see through that, Sister. All right, go ahead. Make her happy so the lodge will be a happy place even after you leave it. Are you intending to leave us, to move to some other lodge, maybe?"

He knew very well that she was, but the gift of horses from Looks Ahead—the formal, solemn proposal of marriage—had not been discussed except in whispers.

"Sometime I may leave, Brother," Antelope replied, pretending embarrassment. "With your permission, if a good man should offer for me."

"We'll see about that," he said with tremendous dignity and became very busy with the arrows he was making. A little later he remarked, as if talking to himself, "In two days I will bring her."

His mother began to scold, as was her right as his mother, but under her breath, because he was an outstanding man in their camp, not to be nagged by women. "How does a man know anything about housekeeping? Does he want to bring in a stranger to think we are slovenly here and don't know how to do things right?"

She began to clean house, moving the many parfleche boxes out from the tepee wall, sorting and tidying the things in them, straightening up bladders of pemmican, hanging bags of dried vegetable food more neatly—and all the time muttering and pretending the job was simply too much for an old woman whose bones ached.

Her daughter, smiling broadly, took the hint and began to do the heavier work of cleaning—dragging out the fur robes that covered the dirt floor, shaking them, piling them up so she could move around and have room to take the layers of robes off the beds and shake them and rearrange them. She said rather loudly, "Of course we can't tidy up at the back of the lodge unless my brother moves off his bed and his backrest. But we wouldn't want to bother him!"

He stood up and threw on his warm fur robe, announcing with a grim look that fooled nobody, "I did not know the woman in this lodge were such bad housekeepers! I can't breathe in all this dirt! Maybe I will find a better place to live."

He strode out with great dignity, meeting Grey Bull and Running Wolf just outside. They had been looking after the horse herd. "Don't go in there," he advised. "It is a terrible place!" All three went away, smiling.

Many Bones Woman remarked, "The baby is sleeping, so I will help, too." She hung the baby's cradle sack on a tripod and began to scour all their dishes and spoons, cleverly made from flat and hollowed-out animal bones and pieces of horn,

18

with warm water and the river sand that they kept by the door on a platter of tree bark for that purpose. The women in her lodge were really very good housekeepers. Now they were going to show off a little to the stranger and set her a good example.

The lodge was big, and there was a place for everything in it. When warmer weather came and they began to move often for the spring hunt and to renew the tepee poles, they would be able to pack all their property on horses and pony drags on very short notice and unpack again and put up the lodge again in time for the evening meal.

Two days later, after due warning to the owner of the captive Crow woman, Eagle Walks led a little procession to the lodge where she was. He wore his best fringed buckskin clothes and a wolfskin robe and rode one of his own horses, leading the one he would use to pay for his new wife. Behind him rode his sister on one of her own horses, leading another on which was tied a bundle. People seeing them pass remarked, "What is this? The captive woman has no rights and no relatives, but see how well they are going to treat her!"

About the same kind of procession, but longer, with more horses and riders and bundles of presents, would accompany a wedding journey to claim an honored girl of their own people, but there was a great difference. Eagle Walks was buying his second wife for the price of a horse. The horses that were exchanged for a Lakota girl were much better and more than one. And her women relatives would exchange valuable presents with the women of the bridegroom, with much gaiety and considerable showing off of their own fine handwork and skill in tanning and quill embroidering.

(One watching woman remarked, "He knows how to treat a woman. It's too bad some other men don't." Whereupon her husband slapped her, which is just what she expected. Those

19

two never did get along very well, but she was industrious and a good cook so he did not divorce her. It would have been easy enough to throw her away, send her back to her family, but he thought he might get a worse wife. So they bickered, to the amusement of their neighbors, but they stayed together in spite of her sharp tongue.)

Eagle Walks entered the tepee when he was invited and sat down at the back beside the lodge master and they smoked ceremonially. One of the women invited Antelope to come in because it was cold outside. They sat quietly by the door and Antelope took her first good look at her new sister-in-law. She was young but looked strong. She might have been pretty, for a foreigner, if she had not acted so frightened. She listened but did not speak.

The other women explained, "She must have learned something of our language in all this time, but she never says anything except in sign talk."

"I have brought her a new dress," Antelope announced. "And a horse to ride on. My brother's second wife should go to his lodge like a wife, not a captive."

The Crow woman understood some of that, all right. Her eyes widened, and she said, "Dress? Horse?" in Lakota, as if not believing. All of them laughed quietly, not wanting to disturb the solemn deliberations of the men.

When the men went out to look at the horse that was to pay for the captive, Antelope hurriedly unwrapped her bundle and shook out the soft tan buckskin dress she had brought. The others got in each other's way helping the captive woman take off her old dress and put on the new one. One woman seized a brush made of an animal's furry tail and began to smooth her hair—very long braids; the Crows were famous for their long hair. The purchased bride stood will-

20

ingly, smiling as if she might cry. All this was so much better than she had any reason to expect!

In the lodge of her new husband, Crow Woman became a different person. She was still quiet, still anxious to do things the Lakota way, and afraid of doing anything wrong, but the other women discovered that she had picked up more of their language than anyone had guessed. Crow Woman worked all the time, whenever she saw anything to do. Winter was a time when there was not so much to do as in good weather—bring in water and wood, keep a pot cooking on the fire, try to keep snug and warm. But there was no butchering to do except of occasional small game (the hunters went out but found no buffalo and did not worry because the camp was well supplied with dried meat from the fall hunt), and the lodge was too dark to permit sewing or embroidery. The only light, with the door shut against the cold of winter, came from the fire.

They had two good steel knives, trade goods brought from a distant trading post. Crow Woman kept them sharp by rubbing the blades against a little stone. Sometimes she rocked the baby when Many Bones felt generous enough to let her, and once they saw that she was crying.

Grandmother Earth Medicine could understand her better than the others. Earth Medicine announced, "She had a little boy, four winters old. She doesn't know whether he is alive. She does not mourn for her husband but thinks he is dead. Maybe he was not good to her. Who knows how those Crows treat their women?"

Crow Woman took great interest in the way their tall lodge was made. She moved around in it, tracing the seams in the sewed-together hides, staring up at the main supporting poles and how they were fastened to hold up the other long poles that made the frame. Sometimes she shook her head, not understanding. When good weather came, and the women had to take down the lodges, move them for miles when the camp moved, and set them up again, she would have to help.

In broken Lakota and much sign language she explained to the other women, "Ab-sa-ro-kee, my people, make another way." With small twigs from the pile of firewood she showed them: the Crows used four poles, not three, as the framework and leaned the additional poles against them in a different way. Then she said something anxiously, and repeated it, hoping to be understood.

This time it was Many Bones Woman who understood. "She says she will try to learn to do it right, the way we do." The four women experimented beside the fire, using twigs and bits of buckskin, with pieces of tough dried grass for fastenings, so that Crow Woman would understand how a proper Lakota lodge was set up. The others had learned in early childhood as part of their little-girl games, long before they helped their elders erect a family-sized lodge.

The two boys, Grey Bull and Running Wolf, swung the door open and came in while the women were manipulating the miniature tepee. They laughed and Grey Bull said, "It is nice to be a little girl and play house! And do the little girls play they cook meals for hungry men?"

He and Running Wolf dropped the still-warm carcass of a fine antelope just inside the entrance.

"Look whose arrow killed it, right in the heart," advised Grey Bull. "See the marks on the arrow?"

"The marks of Running Wolf!" exclaimed Many Bones Woman. "Oh, this is a fine thing!" For he was only ten winters old. The Lakota women began to sing a praise song for Running Wolf, who tried hard to look stern and dignified instead of as happy as he felt. Even Crow Woman tried to join in, but she hadn't learned their music much better than their language or customs.

The only time she got into real trouble was when she wanted to move Eagle Walks' sacred war shield outside one day when the sun came out in his absence. It hung from a tripod behind his backrest at the rear of the lodge. It had been made and painted by a man with great medicine power, at great expense, and because its purpose was to save his life in battle it was holy. The shield should face the sun when the sun was shining.

Among her own people, the Absarokees or Crows, a wife had the duty and privilege of caring for her husband's shield. What Crow Woman had not learned was that among the Lakotas, a woman's touch could profane the shield and render it powerless when a man needed it most.

Fortunately, before actually touching it, she asked Earth Medicine in her awkward, broken talk. The old woman, who had been drowsing by the fire, shrieked and leaped up with the agility of a young girl. She grabbed Crow Woman by the hair and slapped her face, scolding so loudly that she could be heard all over the camp. Crow Woman cowered and began to cry.

Just then Many Bones came in with Eagle Walks. He was very stern and grim about what had almost happened. He moved the tripod out into the sunshine himself, and by the time they all finished scolding, his second wife, although she had not understood all their words, knew that she was never to touch that buffalo-hide shield.

When she tried to explain the customs of her people, nobody would listen. The Lakota way was the right way, the only way. For the Lakotas were The People. Everybody else was inferior, even the tribes that were their friends.

The new wife asked a lot of questions, shyly and without prying, in her broken Lakota and sign language. The other women were usually glad to answer, because she now belonged in the family. Of Antelope Woman—young, attractive, single—she asked, "You—no man?"

Antelope replied, "No man," and made the sign of death to say she was a widow. Crow Woman crooned sympathy and patted her arm.

Almost one moon had passed after Crow Woman's coming before Antelope's widowhood ended. She had begun to think it never would, but it was not seemly for women to try to hurry men, and her brother was conservative; he did things properly—with slow ceremony. Because the weather was so cold, Looks Ahead did not even court her publicly any more by standing in front of the lodge and waiting for her to come out so he could wrap her in his blanket and talk quietly. Once he paid a ceremonial visit to her brother and smoked with him at the rear of the tepee, ignoring the women. They did not say one word about Looks Ahead marrying Antelope.

But the time came at last when two brothers of Looks Ahead visited Eagle Walks and smoked ceremoniously and spoke plainly. The women, silently busy, pretended not to hear. After the two visitors departed, Eagle Walks announced, "Any day now, some presents will come to my sister from the women in the lodge where Looks Ahead stays. There will be a feast over there. A young couple will have their own lodge over there. Maybe we have some things in this lodge to send for presents when our sister sets up her own home?"

His women and the two boys were smiling broadly, and Antelope Woman hid her face in her blanket. (It was unthinkable that she should jump up and embrace her brother as a white girl might have done. Among the Lakotas, such

24

great respect existed between adult brothers and sisters that they seldom looked at each other, even when they were talking.)

"Now," said Grandmother Earth Medicine with boastful satisfaction, "we will show the new wife in this lodge how The People do things—the right way! We have some presents to send. But, oh, how we will miss the girl who will not stay in the lodge of Eagle Walks any more!"

This family was very prosperous, not only in horses but in the fine handwork of furs and embroidered and painted skins that the industry of the women had accumulated. There was no room for most of this in the lodge, so these riches were kept carefully in a small animal-tight shelter just outside. The way to prestige was to give away fine things, and in return fine presents were given to them. These things, and the horses, were the equivalent of a bank account, to be spent lavishly when circumstances called for it.

And so Antelope was married to Looks Ahead, who had waited for her patiently. Because she was a widow, her marriage did not bring her brothers as many horses as when she had married the first time as a virgin. But she rode to her new home on a fine spotted horse with a saddle much decorated, with women singing and laughing, and in her fringed white buckskin dress with a beaver mantle for warmth she looked very pretty indeed.

Chapter 4

Spring came early that year, or it seemed to do so. The sun shone. Would it continue to shine and be warm enough so the people could move from their winter camp, now very dirty, to a clean place? Or would the white wolf of a blizzard come suddenly before they could settle down?

The wise old men of the camp, who met often to discuss the well-being of the people, met and smoked and solemnly discussed the problem. The medicine men, the priest-doctors, sang and drummed and prayed. Everybody was restless.

The council sent out four scouts, *akícitas*, of Grey Bull's warrior society to investigate the condition of a place where they had camped three or four winters before. Grey Bull was one of those honored to be chosen. His society would also serve as police when the people did move, to see that everything went all right. The Kit Foxes competed for honors, in peace and war, with other warrior societies like the Crow Owners, the Badgers, and the Plain Lance Owners.

Around the winter camp, sheltered from the wind by a cliff, firewood was very scarce now, and so was winter-dried grass for the many horses. All the paths used by people and horses were muddy and sloppy.

The scouts returned, waving their bows in triumph. They had examined camping places and had found a good one.

"There is wood and water and shelter for the lodges, with good feed for the horse herd!" they said.

The wise men of the council smoked and asked questions and were satisfied. The priest-doctors believed that the good weather would hold for two days. The village needed only one to move. So the camp crier rode around the camp circle through the mud to announce the move:

"Hear, you men, tomorrow morning we are going to the place where the river talks to itself. Get ready to guard the helpless ones! Hear, you women, pack up and get ready to go as soon as the sun comes up! It is one day's journey to the new camp."

There was great excitement and joy about getting away

from this place that had become so muddy and dirty. Grandmother Earth Medicine said, "Now we decide what worn-out things to throw away. Now we will find out whether Crow Woman can really help tear down the lodge and pack it and put it up again! She will probably only get in the way."

The old woman had never learned to like her new daughter-in-law—a poor scared creature, not like a Lakota woman, and a Crow besides. Earth Medicine had mourned more than one relative killed in battle with members of the Crow tribe.

Many Bones Woman said soothingly, "She will be helpful. She is afraid of you. I think she was badly treated before she came to us. Maybe she had a cruel husband among her own people."

Women all over the camp sorted and packed their things, keeping out enough food for a meal early in the morning and to give everyone something to lunch on during a stop on the journey. Boys came yelling with the horses that would be needed and picketed them near the lodges.

Moving camp was women's work, so Earth Medicine and Many Bones Woman told Running Wolf and Grey Bull exactly which horses of the many their family owned were wanted to carry packs and pull pony drags on which their possessions would be tied, as well as which saddle horses they wanted to ride. Eagle Walks described the good, fast horse he wanted—not his best buffalo-hunting pony nor his favorite war horse, but a good one. The men would do much more riding than the women and children, for the men ranged out from the moving column looking for enemies who might attack the helpless ones.

There was even a pony to pull a basket on poles to transport the new puppies of Earth Medicine's big white bitch. The grandmother wanted those puppies well taken care of, because a fat puppy made a good stew that was a favorite dish for special occasions.

Eagle Walks took care of his weapons, his tough buffalo-hide shield, which was sacred and must never touch the ground, and certain other objects with religious significance which should not be touched by women. Without seeming to pay any attention to what his women folks were doing, he nevertheless watched them and was rather pleased at the skill his new wife showed in preparing to move. He spoke to his mother: "You are not young any more, and sometimes your bones ache. Do you want to ride in a pony drag instead of on a horse?"

Many Bones caught her breath; she had already asked her mother-in-law that and had been scolded angrily. Earth Medicine did not dare scold her son, though—he was the master of the family and was trying to be kind. She said sulkily, "I am not too old to ride a horse. Should I go in the same basket as the puppies?"

He laughed and replied, "They would keep you warm." But there was no more argument. The grandmother would ride a horse of her own, even though someone had to lift her up into the saddle.

The camp crier awakened them all early in the morning: "Warriors, make ready to protect the helpless! Women, tear down the lodges and get ready to go! You boys, help them with the horses! When the sun comes up, we go!"

Earth Medicine continued to be cross with her daughters-in-law. She yelled at them to do this, do that, but her bones did ache and she couldn't do very much herself. Crow Woman hurried and scurried, trying to do everything at once, until Many Bones patted her arm to soothe her. They dismantled the lodge together, untying knots and folding the

28

heavy, buffalo-hide cover in the Lakota way to make a solid bundle.

They took down the long lodgepoles and tied some of them with the slender ends crossed on a horse's shoulders and the heavy ends dragging. On this pony drag they heaved the bundle of tepee cover and tied it, and used other poles to make drags behind other horses to carry other things, including the big hide basket with the new puppies in it.

"We will be late and out of our turn," warned the grandmother crossly, but they were not. The village moved out right on time, in proper order, with the families whose lodges would be pitched at the far end of the new camp going first. Everybody was excited and happy—except Earth Medicine, who was only excited, and the big white bitch, which whined and worried about her puppies.

Up the hill the procession moved, the people and their horses, and their belongings, with a great deal of noise and unnecessary dashing around by the young men and boys on their winter-furry horses. Now and then a horse threw up his heels, trying to argue about carrying his load, but riders had whips to decide that. The tamest, best-behaved horses pulled the pony drags. The young men had taken most of the winter meanness out of the other animals by riding them hard during the past few days.

Many Bones Woman rode happily with her baby on her back in the cradle sack on its rawhide board. The procession did not move fast, and the baby, lulled by the rocking motion, slept most of the time except when she was hungry.

Four times they stopped to rest for a while, at a signal from the wise old men who led the procession, carrying their sacred pipes and a small log with fire in it. One man tended the fire log carefully, feeding it now and then, keeping the coals red, because from this all the lodge fires would be lighted when they reached their new home.

The guardian outriders watched for enemies and for game. During the last rest stop, two young men rode in from beyond a hill to tell the old-men leaders, "Buffalo tracks over there! Not very many, but fresh."

That news spread among the people and there was happy excitement. There would be a hunt the next day. Everybody looked forward to the excitement of it, to feasting on the rich, fresh buffalo meat. There would be heavily haired hides for the women to tan into good warm robes if the sun kept shining. Spring was coming; everything would be different now, with the people no longer shut up in the lodges so much just to keep warm.

Running Wolf and every other young boy in the moving village dreamed of taking great chances in the hunt and bringing down more of the great shaggy beasts with his arrows than any boy his age had ever killed before. Every young man in the Kit Fox Society, who would police the hunt, decided which daring youngsters he would have to watch most closely to keep them from getting badly hurt or even killed.

And so they moved on, that band of The People, noisy and happy, with much shouting and dogs barking and babies crying, through a country rich in game, a land to which their nomadic lives were completely tuned. Now and then someone broke into a short prayer song of gratitude to the Great Mystery and the other spirits, because they were The People, fortunate above all others, and they were happy.

Part II

SPRING AND
SUMMER, 1825
The Sun-gazing Dance

Living in the Lodge:

> *Eagle Walks, 41, head of the family*
> *Many Bones, 30, his wife*
> *Whirlwind Girl, 5, their daughter*
> *Grey Bull, 21, half brother of Eagle Walks*
> *Running Wolf, 15, nephew of Many Bones Woman*
> *Crow Woman, another wife of Eagle Walks, age*
> *   known only to herself*
> *Runs-in-Timber, infant son of Crow Woman and*
> *   Eagle Walks*
> *Sun Goes Down, infant, Whirlwind's full brother*
> *Grandmother Earth Medicine Woman, very old*

Chapter 5

The best time of the year, Whirlwind knew even when she was still a very little girl, was that part of summer when the great ceremony of the Sun-gazing Dance was held. Then all the separate small camps of her people, the Oglala Lakotas, came together in one huge, happy camp to renew the spiritual strength of the tribe. It was a time of rejoicing and fun and feasting and visiting with old friends and making new ones.

It was a sacred time of prayers and awesome rituals and glorious processions. It was when babies old enough to walk had their ears pierced by warriors full of honors, to make them full members of the proud people. And for some brave men it was a time to suffer while they paid the vows they had made to the Great Mystery.

Whirlwind's earliest vivid memory of the great gathering came from the one when she was five winters old, perhaps because so many members of her close family were involved. And because now she felt like a big girl; she had to wear a dress all the time. Like other small children, she had been accustomed to running naked in warm weather. It was a pretty dress, made of soft, tanned deerskin trimmed with fringes, but too warm. When she protested, her mother, Many Bones, and her other mother, Crow Woman, told her firmly that she would get used to it.

The most convincing argument came from her father: "Babies go naked. Are you a baby?"

Of course not. She stopped complaining.

That was the summer when her cousin Running Wolf, now fifteen, went out to cry to the spirits for a vision, to plead with the spirits for their protection so that he could become a man and a warrior. Whirlwind knew something important was going on, because her father and Running Wolf's father and an old holy man had meetings with the boy, who was very quiet and respectful. She knew that men had business they did not talk about much even to women, and certainly not to small children.

Running Wolf was missing from the lodge for several days,

and his mother came often to sit and sew with her mothers, and they seemed worried.

When Running Wolf came back, Whirlwind saw him ride past with his father and her father and the old holy man, toward the council lodge. He sat his horse with his head bowed; he looked sick and even frightened. The women of the household saw him and stood up, watching, not saying anything, so Whirlwind did not speak, either, or even wave.

Whirlwind asked Many Bones Woman, "Where did Running Wolf go and why does he look sick? Did somebody hurt him? When will he come back here and tell about it?"

"He went out on a hill to pray to the spirits for a powerful medicine dream to protect him and bring him good luck. He looks sick because he is hungry and thirsty, and he was afraid. After he tells the old men about it they will tell him the meaning, and then he will come back to our lodge."

Whirlwind answered, "Running Wolf was *afraid*? How can that be? I thought he was never afraid!"

Her mother explained: "He was alone with the spirits, praying to them, and some spirits are bad, very dangerous. When a man faces them all alone at night and talks to them, something terrible can happen to him. Of course he was afraid. But he did it anyway. That is what 'brave' means— being afraid but going ahead anyway. Never forget that."

The sun had moved a long way across the sky before Eagle Walks came back from the council lodge. He looked pleased. Running Wolf did not come with him.

"The boy had a very powerful vision," Eagle Walks said briefly. "The old men agree that it was a true vision, and now he has medicine to protect him. A voice came to him and taught him sacred songs to sing. It was an antelope voice. So his power is the antelope, and he will make his medicine bag with something from the antelope in it."

33

The women said, "Ah, that is good, good!"

"Will he tell me about it?" Whirlwind asked.

"When he wants to tell you, he will. But now he is sleeping in the council lodge, because this lodge is so full of little girls who ask questions." Eagle Walks tugged at one of her braids, teasing her. "You are only one little girl, but you act like many."

After that, Running Wolf was somehow different. He even seemed taller. He was more dignified, no longer a boy but a young man, protected by spirit medicine, eager to take great chances in hunting buffalo, always wanting to go with war parties to prove his courage and begin to make a reputation. He did not go out to steal horses or fight enemies until after the Sun-gazing Dance, because Eagle Walks sternly refused to permit it, but once he broke a hunting law and was punished for it.

A herd of buffalo had been sighted, and the hunters got ready to ride at them. The Kit Fox Society policed that hunt, deciding from which direction the hunters should approach and when they should start at a signal. Running Wolf was too eager. He broke out of the group before the signal. This time it did not matter—they brought down plenty of buffalo —but the law was an important one, for if every hunter did as he pleased, the whole herd could be frightened off and all the people might go hungry.

When the hunt was over, two Kit Foxes rode up to Running Wolf, yelling and abusing him with words. He sat his horse in silence, knowing he had done wrong. Then the two men whipped him hard with their quirts while everyone watched. He covered his face with one arm and sat there, silent, until they had finished.

That was all there was to it. He was punished for doing wrong, and nobody said anything more about it. He learned

34

self-control from that experience. After the skinning and butchering of the buffalo carcasses, he took fine presents of meat to two aged poor couples, because generosity was one of the four virtues by which men of honor lived. The others were bravery, wisdom, and fortitude. Running Wolf was ambitious. He was not going to make any more mistakes.

Whirlwind's village began to move so as to arrive at the sun-gazing camp at the appointed time. All across the prairie the people were moving, excited and happy, to unite for that great ceremony. The young men scouts rode far and fast, watching for enemies, watching for friends. Moving villages met with cries of greeting and traveled on together, camping together as they went.

Everybody was busy, even girls as small as Whirlwind. She was useful in looking after the babies while their mothers packed and unpacked and put up the lodge and cooked and talked to old friends, not seen since last year.

Crow Woman's boy, a year and a half old, was hard to keep track of. Now that he could walk, he was going to have his ears pierced during the ceremony. His name was Runs-in-Timber. Whirlwind's full brother, Sun Goes Down, was ten months old. He objected with loud howls to being confined to his cradle bundle—he liked solid ground under him so he could try to crawl. Whirlwind had her hands full with those two, keeping them out from under foot, but she had time to get acquainted with other little girls who also had babies to mind. Sometimes the babies slept—but never all at once.

Crow Woman spoke the Lakota tongue fluently now. She was one of the family, one of The People, no longer a captive from an enemy tribe.

After the twelve-day ceremony began, the babies were with their mothers, who went to watch and to show off their children. Then Whirlwind was free to watch or to play with her new friends.

There were plenty of exciting rituals for children to watch, but small ones could easily and innocently do something very wrong if they were not prevented, so nobody encouraged Whirlwind and others of her age group to spend much time near the places where sacred things went on. In fact, much of the ceremony was so slow that Whirlwind tired of it and was glad enough, once her curiosity was appeased, to return to the lodge and her grandmother. Old Earth Medicine had to use a staff in walking, so she stayed usually in the lodge or in its shade, leaning against her backrest and making moccasins.

Whirlwind wandered home one day, tired from running, peevish because some older girls wouldn't let her play with them, and puzzled by all the confusion of the ceremony.

"There was a silly old man," she said. "He acts crazy."

"Such people are sometimes holy," her grandmother told her. "What did he do?"

"It is hot in the sun, but he shivered and wrapped himself in a warm robe. A woman offered him something to eat, but he pushed it away. He lives in a ragged old lodge in the next camp—a lodge that faces the opposite way from all the others. We followed him to see."

"Did you and the other children make fun of him and throw things at him?"

"Of course. He acted as if he liked it."

Grandmother Earth Medicine said in a serious voice, "He is *heyoka*, crazy, because of a vision. He is a holy man. The Thunderbird sent him a certain dream, and now he must act like a clown. He has to do things backward, because now he is a contrary. That is very hard for him. Probably he used to be proud, the way a Lakota warrior ought to be, but the

36

Thunderbird gave him a message that he must be humble and foolish."

"Why, do you know him?" Whirlwind asked, surprised.

"No, but I had a brother long ago who was *heyoka*. They have great medicine power. Thunderbird gives them hard duties but big powers. They can dip meat out of boiling soup with their bare hands. Sometimes they can see what is happening at a great distance. Some of them can cure sick people, but when the relatives try to give them presents, the *heyoka* won't take them. So he is always poor. I don't think you should throw things at such a person or jeer at him. He suffers, but he pretends to have fun. He is a holy clown."

Whirlwind considered that. "Yes, it would be hard for a warrior, a proud man, to be humble."

"That's a good girl. Ignorant people jeer. You are not ignorant. You are of a good family." Earth Medicine said in her story-telling voice, "My brother who became *heyoka*—his dream was about a lizard. Lizard, dog, and some other creatures are the *akícitas*, the messengers, of the Thunderbird. After many years my brother tried to get rid of the burden of his power. He was tired of being *heyoka*. He went through a ceremony to get rid of it, but Thunderbird killed him."

"How?" asked Whirlwind.

"Lightning struck him. Thunderbird sends lightning."

Whirlwind shivered. "Now tell me about when you were a little girl," she suggested.

"That was a long time ago, a long time ago. We lived then east of the river and we were all poor. That was before we came here to be near Paha Sapa, the Black Hills. We did not have horses to ride or pony drags to carry our belongings, so we had few possessions, and our hunters could not ride out after buffalo, so we were often hungry. Everything we had, we carried on our backs or on big dogs. Some big dogs could

37

pull a drag but with only small poles. Then we got a few horses, and now we are rich. But when I was your age, I carried a heavy load on my back every time we moved. And we did not have big, comfortable lodges then. Ah, horses made a difference! That is why we call them sacred dogs.

"And now we have furs and robes to buy things from the Wasichus, the traders with pale skins. I saw some of them once. They are very dirty people, with hair all over their faces. They are all men, they don't have any women of their own kind. They take Indian women for their wives.

"The traders are all right in their place, I suppose. We buy iron pots from them, and knives and cloth and beads. But they are nasty people, the Wasichus."

"Tell me something nice," Whirlwind pleaded. "Tell me about the Beautiful One, the White Buffalo Maiden."

Telling religious stories was the duty and the privilege of grandmothers, and Earth Medicine was glad to tell this one again, even though the tired little girl went to sleep before it was over. Whirlwind had heard it before, would hear it many times again, would tell it sometimes to her grandchildren.

"Long ago, two young men were sent to scout for buffalo. They saw a very beautiful woman in lovely clothes of white buckskin. She told them, 'I am of the Buffalo People. I have been sent to bring your people an important message.'

"She told them how to set up a special council lodge. She would be in their village at dawn. One of the young men did not really listen but had bad thoughts about her. There was a loud roll of thunder, and a cloud covered them up. When the cloud went away, the young man was only a pile of bones with snakes crawling on them.

"The Beautiful One told the other man to return at once to his village with her message.

"She came the next morning, beautiful and stately, carrying in one hand a pipe stem and in the other a red stone pipe bowl. She told the people she would be their sister. She said Wakan Tanka was pleased with the Lakotas, and she would give them the pipe, symbol of peace and good faith. She spoke to the women, because they maintain the family and comfort others in trouble and grief. She told the children to respect their parents who love them. She spoke to the men as a sister, telling them to be kind and loving to the weak, and she told their chief how to care for the sacred pipe. She promised that seven sacred ceremonies would be revealed to them. These are Purification, Crying for a Vision, the Sun-gazing Dance, the Ball-throwing, Making a Buffalo Woman, Making as Brothers, and Owning a Ghost.

"When she left the village, walking in her stately way, she turned into a buffalo calf and then into a beautiful, pure-white buffalo cow. Then she disappeared."

The sun-gazing ceremony took twelve days, including the actual dance. Much of this time was spent in ritual preparation, every step of which had to be done in exactly the right way.

There were four days of festival and sociability. Then for four days the men who were going to gaze at the sun stayed in the council lodge with the holy men who taught them what they must do. Whirlwind's uncle, Grey Bull, was one of these dancers. He had vowed several months before to go through this ordeal when he was trying to rescue a close friend during a battle. The friend still lived, and now Grey Bull would pay his debt to the Great Mystery.

In the third four-day period preparations were completed. A sacred tree was carried to the dance lodge and set up there, with rawhide ropes attached to be fastened to the dancers.

Even Earth Medicine joined the great crowd to watch the ear-piercing of her grandson, Runs-in-Timber.

Eagle Walks asked his best friend, Kills-at-Night, to perform the ceremony, and gave him a fine gift of horses. The family, like the other families of the babies in the ceremony, brought gifts to show that they honored the child—soft robes of otter and beaver, beautifully tanned and with the undersides embroidered with dyed quills. These made a bed for lively little Runs-in-Timber. First, Crow Woman arranged the furs on a padding of white sage. Then Eagle Walks' friend counted his coups, recited the stories of the honors he had won for bravery to prove his worthiness to perform this important ceremony. Other men were doing the same thing at the same time, so there was a great deal of shouting.

Then he put a small piece of wood under the baby's ear and pierced the lobe with a sharp bone awl, one ear and then the other. The baby screamed and struggled, as did other babies as the same thing happened to them, and their mothers shuddered. Meanwhile there were men singing.

Kills-at-Night told Eagle Walks to stand beside Crow Woman and solemnly lectured them: this ceremony took the baby into the tribe. They must promise that he would follow the Lakota way, the only right way to live, and that they would bring him up properly. All the other ear-piercers were lecturing parents in about the same way, all of them shouting, all the babies howling.

When it was over, Crow Woman snuggled and soothed her child, and Eagle Walks looked at him with pride and they walked away together, leaving the beautiful furs for poor people to take home.

Whirlwind's cousin, Antelope's little girl, went through the ear-piercing, the taking-into-the-tribe, at the same time.

Whirlwind fingered her own earrings and told her grandmother, "I don't remember when they did that."

"Just as well," chuckled Earth Medicine. "You howled louder than any of them."

Earth Medicine said, "Now we will stay only a little longer. We will see how brave Grey Bull is when they cut his skin and tie him to the tree to begin the dance."

Earth Medicine managed to shove through the crowd, repeating loudly, "Let us see, we are relatives, and I am old. Let us see the brave Grey Bull." They even found his parents and sat on the ground with them.

The first man to be brought out Whirlwind did not know. She stared. He was painted red and blue, and he wore a long red skirt and bracelets and anklets of rabbit fur. He called the name of a man, who came forward—the man had knotted scars on his chest and back, showing that he had gone through this torture himself.

Then Grey Bull was brought out, painted the same way. He called, "Eagle Walks!" and his older brother, Whirlwind's father, came forward. Whirlwind knew his scars; those on his chest she had felt with her cheek when he held her to tell her stories, and with her arm around him she had felt the scars on his back with her hand. Her father was a very brave man—he had danced twice, and the second time was to thank the Great Mystery because she was alive.

One by one the dancers came out and called the names of men they had chosen. These men took the part of their captors, knocking them down in sham battle. Each captor, singing a victory song, pierced the flesh of his dancer with a knife, making slits through which he inserted wooden skewers. While each candidate was being cut, he sang defiantly as if he felt no pain. The skewers were fastened either to several heavy buffalo skulls or to the sacred tree in the center.

41

Then the drums and the slow singing began, and the dancers began to dance slowly, each staring at the sun, each blowing constantly on a whistle made from an eagle's wing bone. Women wailed, and some sang praise songs honoring their brave men.

After a while, Earth Medicine said quietly, "We will go now. It will be long after dark before the last one tears his flesh free."

The next day Whirlwind asked her father, "Why do men do that? It hurts! But nobody makes them do it."

He thought seriously, trying to explain in terms a little girl could understand.

"A man's body is his own, it is the only thing that really belongs to him. And his pain belongs to him. We can give the Great Mystery other presents, but that is where they came from in the first place. So we are only giving back something the spirits gave us. But when we give flesh or blood and pain, that is really ours, it is a real sacrifice."

"None of them cried," Whirlwind remarked. "I would cry."

"Sometimes a man does cry in the Sun-gazing Dance, not from the pain but because he prays so hard. He tells the Great Mystery he is sorry he did some things wrong, he is only a child, he makes mistakes. When a child cries, we forgive it more easily.

"Wakan Tanka, the Great Mystery, is everywhere. We can talk to it and we know it hears. It is not one spirit but many."

"I don't understand," the child murmured.

Her father sighed. "We can't understand everything about religion. We only try."

Chapter 6

When the Sun-gazing Dance was over, Grey Bull did not try to do anything but recover from his wounds and let his sore eyes heal, after the long, painful gazing at the sun. The women of the lodge made a fuss over him, kept the light dim, put strips of cool, wet buckskin over his eyes, fed him the tenderest meat.

His friends visited him often to congratulate him. They helped him when he had to go outside. The young man whose life he had saved and for whom he had vowed the sun-gazing sacrifice brought him gifts and was especially attentive.

The women put small soft cushions against his backrest to make him as comfortable as possible, but he did not sleep very well because of the pain in his eyes and the wounds in his flesh.

He was much honored. Someone was always having to move little Whirlwind out of the way. She just wanted to stare at him in admiration. Sometimes she sang a little praise song that her grandmother had taught her. He smiled and said, "Good, good!"

Early one morning nine men were missing from camp. One of them was Running Wolf, that eager new owner of a medicine bag. He did not come home one night, and the family assumed he had stayed either in the lodge of the Kit Fox Society or with his own parents, Kills-at-Night and River Woman. But Many Bones became suspicious and began to look around.

"His new moccasins are missing," she reported. "And a

bladder of pemmican. He took his shield and weapons and medicine bag to the Kit Fox lodge last night." She caught her breath "Do you suppose he has gone with a war party?"

Grey Bull, who knew very well that he had, pretended to be asleep.

Running Wolf's own mother came running, out of breath. "Some bold young men are missing," she gasped. "Is Running Wolf here?"

Now from all around the camp circle they could hear women wailing as they found out which men had left secretly to meet somewhere.

Eagle Walks came riding in at a lope and swung down off his horse. "The boys at the horse herd have counted. No war horses are missing. So it is not a war party that went out from here. All the horses are accounted for. The young men went on foot. They will come back riding enemy horses. They will come back in triumph."

Or maybe, the women thought, some of them would never come back. This was the way it had always been. Old men, past their brave days of taking enemy horses and gaining glory, drummed and sang prayer songs to the spirits and chanted the tales of their own triumphs to cheer up the worried women.

The women worked harder than usual in the days that followed, trying to keep their minds off their distress. Those who had gone out were brave, but all were young—reckless. Were any of them wise enough to advise the others and help them come back alive? Little girls like Whirlwind stayed close to the lodges. Little boys played war. Older boys guarded the horse herd vigilantly. Even the old men kept their weapons close at hand, because at a time like this the camp might need their protection from enemy attack.

As each day passed and the men did not return, those left

behind worried more. "They must have gone very far," people said.

"Maybe they are all dead now," some woman wailed, and others tried to comfort her: "They will all come back with horses and maybe new war honors. They are brave men. Brave men must do this."

That was true. It was the custom of The People as well as of their enemies. That was why there were always more women than men, because sometimes brave men died proving their courage.

But all these eager, fierce, ambitious young men came back one morning at dawn, stripped to their breech clouts, their faces painted black for victory, their bodies painted. They came in triumph, singing and brandishing their weapons, and driving thirty captured horses ahead of them through the camp. Hearing the triumph song, everyone in camp came running to praise them and sing with them. They had not got away without a fight, and they had lost some of the horses, but they had done very well.

That night there was a feast in their honor, and each one told his story. Running Wolf had the most impressive:

"I saw this fine spotted horse in the moonlight, picketed by a lodge, so I knew it was the best horse of whatever man owned it. I crept between the lodges and cut the picket rope with my knife. The skirt of the lodge was rolled up a little for air, and as I leaped onto the horse a man came out yelling. He jumped up on the horse with his knife in his hand. I hit him with my bow. I counted coup on him! He tried to stab me, but he only cut me along the ribs under my left arm. Then I knocked him off and rode fast to catch up with my friends. Some of the Crows caught up with us, shooting arrows, but we all got away."

The other men who had been with him said, "Yes, it is

true." One of them had glimpsed Running Wolf hitting the enemy with his bow, while he himself was speeding by on a captured horse.

So Running Wolf had covered himself with honor. He had done a brave thing, taking a picketed horse in an enemy camp. He had struck an armed enemy with his hand: he had counted coup, an important coup, because it was very dangerous. That entitled him to wear an eagle feather in the back of his hair, a feather standing up because it was first coup. No other of the party had struck that particular enemy. And of course he was entitled to have his eagle feather dyed red at the tip because he had been wounded.

Running Wolf was on his way to becoming famous for his bravery and his good luck. All his relatives and friends were proud of him.

The women of Eagle Walks' lodge admired the horses that Running Wolf had captured. Fine horses, lots of horses! Running Wolf was especially proud of the gaudy pinto, with great splotches of black on white.

"That was some man's best war horse, all right," Running Wolf boasted. "He was tethered right by a lodge."

Grey Bull agreed. "He will be your best war horse now."

Crow Woman covered her mouth with her hand in token of astonishment. "I know that horse!" she exclaimed. "He was a colt when I saw him before, five winters ago. He was the property of the bad man I was married to. I will not even speak the man's name."

There was great excitement at that.

"I think that man will come looking for his fine pinto war horse," Crow Woman remarked. "He has a terrible temper, and losing that horse has made him very angry. He will come to get it." She added grimly, "I would like to see that man again."

Running Wolf, triumphant enough to promise anything, told her, laughing, "When he comes, I will give him to you."

Eagle Walks asked her with a curious smile, "What will you do with him?"

Crow Woman considered. "First I will show him how happy I am as the wife of Eagle Walks, as a woman of The People. After that—I will think about it."

The old grandmother, Earth Medicine, cackled with laughter. "There is a true woman of the Lakotas!"

The time came, only a few days later. There was no doubt that the Crows would retaliate, because they had lost many horses and two men. Besides, they took pride in being the most cunning and successful horse-stealers of all the Western tribes, and they could not forget an insult like this from the Lakotas. The man whose name Crow Woman would not speak had plenty of help in the return raid.

Every night a strong guard of young men and boys was assigned to watch over the horse herd and the lodges of the people, but they stayed out of sight, waiting to trap the enemy. The best horses of the fighting men were picketed beside their lodges, and Running Wolf used the pinto as special bait. That horse was easy to identify even in the dark.

In the daytime the night guards slept under shady lean-to's and other boys rode among the horse herd, always vigilant. The council sent *akícitas* to watch for enemy smoke from the hills. Women and children did not go far from camp when they searched for vegetable roots to dig or when they brought back water.

But the attack was expected at night, and that was when it came. There was distant yelling from the direction of the horse herd. Every man who was in his lodge leaped from his bed, seized his weapons, and ran out. Every man, that is, except Running Wolf. He lay holding one end of the pinto's rope, suspecting that in the excitement the Crow owner would come through the darkness and try to get the horse. The bottom of the lodge cover was turned up to let in air.

When Running Wolf felt the expected sharp tug on the rope and heard the pinto move, he rolled out with his knife in his hand. The Crow was already on the pinto's back. Running Wolf leaped up and grabbed him, pulling him to the ground. They slashed at each other, yelling and struggling. Both got a few knife cuts, nothing serious, before Running Wolf knocked the wind out of his enemy and tied his hands with the horse rope. Then he remembered to count coup in a loud shout: "I, Running Wolf, have struck him!" He had a first coup. The Crow tried to trip him, so Running Wolf tied his feet together, too, in spite of his struggles.

Nobody got any more sleep that night. The Crows, who had sneaked up on the herd, made off with five horses, each of which had to carry double, but there were two Crows who would never ride again, and some wounded among those who escaped. They had to leave behind two captives, for another man besides Running Wolf had captured one of the enemy, who was yanked off a horse and hit his head on a rock. The village counted five men wounded, but they would recover.

The Sioux won that battle, by a scant margin. Two warriors brought in scalps from the dead Crows and gave them to their sisters as presents, to carry on thin poles like small, ragged banners at the victory dance.

When Running Wolf came swaggering back to the lodge to be praised and have his knife slashes washed, Crow Woman was placidly nursing her little boy.

"I have a man tied up for you," he said with a broad smile. "I don't know whether he is the right one. He's an ugly fellow."

48

"Yes, thank you. He is. I heard his voice. Please leave him out there to worry for a while. Don't let him die. Give him water—if he begs for it."

The captive Crow never did beg for it, so he did not get it. He lay in the hot sun until the sun was high. Then, at Crow Woman's suggestion, two men dragged him to the center of the camp circle and tied him to a post. They tied the other captive with him, back to back. Everybody came out to stare at them, but nobody touched them. Children looked at them and ran away, shrieking with delight.

In mid-afternoon, when the captives had had plenty of time to worry and be thirsty, the whole camp turned out to see what Crow Woman was going to do with the man whose name she would not speak. A kind of procession formed, with her leading it.

She looked very handsome. She wore the most beautiful and valuable dress in the whole camp, borrowed from Earth Medicine, who had treasured it since she was a young woman. The dress was of pure white buckskin with many fringes, a deep yoke of dyed porcupine quills—their colors faded after all these years—and decorated with hundreds of elk teeth. An elk has only two of the big teeth called tusks, but Earth Medicine's men relatives had been mighty hunters and had given her all those teeth to sew on the dress.

Crow Woman wore white moccasins, low cut as the Lakota women wore them, not knee-high like the Crows. She had a knife in a beaded scabbard at her belt, and she held her little boy, Runs-in-Timber, by the hand. He toddled along, big enough now to walk pretty well.

She paraded back and forth in front of the man whose name she would not speak. Now and then she spoke to him in their own language, sneering, and sometimes he grumbled an

49

answer. Then she handed over Runs-in-Timber to another woman so as to leave her own hands free.

The crowd waited with considerable excitement to see what she would do next. Someone handed her a small torch of burning weeds, and everyone said, "Ah!" She strolled up to the man and looked him over carefully, scorching him just a little, scaring him so that he jerked his head back. Then she laughed and threw down the torch.

She marched back and forth with her knife in her hand, threatening, while he tensed his muscles. But she only scratched him with it on the cheek. All the time she was talking Crow.

Then she turned to the crowd and said in Lakota, "Now all women do as I do." As they crowded forward, she spit in his face.

The other women came yelling, crowding, but got themselves into a line and each one spit in his face.

When that was finished, she picked up a piece of horse dropping and said, "Now children do as I do." She threw it at him. The children went shrieking and scrambling to pick up horse droppings.

Finally she stopped them. "Now," she said in Lakota, "I will send him back to his own people, with the other man to tell about it." That was the real turn of the knife—he was utterly disgraced, and he wouldn't even be able to lie about it. The crowd laughed, although a few people were disappointed that she was going to let the two men go.

"But first, I don't want them to be too warm on their long journey." She beckoned to Running Wolf and said, "His clothes are not very good, but don't you want to keep them? Moccasins, too."

The men of her lodge stripped the two captives stark

naked while the women jeered insults, and took their moccasins away. Then they untied the two men and yelled, "Run! Run!"

A couple of *akícitas* on horseback, using whips, hastened their departure.

Old Earth Medicine embraced her daughter-in-law, laughing until she almost cried. "You are a true Lakota, daughter," she crowed. "I couldn't have done better myself! My elktooth dress is yours to keep. I am not going to need it any more."

She was so tired from the excitement that Eagle Walks carried her in his arms back to her bed in the lodge. She lay there chuckling. Suddenly she became serious.

"Many Bones, I do not use my digging stick any more, and it is a good one. You can have it. And my bay horse and my buckskin horse. No, the buckskin is small, he is better for my granddaughter, Whirlwind. Many Bones can have the fine grey instead. The black one—that is for Crow Woman."

She went on, dividing up her belongings among her women relatives, and they thanked her, worrying. She said, "I am well and happy, but I am old. So I give away these things now."

She ate a good supper that night, laughing and joking and —because she was Grandmother Earth Medicine—scolding now and then.

She went to bed early but awakened when the last of the family came home after the victory dance that night. Those whose bed places were nearest to hers heard her chuckle before she slept again. They heard her quiet breathing.

She never woke.

"She knew!" Many Bones exclaimed in the morning. "But how could she know?" She burst into loud wails of grief.

People came running to see what was wrong, to help the bereaved family. Women took the children away to their own lodges, even Whirlwind, who wanted to stay.

All the relatives of Earth Medicine came to help, parceling out their own small children to friends. Eagle Walks sat outside the lodge with his head bowed and did not speak to anyone. He was remembering his mother and how good she had been to him when he was a little boy, how proud she had been as he grew up and brought honor to the family. After a while he went with other men to build her funeral place on a high hill. They erected four stout forked posts. On these they built a stout platform 'of branches, high enough so that wild animals could not reach it.

Back in the lodge, the women unpacked the rawhide parfleches that held Earth Medicine's possessions. She should be dressed in her finest dress, but she had given it to Crow Woman. Crow Woman, weeping, tried to make them use it, crying, "She was good to me!" but they soothed her and refused. There was another beautiful fringed dress for Earth Medicine to wear on her last journey. Many years had passed since she had cared to put on her finery for ceremonies. Her younger relatives did not even know what she had.

"Look," said Many Bones. "She even made her own spirit moccasins to wear!" There they were, carefully packed, fine new moccasins with beaded soles. They were never meant for walking on the earth, but only for the last journey along the Spirit Trail, the Milky Way along the stars, to the Land of Many Lodges.

When she was dressed and her thin grey hair was brushed and braided, they had to call her son, Eagle Walks, because nobody else knew how her face should be painted. She was entitled to marks of honor for her accomplishments in quilling and lodge-making and for the achievements of her husband, dead for many years. Eagle Walks knelt beside her and applied the paints properly, with a red streak along the parting of her hair. Then he went out of the lodge again.

The women placed her beaded awl case beside her, and her knife, worn thin and stubby from much use, and her sewing materials. Then they gently lifted the body and wrapped it in a fine silky buffalo robe, with a tanned skin around that, all tied securely with leather thongs.

Earth Medicine's son, Eagle Walks, and her relatives hacked off some of their hair to show their grief, even her daughters-in-law, even Crow Woman who was one of The People only by marriage-adoption—and she had beautiful hair. For four days they mourned the dead woman, now only a hide-wrapped bundle alone in the lodge. They marched around the camp circle, singing grief songs, or sat under the empty platform where she would lie. One of the *wicasas*, or subchiefs, visited the mourners carrying a ceremonial pipe and advised them sympathetically to work as well as to mourn. The men should hunt and the women should make moccasins or do quill embroidery.

After the four days, older women carried the hide-wrapped bundle out of the lodge, placed it on a pony drag, and transported it to the scaffold that had been built for it. Eagle Walks led the procession, leading a horse that had been his mother's favorite. This one she had not given away. He had painted the white horse with red blotches and covered it with a robe.

Women pulled and pushed the wrapped bundle onto the high platform and tied it there firmly. Eagle Walks' best friend, Kills-at-Night, who had been selected for this honor, then spoke to the horse:

"Friend, your owner liked you very much and now she wants you with her in the Land of Many Lodges. Go joyfully."

He killed the horse with one arrow shot. Then he cut off the tail and fastened it to the top of one of the poles that held the platform. Eagle Walks thanked him and gave him the robe that had been on the horse.

Little Whirlwind watched all this with awe. As the mourners trudged back to the camp, she asked her mother, "But where has Grandmother gone?"

"It is a fine place where she will be happy, with no aches or pains any more. There are the lodges of all her ancestors and friends. There is no end to the good hunting and the fine feasts. There is always abundance of everything good. Everything that ever lived will live there forever, in the Land of Many Lodges."

She did not tell her daughter yet that the spirit must, on the starry road, pass the scrutiny of Tate, the Wind, before being judged by Skan, the Sky. Earth Medicine had been a good woman and would be judged worthy, she was sure.

When the camp moved, they left her there under the sky, Earth Medicine, who was so old she could remember when The People did not have horses but only dogs and their own bowed backs to carry their few belongings.

Part III

SUMMER, 1830

Visit to the Wasichus

Living in the Lodge:

Eagle Walks, 46, head of the family
Many Bones Woman, 35, his wife
Whirlwind Girl, 10, their daughter
Sun Goes Down, almost 6, their son
Covers Up, 3, their son
Crow Woman, wife of Eagle Walks, age untold
Runs-in-Timber, 6, their son
Pemmican Girl, their infant daughter
Running Wolf, 20, nephew of Many Bones Woman
Pushes Ahead, 25, a young man from another band

Chapter 7

The lodge of Eagle Walks housed a big family in the spring when Whirlwind's life had counted ten winters. There were ten persons, five of them children; three hunters; only two women, who had a great deal of work to do. By good fortune, a strong, pretty young woman named Butterfly spent most of her time there and was a great deal of help. She had sisters and was not needed at home, and she had a good reason to help in the lodge of Eagle Walks, because a young man who lived there was courting her.

This was a romance that delighted the other grownups in the lodge. Whirlwind did not know exactly why. The young man, Pushes Ahead, was from another band. He had admired Butterfly so much when he saw her at the last sun-gazing gathering that he decided to join her band. Any family would have been glad to have him—a well-behaved, ambitious man, a successful hunter, one who could boast of war honors.

Oglala girls were so carefully chaperoned that he could not possibly live with Butterfly's family, but there was no reason why he should not live in the home of Eagle Walks—and no reason why Butterfly should not visit there every day to help Eagle Walks' women with their work and to show off her own skills in homemaking.

She seldom looked at Pushes Ahead or spoke to him, whereas he smiled and stared at her often; it was proper for a young man to be bold. While he built a reputation as a good provider, generous and brave, among her people, she tanned hides and sewed and cooked and dried meat, building a reputation as a candidate for wife of such a man. They were never alone together. Butterfly had a chaperon even when she went to bring water; one of her sisters came with her to the lodge in the morning, and one of Whirlwind's mothers walked with her when she returned to her own home at the end of the day. She was a quiet girl, often smiling, strong and skilled. Everybody liked her.

Even with her help, the two wives of Eagle Walks kept busy. Whirlwind had two full brothers, Sun Goes Down, almost six, and Covers Up, who was three. Runs-in-Timber, her half brother, was a few moons older than Sun Goes Down, but they were inseparable in games and fights and lessons. (And they had rigorous lessons with their first bows and in races that made them strong and swift.) Crow Woman had a new baby, Pemmican Girl.

Little Covers Up was everybody's problem. At three, he was not a baby, but he was far too young to keep up with the six-year-olds. They were always escaping from him while he howled in rage. Whirlwind took on the responsibility of trying to keep him happy. Her girl friends had small brothers for him to squabble with, and all the girls were accustomed to keeping an eye on small children.

The lodge was a busy place. There was plenty of meat, plenty of hides to tan, and somebody was always needing new moccasins. The children seldom outgrew them—they wore them out too fast. Covers Up was still so small that he wore no clothing in good weather, only moccasins to protect his feet.

With meat from the successful efforts of three hunters, there was plenty to give to poor people, and the young men earned admiration by their generosity.

Grey Bull had been married now for two years, and with his wife lived in a separate lodge, with some relatives, but they were still close friends, almost family.

As long as there was snow, the children went coasting on sleds made of buffalo brisket kept in the right shape by the strong cords in the animal's neck. After a sled had been broken in with use, its laughing rider could go like the wind down a steep slope.

As the snow melted, women ventured farther out from camp to search for greens to serve as salad or to cook with meat. Whirlwind and her girl friends imitated their mothers and were proud when they found more than their elders did.

The children had sharp eyes for birds' nests, too. They

were proud to take home, very carefully, eggs of wild ducks, cranes, and magpies to be boiled. The girls tried to dodge the boys when they went egg hunting. When men went hunting, they smoked a ceremonial pipe and explained to the spirits of the animals why they must do this—to keep The People alive. Little boys on nest-hunting expeditions smoked a pretend pipe with the proper ceremony but tended to get into arguments that broke eggs.

Their band camped for a while near the base of a cliff where the children enjoyed playing among old buffalo bones. Once an old man, grandfather of some of them, went with them to the top and told them why the bones were down below:

"See those long lines of stones that narrow to a V at the edge of the cliff? Our grandfathers killed buffalo here long ago, before our people had horses. Men in wolf skins would stand along the lines of stones, and other men, behind the herd, would scare the buffalo and stampede them between the rows of wolf-men until they plunged over the edge. The buffalo would break their necks or their legs, and the men and women down below would kill and butcher them and leave the bones there. It is better now when we chase the buffalo on horseback!"

The children spent much of their time on horseback, except those who were still too little, like three-year-old Covers Up. When the camp moved, he had to ride in a basket with the latest litter of puppies between the poles of a pony drag. Moving camp was always an exciting time. Whirlwind had her own small play lodge. She was not yet strong enough to be of much help to her mothers when they dismantled the family lodge and pitched it again in the new camping place, but she could take down her own in a hurry, roll the cover into a tight bundle, fasten the small poles to be dragged by a horse, and put it all together again at the end of the journey.

One day she was carrying a baby in his cradleboard for a woman who simply had too many things to keep track of. Whirlwind and two other little girls were riding on top of the packs on packhorses, with the cradleboard hanging on a projection of the packsaddle. The three decided to race to the nearest tree, quite far away. The race was not fast, but it was bumpy, and when they got to the tree Whirlwind shrieked, "I've dropped the baby somewhere!"

They turned back, riding as fast as they could go, frightened and frantic—and found the cradleboard on the ground with the baby sleeping peacefully. After that they rode very sedately, and none of them ever told anybody about temporarily losing that baby.

Another time that summer Whirlwind was on top of the packs again during another move, dawdling along because the pack mare was old and not interested in running races. This time, through no fault of her own, she tangled with a moving herd of buffalo, running from her right straight across her path. Most of her band had already reached the stopping place. The herd had emerged suddenly from a valley. The *akícitas* and some of the other men were alert to scare the herd away from camp by waving robes and yelling if it turned that way, but it did not swerve, and the huge shaggy beasts came so suddenly that Whirlwind could not turn back, because the herd was wider at the back than at the front and would engulf her. She quirted the old mare until her arm hurt as she tried to ride across in front of the coming herd. But the herd closed around her, and the mare swerved to the left and ran with them—she couldn't do anything else.

A buffalo bull shoved from the right with his great body, and the pack began to turn on the mare's back. Whirlwind threw her weight in the other direction, but she was too light to keep the pack from slipping farther. Suddenly, in the dust and uproar of pounding hoofs, the mare stopped—and Whirlwind went flying over her head. She had been too scared to realize that her father and another man had been riding with the herd ever since they saw her predicament, working the mare over to the thin edge of it. Her father cast a loop in a rawhide rope over the mare's head, stopped her, and scooped up Whirlwind from the ground with one hand.

A friend of Whirlwind's, the same age as she, was not so lucky during another move. Her horse suddenly went crazy, scared by the buzz of a rattlesnake, and dragged her, head down, through a big patch of prickly pear cactus. An *akícita* roped the horse and picked up the little girl. The whole moving village stopped. Women pitched a lodge to keep the sun off the suffering child—her body was swelling from the thousands of cactus spines in it—but she died before they could give her any comfort.

Sometimes boys and girls of Whirlwind's age group played together quite peaceably, but mostly they squabbled and sometimes even fought. Little girls, playing house with their own miniature lodges and looking after babies assigned to them, might have their small play camp attacked by little boys riding in at a gallop on their ponies. The girls defended camp angrily with clubs. Or the boys might surprise them by bringing in small game, like rabbits, and yelling, "Cook a meal, you lazy women!"

The girls took pride in their skill in skinning and cooking such offerings while the boys sat around looking lordly and superior—more so than their fathers did at home.

All this was part of schooling for children, but school for the boys was harder. Groups of them were assigned to old-men advisers who lectured them constantly on behavior for warriors and hunters. They swam in icy water. They ran until exhausted—and then ran some more. After a hunt, when there was lots of meat on the drying racks, boys were sent out to steal some, thereby learning stealth that might save their lives a few years later. A teacher would hold out a branch covered with soft bark and tell a boy to bite it. If he took a big bite, he promised to bring back a big piece of stolen meat, in spite of watchful dogs and wakeful people. A small bite was a smaller promise. Those who returned successfully could boast about their experiences. Those who were caught would be shamed by their captors—to remind them to be more stealthy next time.

Their teachers tested their fortitude under pain. A dried sunflower seed placed on a boy's wrist and lighted burned his skin and made a sore. If he did not flinch, he could boast about the small scar. If he said, "Ow!" the others jeered and called him a woman.

Groups of small boys fought by throwing chunks of mud with willow sticks. Big boys played a serious game that was a battle except that nobody got killed. Naked except for their breech clouts, the way warriors rode, they charged each other on horseback, yelling as their horses collided, rearing and screaming. Riders tussled with each other, and those who fell off were counted dead. When one side had no warriors left, the game was over.

And constantly they improved their marksmanship with bows and arrows.

Whirlwind was glad to be a girl.

Her most exciting adventure came in the fall. The men in the lodge had hunted well, had made much meat, and her mothers and Butterfly had tanned a great many fine furs. Whirlwind felt satisfaction that she had helped by looking after the younger children and doing a great many other things to free her mothers for more useful work. The whole camp was prosperous.

A rumor spread that a party of the men would take some of those fine hides and small, warm furs to a trading post to buy wonderful things. The rumor became fact. Whirlwind's father was one of those who would go. A young woman relative of hers was going, too, with her husband, because she was free, having no children yet, and adventuresome and would be a big help with the cooking and other camp work along the way. Her name was Begins Early.

When Eagle Walks told his household the details of the plans, he asked Many Bones Woman, "What do you want from the trading post?"

"Red cloth for a dress," she answered, with longing in her voice. There had been some cloth dresses on other Oglala women at the sun-gazing gathering. "And an awl of iron for sewing. And a new axe. And maybe some beads?"

"We'll see," her husband answered solemnly. Then he asked Crow Woman, "What do you want from the trading post?"

"Bright blue cloth for a dress," she answered promptly. "And a good knife. And a new iron kettle if we can afford it, because the old one has a crack in it that we can't mend."

"We'll see," Eagle Walks replied. Then he turned to his daughter, Whirlwind: "And what do you want, my good little girl?"

"I want to go with you, Father," she answered promptly. "If I can go along, I can be happy without presents."

"Go with me?" He sounded shocked, and he was, but he got over it. "It will be a hard trip for a little girl," he warned, "but otherwise I see nothing much wrong with the idea."

"I see very much wrong with it!" Many Bones Woman exclaimed. She was a calm person, but like any self-respect-ing Sioux woman she said what she thought. She proceeded to tell why this was a bad idea. She gave a dozen good reasons, speaking firmly and loudly, and when she ran out of reasons she started all over at the beginning. By that time, Eagle Walks had his hands over his ears and was laughing, his daughter's mouth and eyes were wide open, and Crow Woman was shivering with terror, because Many Bones had never made such a fuss about anything before.

Having talked herself out, Many Bones felt better. She put her hands on her little girl's shoulders and looked into her face and said, "Just the same, you can go, and your father will take care of you, and you will be a good girl and do exactly what you're told."

Then she turned, slipped out through the lodge doorway, and walked away with great dignity to spread the news that little Whirlwind was going to the trading post.

The horseback journey of eight days was miserably uncomfortable. The sun never came out from behind clouds. It rained most of the time, and although the grownups built a lean-to each night to keep the rain off, they were wet as they rode. They rode fast all day, careful to keep the fire in their small iron pot from being extinguished. Sometimes it was hard to find dry firewood, and they ate pemmican or half-cooked fresh meat.

The men grumbled, the woman murmured sometimes, but Whirlwind was as happy as a meadowlark in the spring. When she wasn't happy, she kept it to herself. Most of the time she pretended she was a big boy going with a horse-stealing party of warriors as their water boy. She rode her own pony and led a packhorse. She gathered firewood and carried water and helped Begins Early dress out an antelope that one of the men brought down with an arrow.

As they neared the big river and could see the buildings of

the Frenchmen's trading post, surrounded by a stout palisade of heavy posts standing on end, the whole party felt better. The sun came out from behind a cloud. One of the men, in sudden good humor, remarked, "It is a good thing we brought two women along. The traders will know we come in peace."

Whirlwind hardly heard the compliment of being called a woman. She was staring at the palisade and the log buildings inside. She had never seen permanent buildings before in her life. Her people had none; they moved camp very often.

How, she wondered, do they keep their camp clean if they never move it? She found out soon that they didn't keep it clean. It was dirty and smelled bad. The white men simply didn't know how to live, she concluded.

The whole party rode back and forth in front of the closed gate, yelling greetings, so the wary traders could look them over, see they were not dressed for war, see they had pack-horses and pony drags piled high with furs and robes to trade.

The gate opened, and two men came out, carrying guns but making the sign for peace, and the visitors made the same sign. Then there were loud greetings, and they were allowed to come partway inside, while the Sioux and the traders alike shouted "*How, kola!*"—Greetings, friend.

That was how Whirlwind saw white men for the first time. She remembered that her grandmother had described them as dirty, with hair all over their faces. Whirlwind agreed completely. Sioux men did not have much hair on their faces, and they pulled the hairs out, one by one, because they wanted to look nice.

These were French Canadian traders, with Indian wives if they had women; some of the traders were part Indian. They talked the sign language that all the Plains tribes knew, and a little of several Indian tongues. Among themselves they spoke very fast in another language, French.

What the traders wore fascinated her. All of them had shirts like her father's, made of soft buckskin, fringed and decorated, but two or three wore long pants made of heavy cloth, and these were like nothing she had seen before, because although they had separate places for the legs, the garment was all in one piece. Men of her people, when cold weather required so much clothing, wore long leggings but these were separate, covered and made decent at the top with a breech clout. Whirlwind shook her head in amazement. What peculiar people these were! They didn't do anything right.

Her people made good trading at the fort, each man keeping track of the furs that were his and those that belonged to his brother or his friend, and how much in furs he had to pay for every knife or axe or kettle or piece of cloth he bought and who had ordered it.

Whirlwind took the greatest pleasure in helping her father choose the beautiful red cloth for her mother, the beautiful blue cloth for her other mother, and all the other things they wanted. He himself bought a gun, and lead balls and powder for this dangerous thing, and pretty things for all his children, and a handsome red blanket to wear when he dressed up. Then he picked up something that frightened Whirlwind when he showed it to her, smiling. It was flat and smooth, and when she looked at it, a little girl with mussed black braids looked back.

She wanted to throw it away, as a magic thing and probably dangerous, but The People are brave, and she faintly remembered seeing something like it before, only smaller.

Her father wasn't afraid of it. He laughed at her. "That is you," he said. "But when I hold it this way, it is me. When your mothers look in it, they will see themselves."

"How much nicer than a pond of water!" she exclaimed. "With that, you can put on your paint so it comes out just right on both sides of your face!"

He bought the small mirror and packed it very carefully because it was easy to break.

The trader-men, some of whom had part-Indian children of their own, were amused by Whirlwind. She refused to play with the other children—she couldn't waste her time that way; there was too much to see and learn. She clung to the fringes of her tall father's leggings and when one of the strange men came near, she ducked behind Eagle Walks for safety, but kept on staring. She was careful every minute to be a *very* good girl. When she sat down beside Begins Early to wait for her father to conclude a transaction in sign language, she even sat like a lady, with her knees bent and both feet together toward the right. Her mothers often chided her for sitting any old way, with legs crossed or feet straight out in front of her, the way boys and men sat, or women who were scorned as having no reputation.

One of the trader men, older than the others, sometimes got tired and sat down on a strange contraption that to Whirlwind looked uncomfortable. It was made of poles, cut short and tied with rawhide, and it had a flat seat of rawhide. She couldn't keep from staring at him. He leaned back against the short poles—surely nowhere near as good as the comfortable backrests in the lodge at home—with his knees bent and his feet on the floor.

She whispered, "Father, what is that and why does he sit that way?"

"It is their custom," Eagle Walks said, and asked the man in sign talk for the name of the thing.

"Shez," the old man said. "Shez. Oo see-ezh, see-ezh." [In French, *chaise* or *siege*.] He stood up and bowed, gesturing toward the object, inviting her to sit. Whirlwind looked up at her father for permission. He picked her up, smiling, and seated her in the crude chair. How uncomfortable, with her feet hanging down and no nice limber backrest as on her bed at home! She slid down and hid behind her father again.

The trade ended with everybody satisfied. The trader-men even bought the extra packhorses. There were plenty of fine things to load onto the horses that remained—blankets, guns, ammunition, cloth for dresses for many women, sashes for many men, beads and paints and dyes, metal tools and knives and axes, very expensive, very useful. These were all things that the Indians could not make at all or, in the case of coloring materials, could not make so well. They bought small sheets of iron for the making of sharp, lethal arrow-heads.

The traders made a feast for them in farewell, to encourage them to come back. For the first time in her life, Whirlwind tasted rough brown sweet lumps of sugar, bread (which she did not care for very much—but by this time she was homesick for the cooking back in her parents' lodge), strong black hot liquid called *cah*-fay, and plenty of salt on her meat.

Her people liked seasoning and strong flavors—buffalo gall on raw buffalo liver was good—but they seldom found salt springs and did not expect to have salt all the time. Eagle Walks bought some chunks of salt to take home, and one of the traders warned him to keep it protected in a parfleche box so it would not get wet.

There was rain all the way back to camp—which they had no trouble finding, although it had moved to a new place— but nobody grumbled. The trading party rode into camp yelling and showing off, almost like victorious warriors. Everybody was happy.

The things Whirlwind remembered most vividly about that journey were the foolish man who liked to sit in his uncomfortable shez instead of on the ground, like sensible people, and the great treats of sugar and plenty of salt.

Part IV

SPRING AND SUMMER, 1833

The Buffalo Maiden

Living in the Lodge:

Eagle Walks, 49, head of the family
Many Bones Woman, 38, his wife
Whirlwind Girl, 13, their daughter
Sun Goes Down, 9, their son
Covers Up, 6, their son
Crow Woman, wife of Eagle Walks, age untold
Runs-in-Timber, 9, her son by Eagle Walks
Pemmican Girl, 3, her daughter by Eagle Walks
Running Wolf, 23, nephew of Many Bones Woman
Swims Under, 15, an adopted youth

Chapter 8

The people who lived in the lodge of Eagle Walks changed
from year to year, as children were born, relatives moved out
because of marriage or because of death or divorce of a husband or wife. When Whirlwind was thirteen, the lodge
housed three hunters—her father, her cousin Running Wolf
(who was courting two or three girls and would probably

marry and set up his own lodge before long) and a fifteen-year-old orphan youth named Swims Under. He was a fine boy, and half a dozen families wanted him, but Eagle Walks needed him because there were many mouths to feed in his lodge. Pushes Ahead had moved out when he married Butterfly and they set up their own home, but they visited often and were the best of friends.

Whirlwind was still a little girl who played girl games, but she was ready to become a woman, even though it meant being more dignified and remembering always to sit like a lady. She already spent much time doing skilled women's work with her two mothers. When the time came, there would be a great ceremony in her honor. Not all girls could have the Buffalo Maiden ceremony. It was expensive because many gifts had to be given. Her father had promised it, though, and he could afford it—he had plenty of horses to give away, and her mothers and aunts had been tanning and sewing and embroidering for a year now.

Sometimes her mother, Many Bones, exasperated at her hoydenish ways, reminded her, "When you are a woman, especially a Buffalo Woman, your manners will have to improve. You won't chatter so much, and do be careful not to stare at boys or men who might marry you because you're not related. You must not stare into the eyes of other people, either, even your best friend. I keep telling you it's rude. And don't sit that way. Sit like a lady."

The fact was that she had practiced sitting, with two or three friends, when they were minding babies out of sight of camp. They had practiced so much that they could do it perfectly, sinking as gracefully as a butterfly to a flower, sitting with both feet modestly to one side, and rising just as gracefully, never touching the ground with their hands. But they didn't do it at home. They were saving this lovely skill to surprise their families when the right time came, when they changed from little girls to young women old enough to be courted.

When the change came to Whirlwind she was not shocked or puzzled, because her mother had warned her what to expect. She said quietly to Many Bones Woman, "It is time for me to go to the little lodge," and Many Bones hugged her.

Near the family lodge was a special small one to which both her mothers retired at certain times of the moon, because neither was pregnant or nursing a baby. It was dangerous to remain in the home lodge, because who knew what harm might come to a man's weapons and shield and protective medicine if a woman under the moon's influence came near them?

Many Bones Woman proudly took her daughter to the little lodge to remain for four days. Crow Woman brought their food and anything else they needed. The men and boys stayed strictly away, but Eagle Walks began at once to prepare for the Buffalo Sing ceremony to honor his beloved daughter.

He smoked ceremoniously with a medicine-priest who was also a Buffalo Dreamer, for the Buffalo God was the protector of young girls and the patron of the virtues that women should have, such as industry, generosity, and the love of children. They arranged for the day of the ceremony. Eagle Walks invited the families of relatives and friends. Meanwhile Whirlwind's female relatives erected a big ceremonial lodge, decided on the many presents they would bring for the giveaway, and began to prepare a great amount of food.

In the small special lodge, Many Bones spent all the four days teaching her daughter how to embroider with dyed porcupine quills, and Whirlwind worked at it constantly. She already knew, but this teaching was part of the ceremony of becoming a woman. If she applied herself to quilling now, she would always be industrious, a great virtue.

The day before the Buffalo Sing ceremony, the invited guests—some from bands many miles away—came riding in joyfully and set up their lodges near that of Eagle Walks. They visited and drummed and sang and danced until late that night. It was a joyful social occasion.

Whirlwind's mothers and other women dismantled the newly erected ceremonial lodge and set it up again. This drove out any evil influences that might have got in. Eagle Walks built an earth altar in the lodge near the fire, placed a buffalo skull on the altar, and spread sagebrush over it, with the Buffalo Dreamer supervising everything.

Outside the lodge the women built a fire of cottonwood, because this wood chases away Anog Ite, the bad Double-faced Woman, half beautiful and half ugly, who causes bickering. The fire was on the north side of the lodge to guard against another bad spirit, Wazi the Wizard. Many Bones Woman sang a protective song:

> The spirit of the dry wood,
> Those coming are pleased.
> The spirit of the dry wood,
> Wazi is going away.

The Buffalo Dreamer priest was very busy overseeing all these activities to be sure everything was done exactly right. He prayed to Grandfather the Sun and asked the spirit of the West Wind to keep the Winged God, the dangerous Thunderbird, away.

When the Buffalo Dreamer entered the purified ceremonial lodge, he wore a breech clout, leggings, and moccasins. His body and face were painted red. Men and women

72

entered and sat on facing sides of the lodge. The Dreamer carefully placed purifying sweet grass on the fire outside and entered to walk around, peering into the faces of all the guests to see that they were worthy and not evil spirits trying to sneak in.

Eagle Walks brought coals and made a fire by the altar inside. The Dreamer lighted his pipe and blew smoke into the nostril cavities of the buffalo skull. All the guests did the same thing in turn.

Then the dreamer painted the skull's forehead red, placed it reverently on the altar, and sprinkled sweet grass on the fire. With his ceremonial pipe he invoked the Buffalo God and the Four Winds. He sang:

> Buffalo bull in the west lowing,
> Buffalo bull in the west lowing,
> Lowing he speaks.

Now, for the first time, the honored maiden herself appeared. Whirlwind was led in by her mother and sat down where she was told—with her legs crossed, for the last time. Everyone stared at her. This was her day, she was being honored greatly because her parents loved her.

The Buffalo Dreamer, first sprinkling sage on the small fire, banished the evil spirits that might tempt or harm her:

"Iya, go away so that this may not be a lazy woman. Iktomi, go away so this young woman may not do foolish things. Anog Ite, go away so this young woman may not do shameful things. Hohnogica, go away so this young woman may not be troubled when she is a mother."

He spoke directly to Whirlwind: "Do not sit any more as a child sits, because you are now a woman." Her mother arranged her so that she sat modestly with feet and legs together on one side.

She sat with her head bowed as the Buffalo Dreamer walked four times around her, singing explanations, advice, and warnings:

"The Buffalo in the west has sent a messenger. He mentioned a spider, a turtle, the voice of a lark, a brave man, children, a lodge smoking. Now here is the meaning: The spider is an industrious woman who gives her children a home and plenty of food. The turtle is a wise woman. She hears much but says nothing. Her skin is a shield. The lark is a cheerful woman who does not scold.

"If a brave man takes you for his woman, you may sing his scalp song and dance his scalp dance. He will kill plenty of game. You will bear him many children and be happy."

Very solemnly the Buffalo Dreamer continued with admonitions about how she should live as a woman: "Be industrious like the spider, wise like the turtle, cheerful like the lark. Then a brave man will choose you and you will have plenty. You will never be ashamed. But if you listen to the bad gods, you will be lazy and miserable and poor. No brave man or good hunter will even give a dog for you!"

Whirlwind listened and resolved to be good.

The people all sang to the fast pounding of drums and the sound of rattles, briskly shaken. The Dreamer seemed to become a buffalo bull. He pawed the earth and made guttural noises while he danced frantically. He even pushed against her. Her mother, for protection against evil, put sagebrush under her arms and laid some in her lap, so the symbolic buffalo had to stop tempting her.

The Buffalo Dreamer sat down, out of breath for he was an old man, and told her, "That is how the Crazy Buffalo will approach you to tempt you to do things that will make you ashamed. Your mother will show you how to drive away evil things. If you do, a good man will ask for you and pay a high bride price for you, and you will be proud of your children."

Six fine buffalo robes constituted a good bride price. A wife who brought that many could boast about it for the rest of her life.

Among the things the Buffalo Dreamer had brought in and consecrated was a wooden bowl filled with water and buffalo berries. He now offered it to Whirlwind, who drank from it. He drank, and then passed it to the audience.

"Now you will dress like a woman," he commanded. Many Bones Woman helped her daughter take off her dress and laid it on the buffalo skull. A poor woman in the audience called, "Will you give me the old dress?" and it was handed to her.

Whirlwind put on a new dress that her mother had brought. At a signal from the Buffalo Dreamer she sat down —gracefully, all in one motion, as a good woman sits—and her mother arranged her hair the way a woman wears it, parted neatly in the middle and in two braids that hung down in front prettily on her shoulders instead of down the back like a little girl's. While Many Bones was doing this, Whirlwind chewed sage leaves and sweet grass to make her breath sweet. The Buffalo Dreamer painted the parting of her hair red and also her forehead, for red was the sacred color.

The Dreamer chanted loudly: "You are a relative of the Buffalo God. He is pleased with an industrious woman, a generous woman who gives food to the hungry. He will cause brave men to want you, and you may choose the man you want. If he has other wives, you will still be foremost. You will be his sits-beside-him wife and your place will be next to the place of honor at the back of the lodge. The others will carry wood and water while you mend moccasins."

But Whirlwind resolved never to be considered lazy, in spite of the honors to which she was now entitled. She would carry wood and water too, because that was woman's work. She would do her full share.

The Dreamer tied an eagle plume to her hair, giving her the spirit of the eagle and the blessing of the Sun and the South Wind. He handed her a staff of cherry wood, saying, "This will help you find plums and chokecherries to make plenty of pemmican."

He stood away from her and shouted, "You are now a woman. Go forth from this lodge."

So she walked out first, feeling proud but with her eyes lowered for fear she might look into the eyes of a man who might become her husband. She walked out into the bright world a woman, with all the others from the lodge following, cheering and talking and happy.

Her proud father made a speech and gave the Buffalo Dreamer a horse as payment for his work in the ceremony. There were presents for everyone—large robes and small furs and beaded things and embroidered things. Most of them were from her relatives, who called out the names of the recipients, but many were from friends to other friends.

The giveaway was a joyous, noisy, confusing affair. Three or four men and women might all be shouting at once the names of the friends to whom they were giving something. People burst into song, greeted old friends, laughed at jokes. Whirlwind, the honored woman, was always surrounded by well-wishers, the women hugging her and sometimes weeping for joy. Without looking directly at anyone, she was well aware of many men staring at her with admiration. Several of them were distinguished warriors with considerable prestige. More were young and better looking, who had been noticing her even before the ceremony that announced formally that she was now ready to be courted.

She kept reminding herself happily, I can choose for myself among those who may want me. Not many girls have that privilege. How lucky I am to have a family that loves me and will advise me wisely! But not yet. I am not going to choose yet.

The women of her family began to shout, "Come and eat in honor of Whirlwind the Buffalo Maiden!" and people began to move toward the feast. The principal dish was tender boiled puppy, and there were plenty of other good things, too.

The feast and the merriment continued late into the night. All the following day visitors from other bands came to say good-bye and begin the return trip to their homes. They would meet again soon, at the Sun-gazing Dance.

Now that Whirlwind was no longer a little girl, she had to remember to be dignified toward certain people, like grown-up brothers. She had no real brothers older than herself, but her uncle Grey Bull seemed like a brother; Running Wolf, her cousin, was a proved warrior looking around for a wife, and the adopted youth, Swims Under, lived in her lodge. She spoke now to them with less frivolity than before and did not look straight at them any more.

Her family was always pleased when Grey Bull came to call on her father. They smoked the ceremonial pipe together and talked about serious matters, but Grey Bull also played and laughed with the little boys in the lodge, gave them advice about how to shoot straight, and admired the small game they proudly brought home.

At twenty-nine, Grey Bull was one of the outstanding hunters and warriors of his band of Lakotas. He was noticed with approval by the entire tribe at every sun-gazing ceremony. Wise and thoughtful older men sometimes asked his advice when something important had to be decided for the good of the people. He was an ambitious man, on his way up to a position of great responsibility.

Everyone admired his courage. Boys imitated the proud way he walked, the vigor and strength of his dancing at ceremonies, and his great dignity. He had counted coup twenty-six times in battle and as a result was often honored by being asked to take part in ceremonies, such as the painting of a new lodge or the ear-piercing and naming of babies.

When Grey Bull invited men to join a war party that he was going to lead, they accepted, because his medicine was strong and his success was talked about in all the lodges. In council, he was a fine, persuasive orator. He was known for his generosity in giving meat and robes and horses to the poor. Like most Lakotas, he was tall and striking in appearance.

He was successful with women. Young men sometimes paid a high price to a medicine priest for an eagle-bone whistle that carried so much power that a girl, hearing it, could not resist. She felt she had to come out of the lodge to be with the man who courted her with the charmed whistle. But Grey Bull never bothered with a whistle like that. He used an ordinary one, less expensive, and for a long time he courted every pretty girl in the village. Even those best protected by their parents, most closely chaperoned, stepped outside their homes when they thought he was there—several men might be blowing whistles at the same time, lined up out there—and went to him, let him wrap his blanket around them, and stood and talked for a while.

But he never made an offer for any of them, and they married other men. Grey Bull ran away with a girl from a

Brulé camp and took her home with him, causing great distress among her relatives. She was a good girl, industrious and well behaved, but he did not give any horses for her, and she came without any dowry of lodge or furnishings or pretty clothes. His own women relatives provided what was needed for the couple to set up housekeeping. They were startled by his boldness and rather proud of him. There was a man!

Chapter 9

Everything Grey Bull undertook turned out well for him—until he went out to seek a vision in the spring when he was twenty-nine years old, because he was ambitious. He wanted the additional spirit power that another successful vision quest would give him. He had gone out on a hill for a vision twice before, receiving power both times.

He went humbly to a holy man named Cottonwood, carrying a filled pipe, and asked his help: "I want to lament and pray to the Great Mystery. Will you send your voice for me to the Powers?"

Cottonwood was pleased to be asked. They went into the open space in the camp circle and the holy man made the announcement, with a ceremonial prayer to all the Powers. Many men came out of their lodges and sat in a circle on the ground while Cottonwood prayed again, and they took turns smoking the pipe ceremonially. The holy man announced the day on which Grey Bull would go to seek his vision.

When the selected day came, Grey Bull went to the holy man's lodge, carrying his sacred pipe and wearing only a breech clout, a buffalo robe, and moccasins. "Be merciful to me and help me," he implored. "I want to lament on the hill for three days."

Cottonwood gave him solemn instructions and warnings. First he must build a sweat lodge in which to purify himself, with every detail of the ceremony carried out exactly right. A few other men took part in this ritual of prayers, sweating, and purification, during which water was poured on heated rocks to make steam in the tiny dome-shaped lodge. Cottonwood prayed to all the Powers, over and over asking their aid for this suppliant who came to them in humility, seeking wisdom and help.

When that was finished, Grey Bull left the sweat lodge first, crying pitifully to the Powers everywhere. Three horses were ready, two of them loaded with paraphernalia for the lamenting on the hill, and Grey Bull, wailing constantly, rode the third. The old holy man and a helper walked with him to the faraway mountain Cottonwood had chosen.

Grey Bull stayed at the base of it, weeping and praying, while the other two climbed to a place that they made sacred for him. They set up five tall poles with offerings tied at the tops. One pole was the center, the others to the west, north, east, and south. They made a bed of sage where Grey Bull could lie down with his head against the center pole and his feet toward the east. Then they went down to tell him that everything was ready.

He took off his moccasins and even his breech clout, to be naked and poor before the Powers everywhere, and climbed the mountain carrying only his pipe and the buffalo robe he would need at night.

He cried out constantly, "Great Mystery, be merciful to me that my people may live!" He prayed at the center, at the western pole, returned to the center and prayed, slowly walked to the north, and so on, always lamenting, crying for

80

mercy, humbling himself, as always returning to the center.

By evening he was very tired but alert to everything—winds and sounds and living creatures and changes in the light, for anything might have a message for him. He was also very thirsty. He would not eat or drink during the whole time of his lamenting. He cried until his voice was feeble. Then he lay down on the bed of sage and covered himself with the buffalo robe, because the night was cold. It was all right to sleep when he could, because the vision might come whether he was awake or asleep.

On the second night he was in misery from thirst and light-headed and dizzy from hunger and fear of the Powers. He continued to lament and pray, feeling very humble indeed before the vastness and mystery and unknown terrors of the universe. He was more afraid than he had ever been in battle, because in a battle one fights living men, but he was now subject to unpredictable powers and he could not fight. He could only cry and pray for help. He heard strange sounds and sometimes sneering voices that threatened him. A sudden storm came up when the night was blackest, and the Thunder Beings roared and flashed. There was heavy hail, but none of it touched him although he had nothing to shelter him from the sky. In the morning he saw hail in little drifts outside the sacred spot where he prayed—but none inside.

"Something holy has happened here!" he exclaimed, and cried out again to all the Powers.

He was lamenting at the center pole, facing west, when the first part of his vision came. Suddenly he could see his home village, although the mountain was between it and him and it was miles away. He could see far beyond the village, even, to a valley where two men were hunting buffalo. Close to him, all around him, he heard dogs barking. He was overcome with terror so that he had to hold fast to the center pole to keep from falling. Because the dog was one of the *akícitas*, messengers, of the terrible Thunderbird, which had already been so close during the night.

The dogs howled frantically, and spoke in words: "Grey Bull, somebody is in trouble over there! You had better help him!"

Grey Bull cried in fear and anguish, "I am only a man, as weak as an ant. Help me, all you Powers! Help me to obey!"

Then he could see the dogs, four of them—the sacred number four—all different colors. They were around him, showing their teeth. He cried again: "Help me to help whoever is in trouble!"

They sped through the air, the four dogs with him among them, faster than arrows fly, as fast as lightning, toward the two buffalo hunters. He could see that one man had been thrown from his horse and was right in the path of a charging buffalo bull with an arrow sticking out of its side.

Now the dogs howled, "Grey Bull, be humble in your power!" and dived through the air down toward the hunters. Grey Bull dived with them to the ground straight in front of the charging bull, and the animal swerved and fell. The hunter who had come so close to death stood there staring at the dead animal.

The Powers of the earth and sky roared and crackled and swirled about Grey Bull, and he lost consciousness.

He did not awaken until he heard the voice of Cottonwood saying, "It is finished. Get up and come with me." He was right where he had been before, in the sacred spot, with his hands still clinging to the center pole. The old holy man helped him stand up and gave him support as they walked slowly down the mountain.

Whirlwind's nine-year-old brothers were hunting (for

rabbits or anything else they could shoot at to improve their skill) when they saw three men ride slowly toward camp. The boys could run faster than those three horses were moving, and they did. They passed their younger brother, Covers Up, who was playing with some other boys of his age and had not forgotten that he was angry because he had been left behind. He yelled at them, but they paid no attention. Now Sun Goes Down and Runs-in-Timber were playing a game of their own. They were racing to warn the camp of enemies approaching, but neither won the race.

Their mothers were scraping a buffalo hide staked out on the ground. Sun Goes Down reported, "Grey Bull is coming back from his vision," and Runs-in-Timber added, "He looks sick."

"Go and tell your father," Many Bones advised Sun Goes Down. "He is in the village somewhere. But don't yell for him. Remember your manners." She pointed at the other boy and said, "Go tell Grey Bull's wife. Your sister is with her."

The boys sped away like antelope.

Eagle Walks was talking to another man, and his son did not dare to interrupt but was so excited that he danced up and down to get attention. Eagle Walks answered, "Ah, thanks. You are my good little *akícita*. Grey Bull will go to the sweat lodge. I will purify myself, too."

At Grey Bull's lodge when the message was delivered, his wife said at once, "I must make everything comfortable for him," a polite hint that Whirlwind should leave soon. They had been quilling moccasins out-of-doors. The others who lived there had already moved temporarily to other lodges, because a man who had gone to lament on a hill, to seek a vision, was physically weak when he returned and also needed privacy to think about what the Powers had told him.

"Is there anything I can do to help you before I leave?" Whirlwind asked. "You have everything tidy and nice for him, and soup ready on the fire. Shall I bring fresh water? There is plenty of time."

Runs-in-Timber walked with her to the creek for water. Now that Whirlwind was a woman, it was not proper for her to go that far alone. Then they went home, because Grey Bull's wife, nervous and worried, preferred to wait alone.

Eagle Walks quickly found three other men of consequence, and they were preparing the necessary things at the sweat lodge when Grey Bull and his sponsor, Cottonwood, and their helper arrived.

Cottonwood told the men gathered there, "We need two of you to keep people away while Grey Bull tells what happened. Nobody but us should hear this great vision yet. But you guards can hear everything from outside."

After prayers and the smoking of the pipe, Cottonwood instructed Grey Bull to tell those present exactly what had happened, omitting nothing. This he did, humbly—relating everything he had seen or heard or felt or done or feared. He told his dream, every detail, and he shivered as he talked, because he knew it was a very powerful one. It was a dream he did not want but could not erase.

He told how the four dogs had warned him that someone was in trouble and he had implored them to help him help that person. He told of the man he saw from afar, about to be gored by a wounded buffalo, and how the dogs had howled, "Grey Bull, be humble in your power!" as they shot with him through the air to save the man. And how the earth and sky roared and he fell unconscious.

The men in the sweat lodge gasped, "*Wakan*! Holy!"

Hot rocks were handed in through the doorway and the

sweating began. Grey Bull, that man who had been so arrogant, so ambitious, bowed his head and wept as the prayers of thanks to the Powers went on.

The holy man then told him, "You have had a very powerful vision. The dogs are the *akícitas* of the Thunderbird. This vision gives you wonderful power to help your people, and terrible responsibilities. You can never again live as other men do. You must be a sacred clown, for you will be *heyoka*. You have been a proud man, but now you are humbler than the tiniest ant, and you must always be so, out of gratitude to the Powers."

Grey Bull knew it was so, and accepted his fate with bowed head and tears on his cheeks. From that day onward, he would have to be a different man.

Cottonwood helped Grey Bull to his lodge. Just before they reached it, two men rode past carrying much meat on pony drags. Grey Bull said quietly, "Those are the hunters. I recognize their horses. The bay horse has a scar that we cannot see with the rider on it. Ask them what happened on their hunt."

Cottonwood exclaimed, "*Wakan*! *Wakan*! They left camp early this morning, but your dream came in the dark of night!"

In his lodge, Grey Bull's wife greeted him softly, made him comfortable on his bed, and brought him a horn cup of soup, then plenty of water. She sat by him and bathed him tenderly with a piece of buckskin dipped in warm water as she sang a little prayer of thanks that he was back. When he asked for food, she fed him bits of meat.

Old Cottonwood followed the two hunters and heard the story they told while they unloaded their meat: How Ice had come close to death when his horse, moving at great speed, caught one foot in an animal burrow and threw him in front of a charging, wounded buffalo bull, but the bull fell dead just as it almost touched him.

Both hunters agreed that the narrow escape must be the result of something *wakan*. Cottonwood looked at the bay horse, and there was the old scar that was not visible when a rider was on his back.

"It is indeed *wakan*," Cottonwood told them. "The Powers saved your life through a man you know, although he was far away. A little later you will know how this happened."

They covered their mouths with their right hands in token of astonishment.

"I think you owe the Great Mystery a sacrifice," he advised Ice. "You should give your buffalo horse to the Powers."

Later in the day, Ice took the bay horse up on a hill and sang a long prayer of thanks to Wakan Tanka and all the other Powers because his life had been saved. He patted the horse's neck and rubbed it all over with a piece of soft deerskin. The horse nuzzled his shoulder. Then he told the animal:

"We have been good friends. You are the best buffalo horse I ever had. You have gone into danger with me many times. Now we must walk on separate trails. It was not your fault that I was dismounted when the wounded bull charged.

"But you are going to the Land of Many Lodges, because I owe a debt to the Powers. It is a good place for horses and people and all things that ever lived. Sometime we will meet again there. Now forgive me for what I must do to pay my debt."

As he stepped back, the horse bent its head to graze on succulent grass. Ice put an arrow to his bow and, from a short distance away, pulled the bowstring powerfully and shot the animal in the heart so that it would die fast. He sat beside it until it was dead and then walked back to camp with his head bowed and his own heart hurting.

After Grey Bull had eaten and drunk more water, he slept for a while, sometimes faintly hearing the voices of friends who came to ask his wife how he was getting along. He heard her say softly, "I do not know what he dreamed, but I think it was a dream of great power."

Friends were puzzled; there was some mystery here. Usually the news of what a vision seeker told the holy man and the attendants in the sweat lodge spread fast and everybody talked about it, but this time none of them had told. There were only rumors.

After he had rested, he said gently to his wife, "Will you come and sit down by me now? I have to tell you something. I dreamed of dogs, a Thunderbird dream. So I am going to be *heyoka*. I am going to be a sacred clown and very poor. I cannot live the way other men do. I must be a holy fool, to keep showing the Thunderbird that I am unworthy, I am nothing."

She was shocked, but she took his hand in both hers for comfort. He shook his head. "I do not deserve you. I did wrong when I persuaded you to run away with me. I was wrong and bad. You have suffered for it, and now your life will be worse if you stay with me. You must go home to your family among the Brulé people. I will take you to them, with many horses and gifts, and ask them to forgive me, and you will be free."

She answered quietly, "But I love you. I will not leave you unless you throw me away, and you will never have any reason to do that. We will be poor together as long as we both live."

He groaned, "No! No! I do not deserve you. I am nothing, less than nothing."

His wife smiled as she said, "You are to be *heyoka*, and you must be humble. But I am not *heyoka*. I am your wife who loves you, and nobody can stop me from being just as proud of you as I ever was."

He turned his head away, saying, "I am not worthy."

"That is not my opinion," she answered firmly.

He slept again, exhausted. She sat beside him, gazing at him with love.

Chapter 10

The Thunder Dreamers Society was the most powerful among The People, although all the members were humble and poor and foolish-acting. In this camp there were no members, no *heyokas*, and so what must be done soon could not be done yet. Cottonwood, the old holy man, made a ceremonial visit to Eagle Walks, in whose lodge Grey Bull had grown up, their father being dead. After everyone else left the lodge, Cottonwood and Eagle Walks smoked the sacred pipe and then the old man explained:

"In Grey Bull's vision, dogs helped him save the life of Ice. You know dogs are among the *akícitas* of the Thunderbird, so now Grey Bull must be *heyoka*. He must join the society soon. Until he does, he is in terrible danger of being killed by lightning."

Eagle Walks understood at once. "We have no *heyokas*, and he cannot go through the ceremony until some of them come to help him. But it may be too late if we wait until all the people gather for the Sun-gazing Dance."

"All that is true. Let us ask the members of the council to send out young men to other camps to invite the *heyokas* to come here right away."

"Of course. We will talk about this important thing right away, without sending the old-man crier. This must be a very private meeting."

Just as the sun came up next morning, six young men rode out, with the blessing of Cottonwood, to go in various directions and find villages where there were *heyokas*. Everyone knew now that Grey Bull had had a very *wakan* dream.

If *heyokas* were needed for a ceremony, then Grey Bull had dreamed a Thunderbird dream and must join the Thunder Dreamers Society as soon as possible. There was quiet rejoicing in the camp, because he would have great power to help all the people. There was deep pity, too, because of the sacrifices he would have to make for the rest of his life.

In many battles Grey Bull had never admitted he was afraid, but those battles were against mere human enemies. Now he was at the mercy of the tremendous Powers of the universe, and it was proper to admit how much afraid he was.

He told his wife, "I am in danger from death by lightning every moment until the ceremony is held, and you are in danger when you are near me. So I want you to live in the lodge of Eagle Walks for a while, to be safe."

"I will stay with you," she answered, "and be afraid with you, and if the lightning strikes, it will take us both."

The *akícitas* rode hard, in different directions, using their skill in tracking and their keen eyesight to look for the smoke of other camps. They brought back four Thunder Dreamers at the end of seven days. One of these men rode painfully because he was not yet recovered from a wound. Another was all ready to travel before an *akícita* reached him. He had

had a vivid sleeping dream that he was wanted somewhere.

Moving somewhat more slowly, because they carried baggage and food on pony drags, came families from two of the camps the *akícitas* had visited. It was good for everyone to be present at a *heyoka* ceremony. Protecting the women and children were four young warriors and three men a generation older. One of the young men, White Thunder, rode on ahead to tell the camp that others were coming so nobody would be startled by strangers. He was directed to the lodge of Eagle Walks, older brother of Grey Bull. The first person he saw there was a young woman chopping firewood. He stayed far off, to avoid scaring her, and stared with admiration until she looked up.

That was how Whirlwind first saw him, sitting on a spotted horse, a handsome young man, though dirty from travel, looking at her and smiling. For a moment she froze, wanting to keep looking at him. Then she ran into the lodge, and her mother came out to greet the visitor.

Grey Bull had hung an offering to the Thunderbird at the top of his tepee poles as a preliminary announcement that the *heyoka* ceremony was going to be held. He had asked the old-man crier to ride around and announce that Grey Bull would join the Thunder Dreamers Society, the fraternity of fools, two days after all the *akícitas* returned.

The two little boys who had first seen Grey Bull coming back from his vision naturally took a great deal of credit, feeling responsible for having set off this excitement. But since they didn't understand it, they went to Eagle Walks. One said, "Father, what is *heyoka*?" The other asked, "What is the Thunderbird?"

Eagle Walks was always concerned with the proper education of his children, so he promised, "I will find someone to tell you the story. All your age-group friends can come." He added severely, "Your little brother can come too, whether he is big enough to understand or not."

The first Thunder Dreamer to arrive was a very old man, so old that his braids were thin and white. His clothing was ragged and patched. He refused the hospitality of Eagle Walks and everyone else who offered it, repeating, "I am not worthy. I am nobody, less than nothing. I must not sleep in a fine lodge, but if you want to build a shelter of boughs such as men use on war parties, I will sleep there and so will the other Dreamers when they come."

The women of Eagle Walks' family had the privilege of taking him food, which he ate from his own plate and horn cup. They treated him with the utmost respect and kept the children from crowding around to stare at him.

Although he was very tired, he went to see Grey Bull and began to give instructions: "The new Thunder Dreamer will live in an old, ragged lodge and wear shabby clothing. This man lives in a new lodge and wears fine clothes that his wife has made."

The meaning of that was clear. Grey Bull asked Eagle Walks to find the poorest man in the village. He gave him his new lodge and good clothes in exchange for the poor man's ragged lodge and old clothing. The poor man, who had had bad luck all his life, blessed him for it.

"Now the women should set up the ragged lodge in the center of the camp circle and we will use it in the ceremony. Later the new Thunder Dreamer will live in it, in his proper place in the camp circle, but the entrance will face the opposite direction from all the rest."

The small children kept waiting for the visitor to do something ridiculous, like the sacred clowns they had seen at Sungazing Dances, but he was not funny yet. He was only humble. Still, he wore on his lean old body the knotted scars that proved his courage and endurance. Even children could identify the scars that showed he had taken part in the most agonizing form of the Sun-gazing Dance, and scars from battle wounds besides.

As other members of the Fraternity of Fools rode in with the *akicitas*, they took over parts of the preparation and the old man rested.

All the specially learned priests and holy men were busy helping to prepare for the ceremony—someone was always drumming and chanting, day and night—but Eagle Walks found a medicine woman whose older brother had been a Thunder Dreamer, and she was free to tell the group of children who gathered. Eagle Walks and his wives stayed in the background, hoping their children, at least, would behave well. They did. So did the others. The old medicine woman had cured some of them, or their relatives, when they were sick, and besides they were afraid of her.

The little boys, practicing stealthy approaches to an enemy, often tried to steal strips of meat from her drying racks just because it was almost impossible to do so without being caught. None of them had ever been slapped or spanked as punishment for anything; The People never struck children. The old medicine woman never slapped, either, but when she caught a boy she pinched him, hard, warning, "If you get caught in an enemy camp, you'll get worse than that."

And so the boys in her audience were quiet, remembering pinches, and the girls acted like little ladies. Even the babies some of them were tending did not cry.

She told them what the Thunderbird looked like: "He is the winged god, Wakinyan. He has no shape, but his wings have four joints. He has huge talons—but no feet. He has a

92

huge beak with teeth like a wolf—although he has no head. His voice is thunder. His glance is lightning, and he kills with it."

She told how he lived: "His lodge is on the top of a mountain where the sun goes down. His young constantly come forth from a great egg, and he eats them. He is very terrible.

"His messengers are the dog, the shore lark, the swallow, the night hawk, the lizard, the frog, and the dragonfly. These are his *akícitas*, which he sends in dreams. When a man has a vision of one of these, that man becomes *heyoka*.

"Now do you understand all that?" the old woman demanded.

Some of the children said they did, because she scared them and they wanted to get away.

"You lie!" she shouted. "You can't possibly understand it." She glared around at them. "Tomorrow Grey Bull and the visiting *heyokas* will re-enact his holy dream. That is part of the ceremony that makes him a member of the Society of Thunder Dreamers. You won't understand that, either, but most people won't. That is all I am going to tell you."

She turned and stalked away, and at a nod from Eagle Walks the frightened children scattered.

He told his wives, "I think I paid her too much."

The next day was cloudy, but musicians kept drumming and singing, hoping to keep the rain away—or, if it had to come, to keep away thunderstorms. Lightning and thunder would be very bad, very frightening to the people, especially dangerous for this ceremony. But all the *heyokas* had pledged it. They could not put it off, even if the Thunderbird meant to kill them.

Everyone in camp had by that time heard about Grey Bull's dream over and over, so most people could understand the re-enactment, more or less.

All four Dreamers came out on horseback, dressed in ragged clothing, with their hair hanging loose and tangled. They rode around fast, acting foolish, pretending to fall off. They all retreated, and Grey Bull rode forward alone with his head down as if sleeping. He awoke and put one hand to his ear, listening clownishly. Another *heyoka* rode out, howling and barking, with the other three following.

People—some people, but only the ignorant—began to laugh at the silly men acting like dogs. Grey Bull mimed seeing something happen very far away. He clowned, pretending horror, yelling nonsense. He leaped from his horse and pretended he was a charging buffalo. Then he dropped and played dead.

The sacred fools kept clowning, shooting crooked arrows from useless bows, entertaining the people, abasing themselves before the people, proud men once who could be proud no longer because the Thunder possessed them and they were nothing, weaker than an ant.

Almost everyone was laughing; it was hard not to laugh at this foolishness, even while pitying the clowns.

Meanwhile, a pot had been boiling over a fire, cooking a buffalo tongue and a tender puppy. Rain began to fall, but nobody left the crowd to seek shelter, because now the *heyokas* would prove their power. Many of the people of Grey Bull's village had never seen this ritual.

The clowns gathered around the kettle and wiped their hands and arms with certain herbs, slowly and carefully, singing prayers while a drum sounded. Then each one plunged his bare hands into the boiling soup and pulled out a piece of cooked meat, calling, "This is for the poor!"

A few old, ragged men and women came forward as fast as they could, and as the clowns kept dipping out meat, each poor person got a piece of it. Some had come prepared with a plate of bark or a bone bowl. Those who had nothing to put the meat in dropped it in the dirt because it was too hot to hold. They cleaned it off when it was cooler and took it home to eat.

Whirlwind took a look at her uncle Grey Bull's hands and arms as soon as she could get close enough. They were not scalded. The skin was not even reddened. The Thunder had indeed given him great power.

The ceremony ended just when rain began to pour down. The five *heyokas* capered around and dumped water over one another's heads.

Chapter 11

Later that summer Whirlwind was invited to a Night Dance for the first time. The hostess, who invited her, was newly married. She would provide the feast.

The Night Dance was the only social dance among The People in which there was mixed dancing with both men and women—all the others were for warriors only, with their female relatives, or the *akícita* societies, or women only. The Night Dance was a formal party for courting-age men and women with a few newly-wed couples.

Whirlwind was nervous as she prepared for it, and both her mothers were excited as they helped her dress and do her hair. She wore her very best dress of white buckskin, with much quill embroidery, and Many Bones and Crow Woman took forever deciding which shell and bead jewelry she should wear. Her father was much amused.

"Anyone would think," he remarked, "that no girl ever

went to a party before. Anyone would think my daughter is frightened."

"I am," she admitted.

"The party will have chaperons," he reminded her, "and you have watched such dances often enough. You know what to do."

"But then I was a little girl, watching from outside," she said. "Now I am grown up and everything is different!"

"We will all be watching," Eagle Walks told her, smiling, "and you will have a good time. Now your mothers should dress up."

Everyone wore his or her best clothes, including the audience. Whirlwind walked to the big dance lodge with her mother and three girl friends and their mothers, eager but a little timid. A fire was burning in the middle of the lodge, for illumination, and the sides were rolled up so everyone outside could watch. Besides, the night was fairly warm and the dancers needed air. Near the fire were two cooking kettles, each with a cut-up fat puppy stewing for the feast to follow.

The orchestra, four good singers with drums, sang as the participants entered. Young women sat on one side of the lodge, young men on the other. The men had taken as much pains with their appearance as the girls had. Their hair shone in the firelight, and their braids hung long, with fine fur wrappings. All of them had painstakingly pulled out their facial hairs and put on their face paint with great care. Several wore sashes hung with small deer hoofs that clicked and tinkled. With fringed leggings and new embroidered moccasins and dangling bits of fur and necklaces of animal claws and teeth, they were handsome indeed.

And how they stared at the young women, smiling and eager!

For in the first dance, the girls had the privilege of choos-

96

ing partners. At a signal from the musicians, the girls stood up (gracefully, not touching the ground with their hands).

Whirlwind had no special young man yet, and her head swam with trying to remember which couples were really courting. She thought of waiting until they had paired off, but she had a sudden idea for a good joke. She waited only until one girl had crossed over and kicked the sole of her man's moccasin. Then Whirlwind darted around the fire straight at Black Plume, who was courting a girl two years older than herself. She kicked his moccasin sole and heard her father, outside, shout with laughter. Black Plume, grinning, leaped up and stood at her left. His girl glared but chose another man.

The singing and drumming began; each dancer grasped the belt of his or her partner, and they bent their knees to dance in a gently rocking motion around the fire.

After an intermission, the men chose partners. Whirlwind heard her father laugh again when two young men leaped toward her at the same instant. Neither of them was Black Plume. One of them slyly tripped the other.

Even the serving of refreshments involved dancing and choosing partners. First the girls came forward, each with a bowl, and each danced toward a man, offering the dish four times but withdrawing it until the music of the drums signaled her to give it to him. Then the men did the same, offering bowls to the girls four times.

After everyone was served, the hostess chose four men who had won honors in war. They sat in the middle, with bowls of meat. When everyone had eaten, the four warriors took turns counting coup—each telling of a brave thing he had done in a battle.

Whirlwind had forgotten, by this time, that she had been timid. The party was wonderful. After more dancing, the

97

couple acting as chaperons danced out of the lodge—the signal that the party was over. It was very late. The girls reluctantly filed out to where their mothers waited, and the men got together in little groups to stroll around the camp, talking it over, teasing one another, laughing.

It wasn't until far past getting-up time next morning that Whirlwind realized she was tired and very, very sleepy. One of her little brothers was standing beside her bed place, staring at her with a big grin and dripping cold water on her face. She grumbled at him and pulled up the light summer bed robe to cover herself completely. Then she leaped up and pinched his arm and he ran away, laughing.

Part V

SUMMER, 1836
The Courting of Whirlwind

Living in the Lodge:

> *Eagle Walks, 52, head of the family*
> *Many Bones Woman, 41, his wife*
> *Whirlwind Girl, 16, their daughter*
> *Sun Goes Down, 12, their son*
> *Covers Up, 9, their son*
> *Crow Woman, wife of Eagle Walks, age untold*
> *Runs-in-Timber, 12, her son by Eagle Walks*
> *Pemmican Girl, 6, her daughter by Eagle Walks*
> *Swims Under, 18, adopted youth*

Chapter 12

When Whirlwind was sixteen, her people had been living for
almost a year in country different from that in which she had
grown up. They had lived before near the Black Hills and
had hunted on the plains east of there; they did not camp *in*
the Black Hills because those mountains, Paha Sapa, were
sacred. They went there for new lodgepoles and sometimes
to hunt.

But in the fall of 1834, some of the Oglalas had moved
down to be nearer the North Platte River, because there was

a fine trading post there on the Laramie River, and they had come to depend on the things they could get from traders but could not make for themselves. Just before the fall hunt of 1835, two thousand more Oglalas moved down to live in the area of Fort Laramie, and this big bunch of people included Whirlwind's band.

In this new country they sometimes encountered a new enemy, the Pawnees, and old friends, the Cheyennes. The Pawnees were a hated people, because they sacrificed human beings to their god, Morning Star, and in 1833 they had burned a captured Cheyenne girl and shot her full of arrows in this revolting worship.

Whirlwind's family was having a hard time now. They were not poor, but her father, Eagle Walks, was fifty-two, and the violent work of buffalo hunting was almost too much for him. The adopted youth, Swims Under, was a hard-riding, effective hunter. But these two had to provide meat for nine persons, including two growing-up boys who seemed to have no bottom to their stomachs, and quantities of robes and furs as well, if they were to have anything to trade at Fort Laramie.

The boys, Sun Goes Down and Runs-in-Timber, were too daring for their own good; they had to be restrained from the kind of chances they wanted to take. Neither of them had his full growth or strength, but they took great risks in the highly dangerous business of buffalo hunting. A full-grown man could drive an arrow clear through the huge body of a racing buffalo bull, but the boys could not. They were likely to have the wounded bull turn and knock their horses over. Eagle Walks tried to make them stay on the edges of the racing herd, but he worried about them all the time.

Whirlwind had problems too. She was being courted by four or five fine young men, and her mothers kept saying,

"This is the happiest time of your life, daughter," but she was often melancholy. White Thunder was the only young man she could think about. Sometimes it seemed she could think of nothing else. But he had not asked for her.

She well remembered the first time she ever saw him. She was picking up an armload of firewood right outside her father's lodge when she heard a horse stop. She looked up, over the load of wood, and saw a stranger on a spotted horse smiling down at her. He was a very handsome young man, with scars from a Sun-gazing Dance on his chest and an eagle feather in his hair in the position that showed he had counted first coup in battle at least once. She was embarrassed to realize that she was staring. She averted her eyes and ran into the lodge without piling any more firewood on her left arm. That was the first summer she was a woman, the summer her uncle Grey Bull joined the Thunder Dreamers.

She remembered the second time she saw White Thunder, too, the summer she was fourteen. She had a glimpse of him in a crowd at the Sun-gazing Dance but did not know whether he saw her. Until small miracles began to happen, she did not even know his name.

Next morning Swims Under, who naturally circulated among the great crowd of people assembled for the big annual ceremony, remarked to the family that he had become acquainted with a man he admired, White Thunder, a bachelor twenty-four years old, with war honors, well thought of in his own camp. They were going to walk over to the preliminary festival. When White Thunder came and called "Hey, Swims Under!" outside the lodge, Whirlwind took a quick look at him—and behold, it was the man who had smiled at her.

The day after that, the men took the younger boys along, Runs-in-Timber and Sun Goes Down. The boys, flattered by the friendship of so admirable a man, couldn't stop talking about him—and Whirlwind couldn't stop listening, although she didn't say a word.

The next day they brought him back to the lodge to smoke with their father. Eagle Walks was favorably impressed with his manners, his conversation, and his honors. He commented later, "There is a man who is going to amount to something."

Whirlwind had not once looked at him, but she could have described every move he made, she could have repeated every word he said. Both her mothers thought he was a fine man. Many Bones said, "I wish he lived in our camp." Whirlwind wished it too, silently.

There was much talk during the Sun-gazing Dance about moving to be closer to Fort Laramie; the decision was made that most of the Oglalas would go just before the big fall hunt. The band with which White Thunder's family lived was not going; Whirlwind felt sick when she learned that. Then the boys brought good news; he and his family were going to go anyway, leaving their band. Her heart sang.

Right after the Sun-gazing Dance, White Thunder and Swims Under went on a hunt of their own and took the two younger boys along, to their great delight, for special tutoring in buffalo hunting and how to bring down plenty of meat without getting hurt. All the meat and all the hides came back to the lodge of Eagle Walks. White Thunder had brothers to take care of his family's needs.

When the horses brought in all that meat, packed on their backs and on pony drags, Whirlwind's two mothers screamed with delight and covered the four hunters with praises. Whirlwind herself spoke her first word to White Thunder. Smiling, but without looking up, she said, "Thanks."

After the people moved down to the area of Fort Laramie,

102

and after the great fall hunt, the young men had time to go back to their courting. Every time Whirlwind heard the shrill sound of an eagle-bone whistle outside the lodge in the evening, she jumped, and her family laughed. When she heard at least three whistles going at once, she considered it worthwhile to stroll out to see who was there. If she cared to, she could stop in front of one of the men and he would wrap his blanket around her and they would stand there talking. If she saw White Thunder, she stopped.

But he never said, "I am going to ask your father for you," or "I want to give your father some horses." The suspense made her nervous and irritable, especially after Swims Under said, with a broad smile, "I heard that a certain warrior paid a big price to a medicine priest for a special whistle because he wants you so bad. When he blows it, you will have to go out—no girl can resist a medicine whistle."

"Who is it?" she demanded eagerly.

"You'll find out when he blows it, because you will have to go. He is forty years old and has two wives already, but he's a great man."

She lost her temper and threw a stick of wood at him. It struck his knee and he danced around yelling, "Ow! Ow!" holding his hurt knee.

The whole family laughed. Whirlwind sulked.

She tried sometimes to persuade one of her brothers to go out and see what men were blowing whistles, but they refused and teased her.

A month before the Sun-gazing Dance she was greatly honored. Several months earlier a relative had lost a fine little girl who died from being kicked in the head by a horse. The parents had resolved to undertake a long, expensive mourning ceremony in order to keep the child's spirit with them for a certain period, which was now ending. In all that time, the grieving father could not hunt or go to war or take part in social activities. His lodge was sacred. He and his wife lived very quietly, spending all their time taking care of a bundle that represented the dead child's spirit. They had to depend on other people for all their food.

Now the spirit was to be released with a great feast and a giveaway, to which their relatives brought presents they had worked hard and long to prepare. Four virgins had an important part in the ceremony, and Whirlwind was honored by being asked to be one of this group.

When it was finished, the spirit keeper and his wife gave away everything they possessed except the clothing they wore. Even their lodge was cut up by women who came running with knives.

But later that evening a relative came to tell them they had a new lodge, and others brought kettles, food, blankets, clothes, tools. So they started life all over again, rejoicing that they had been able to honor their dead little girl.

Whirlwind still brooded, however, about White Thunder's long courtship and his failure to ask for her. Then her cousin, Running Wolf, who seemed like a brother, asked her to attend him in the Sun-gazing Dance. He had vowed the sacrifice when his wife was very sick. She had lost the baby she was carrying; she was mending now but not completely well.

Whirlwind told Running Wolf, "Of course! I am honored that you ask me. You are doing a great thing. You will have other children."

"You will have children, too, sister," Running Wolf said.

She almost cried. "But a certain man does not ask for me. And he is the only one I want. I could make him happy."

Running Wolf smiled. "I'll tell you a secret, little sister. He has asked for you. So have some other men. Fine men. You will have the one you want. But your father and mother want you to be young and free for one more Sun-gazing Dance. After you are married you will live a different life. You have never paired off with a young man in the Buffalo Dance procession. This year you can do that."

She could not answer in words. She simply stared at him—a breach of good manners to an almost-brother now that she was grown up—in speechless joy.

After Running Wolf went home, she had to find release for her joy in doing something nice for someone, so she took a new pair of moccasins to the lodge of her uncle Grey Bull, the *heyoka*, and left them outside the door. She took Covers Up along—he was only nine, but he would do for a chaperon. On the way home she noticed a sharp-eyed old woman, a vicious gossip, watching her and was glad that her excitement and happiness hadn't caused her to give anyone cause for spreading any bad rumors about her. She hoped the woman had observed her errand of mercy but doubted whether that was the kind of news the gossip would care to pass along.

During the first four days of preparation for the great dance, Whirlwind and other young women spent some of their time hunting for grama grass with four heads, calling out gleefully when they found one, because it brought good luck in love. Whirlwind had done this in other years, but this time it had more meaning. One of her friends whispered, "Are you promised? Your eyes shine."

She answered, smiling, "No, I'm not promised, but I'm happy," and let the girl figure that out for herself.

The holy men chose those who would help them in the long, complicated ceremony. Being chosen was a great honor. Four virtuous mothers, of spotless reputation, were called out; they would chop down a cottonwood tree for the sacred pole around which the vow-payers would suffer. The

105

names of the virtuous women relatives who would attend the sun-gazers were called out, Whirlwind's among them. There was feasting and laughter and much socializing when these sacred things were not going on.

During the second four-day period, the candidates for the dance were not seen by the rest of the people. They were isolated in the big council lodge with the holy men, receiving instructions.

The final four days were full of ceremony. On the first of them, a dance arbor of poles covered with leafy boughs was erected. East of it, the sacred lodge was made; there the candidates would receive their final instructions. A brave man designated as the hunter scouted for a forked cottonwood tree that would be the dance pole. The Buffalo Dance procession then moved four times around the camp, with families marching together—except that couples who were courting could go in pairs, the girls carrying the four-headed grama grass they had found. Everyone shouted and praised two gods, the Buffalo and the Whirlwind, patrons of the home and of lovemaking.

Whirlwind, flushed with happiness, walked beside White Thunder, who looked proud and teased her because of her name. "We are all praising you and the Buffalo," he said. She smiled and said, "Hush. Are you irreverent?"

"Oh, no," he said, "I worship Whirlwind and the Buffalo."

Before they separated, he told her, "Meet me by the cutbank down the creek after the sun goes down."

She gasped, but on this one day of the year such a meeting would be all right. That was custom.

They met at the cutbank and talked freely, informally, like friends, for the first time.

"I am going to offer for you again pretty soon after the dance," he said, holding her hands in his hands.

She answered, "I am glad."

Meanwhile in the family lodge, her mother worried and could not think of anything but what might be happening to Whirlwind, alone in some secret place with an ardent suitor. She need not have fretted. Six other men had chosen the cutbank as a trysting place with their sweethearts. All the couples ignored all the other couples with dignity, but the men sometimes glared at one another.

On the second holy day, the four chosen, honored women pretended, in a long ritual, to capture the cottonwood tree. Four warriors counted coup on it, and the four women chopped it down. Everyone shouted with joy. The tree was carried to camp carefully with carrying sticks; it was now dedicated to Wakan Tanka and could be touched only by priests or men who had already been through the Sun-gazing Dance.

There was a great procession on the third holy day, but no children took part. The women marched together, with the men behind them, four times around the inside of the camp circle, singing.

On this day candidates for the dance, who had been praying and meditating and taking instruction in the rites to follow, could drink water, but they could not eat again until their ordeal of suffering was ended.

Certain men lifted the decorated sun pole by degrees so it stood in the center of the sun lodge. The whole sacred area was an anthill of activity; drummers came, and warriors who performed a victory dance to smooth the ground in the sun lodge; other men got things ready for the dancers. They brought heavy buffalo skulls, which some dancers would have attached to their bodies with thongs through the flesh; they set stakes upright in the ground for another form of the dance, and attached thongs to the sacred pole for still another. A bed of white sage was made for babies whose ears were to be pierced. Following a big feast for the holy men, who still had to drive evil spirits out of the dance lodge and visit the dance candidates in the sacred lodge, the people went quietly to their homes.

Part of the final sacred day's ceremony was the calling out and testing of the virtuous women who would attend the dancers in their pain. They might be wives or maidens. Whirlwind was the only unmarried girl among those attending the dancers.

As each was called out, anyone who knew anything bad about her was expected to announce it—and it need not be very bad. The accuser must be willing to bite the knife, that is to swear solemnly to the truth of the accusation, and the accused could bite the knife to defend herself. There had been a small scandal three years before; a girl had had a brief flirtation with a young man, nothing bad, but not quite right either, and had been ruled unfit to attend her brother in the dance. People were still talking about that.

Whirlwind's was the fourth name called. She stepped forward. A gossipy old troublemaker yelled shrilly, "She was alone in a trysting place with White Thunder, although she is not promised to him or anyone."

Everyone gasped. The old holy man in charge asked, "Will you bite the knife?" The old woman said, "Oh, yes, I will," and began to push through the crowd.

The old priest said, "If they were alone, how did you happen to be with them?"

"I saw them leave," the gossip claimed. "I saw them come back."

Whirlwind stood rigid with embarrassment—more than embarrassment, it was horror.

Before she could summon up her voice to say it was not

108

true, that she would bite the knife and hope it killed her if she lied, men's shouts arose. Seven warriors came pushing through the crowd, yelling, "It is not true! Where is the knife? Let me bite the knife!"

One of them was White Thunder. The others were the six who had been in the same trysting place with their girls. The priest might not have believed White Thunder—who was prejudiced, of course—but when the rest of them finished their shouting and explaining, and each one angrily bit the knife in defense of Whirlwind's virtue, who could doubt?

The other six maidens were coming forward now, quietly but with determination. There was a confusion of their cries: "She did nothing wrong—she was not alone with any man. I was there! I was there! Let me bite the knife!"

There was no possible doubt. The old gossip was nowhere to be seen. She had slunk away, while a few people threw stones at her.

Thus Whirlwind was vindicated. It was well that she and White Thunder had not found the brief privacy they had a right to seek on that one evening of the whole year!

On this final day, every person was dressed in his or her best, with ornaments and finery. Warriors wore their insignia of valor. Whirlwind and the other attendants had brought little bundles of whatever things they hoped might be of some comfort to the suffering dancers. Whirlwind had painted the parting of her hair red, as was her right because she was a Buffalo Woman.

The dance candidates were painted by the priests in various ways to indicate which form of the Sun-gazing Dance they had chosen. Running Wolf had his hands and feet painted red, and there were blue stripes across his shoulders and chest. These indicated that he was going to dance with heavy buffalo skulls, four of them, hanging from thongs attached to skewers passed through slits cut through the skin under his shoulders.

All the candidates performed a Buffalo Dance in four parts in which they imitated the way an angry buffalo bull acts. Then they rested while the children's ears were pierced. After that, each candidate called on the man he had asked to be his captor—a warrior who had many war honors.

Running Wolf had chosen to perform the gaze-at-the-sun buffalo version of the dance. He was brought out first to the sacred pole, where he called the name of the man who would help him—Grey Bull the *heyoka*, who was not expected to act like a fool on this holy day.

Grey Bull stood and shouted the story of some of the brave deeds in battle that qualified him to act now. Then the next man, and the next, until the helpers were all finished. They moved back and then, all together, attacked the dance candidates in a sham battle and threw them to the ground, thus capturing and humiliating them.

The women attendants came forward then, as the captors began the ritual of piercing the candidates' flesh. Whirlwind knelt near Running Wolf, out of the way but able to reach him. She gritted her teeth as Grey Bull slit the skin below Running Wolf's shoulder blade twice, then twice on the other side. Blood ran down his back, so Whirlwind wiped it away with bunches of sweet grass, wailing like a mother whose child is hurt. (Later she would burn these bunches of sweet grass as incense, because it assured that love would endure.)

Running Wolf, meanwhile, sang a song of defiance. Grey Bull pushed sharpened skewers of wood through the slits in the skin; when blood obscured the area, Whirlwind wiped it away gently.

The other "captors" were working with knives and skewers

on the backs or chests of their candidates, and women attended them. Most of the "captives" shouted defiance songs (one was silent because he was biting down on a piece of wood between his teeth), and their women attendants all wailed as they encouraged them and wiped away blood. The other candidates had undertaken even greater torment than Running Wolf, but his was very bad. When he stood up, four heavy buffalo skulls hung from the skin of his shoulders, with their knifelike edges and horn tips clawing his back.

When all of them were ready, other persons came forward, including a woman; they would dance only the Gaze-at-the-sun Dance, painful for the eyes but not requiring wounds. The drummers began to beat slowly, and all the dancers danced slowly, each blowing a bone whistle continually while staring constantly at the sun. The crowd, the people, sang encouraging songs. After four slow songs there was an intermission; Whirlwind and other attendants comforted the men. The next dances were faster and the sufferers began to struggle to free themselves by tearing the sticks through their skin, which stretched out like rubber.

As the music became faster after each intermission, the dancers struggled more violently, always staring at the sun in worship and blowing their whistles. In intermission, when the dancers rested, their attendants cleansed their wounds and wiped away sweat with sprigs of sage. Whirlwind was even able to give her almost-brother a little water that she had surreptitiously put into her own mouth from a cup.

The sacrifice of pain had been going on for many hours when Running Wolf's bone whistle stopped shrilling—with a mighty effort he plunged forward and one of the skewers tore through his skin and flesh, so that two of the buffalo skulls came loose. He fell forward, fainting.

This was a bad moment. His captor could cut the other

111

skewer loose, but if he could go on dancing to the end he would earn much more honor. Whirlwind ran forward to wail for him and praise him, to wipe away his blood and sweat. His captor hesitated.

Then from the crowd Running Wolf's sick young wife came forward, singing:

> "Running Wolf said this:
> 'Wakan Tanka, pity me
> From henceforth.
> For a long time I will live.'
> He is saying this, and
> He stands there, enduring."

Her voice was not loud, but there was pride in it, and the people cried out to reinforce the praise. Running Wolf pulled himself to his knees, then to his feet. Staring at the sun, he fumbled for the whistle on a thong around his neck. Then he went on dancing.

At noon the following day he fell free of the other skewer and the weight of the other buffalo skulls. A roar of prayer and praise went up from the assembled people. He had gone through this for the good of all of them, to bring them closer to Wakan Tanka.

Before the fall hunt, two of White Thunder's brothers met Whirlwind's father and Running Wolf, her cousin and almost-brother, for a ceremonial smoke. By prearrangement, the women had been invited to visit White Thunder's married sister, whom they liked. They knew very well what was going on, but nobody mentioned it. White Thunder's brothers were formally asking for her and making an offer. He was not present. He spent the evening in his warrior-society

112

lodge, where all his friends guessed what was going on and kept joking, asking why he was nervous.

The bride price agreed upon was eight fine horses—a very high price, but so outstanding a girl as Whirlwind was worth it, and it brought much honor to both families concerned. The men decided also where the newly married couple would live—in their own lodge, of course, and right in front of that of Eagle Walks, because his family needed this good hunter. White Thunder's parents had other grown sons, and married daughters near them to help their mother.

A marriage was a civil contract, without any religious vows, so no promises were made and no holy man officiated. But all the relatives took part in the grand procession that announced the marriage.

A day or two after the arrangements had been agreed upon, White Thunder's brothers, dressed in their finest clothes with their feathers waving, rode their gaudiest horses to the bride's lodge, driving the gift horses before them. Her younger brothers took charge of them, crying out their admiration, and her father came out, dressed in his best, to thank them with dignity.

From many lodges came relatives carrying gifts, shouting joyfully. They mounted their horses. White Thunder rode to his bride's lodge, in fine new clothing. Her two mothers brought her out and helped her mount a horse. She wore fringed white buckskin with a short cape of the finest quill embroidery and elaborately quilled moccasins. The bride and groom rode at the head of the procession with relatives and friends following, shouting and singing. The procession wound four times around the camp circle. When it passed the ragged lodge of Grey Bull the *heyoka*, he was sitting in front with his wife. He was beating a small drum with his fingers and singing a prayer.

As the wedding procession moved, Whirlwind pretended not to notice that her two mothers were erecting a brand-new small lodge (she herself had helped to make it), and when the parade had gone four times around, that was where it stopped.

The wedding presents that had been carried by the riders were enough to furnish their new home. There was plentiful food, too, and the bridal feast was long talked about. So were the generous gifts of meat that White Thunder sent to the old and poor of the camp.

Such was the wedding. The couple had two or three days to be alone—but it took longer than that for Whirlwind to get used to the idea that now it was all right for her to speak to the man she loved, to look at him, to be held in his arms.

Two persons could hardly live alone, unless they were very old and depended on the bounty of others. There was too much work to be done. So it was arranged that a widowed sister of White Thunder should live with them to help Whirlwind with the heavy work of homemaking; her own nine-year-old brother, Covers Up, would also live with them. There were plenty of small jobs for a small boy to do.

Of course this choice did not at all please Sun Goes Down and Runs-in-Timber, who thought they should have the privilege of living with White Thunder. They came with their arguments, and he listened patiently.

"You will both be strong speakers in council some years from now," he told them. "But what we are going to do now has been decided by older men, so that is what younger men will do."

They went away glowing with pride. He had called them men! They even treated Covers Up in a more friendly way after that, teaching him some tricks about looking after the pony herd.

The reason the young couple could not move in with the parents of either was that by ancient custom a man must not speak to his mother-in-law and a woman must, in the same way, totally avoid her father-in-law. This was simply a matter of showing great respect. Sometimes it made life very complicated. But the custom was tribal law, and it had to be observed.

Whirlwind had been the wife of White Thunder for only three weeks when an older man carried a pipe to him, asking him to join a war party against the Pawnees. He accepted, because it was his duty. Until he returned, ten days later, with his face painted black for victory, his bride knew for the first time the real suffering a wife must endure while her man is far away in danger. It was suffering that she experienced many more times during their life together. It was part of being a woman who loved her man.

Part VI

SPRING, 1845

Brings Horses Girl

Living in the Lodge:

> *White Thunder, 35, head of the family*
> *Whirlwind, 25, his wife*
> *Morning Rider, 5, their son*
> *Sun Goes Down, 21, Whirlwind's full brother*
> *Covers Up, 18, Whirlwind's full brother*
> *Runs-in-Timber, 22, her half brother*
> *Pemmican Girl, 15, her half sister*
> *Crazy Bear, 20, White Thunder's younger brother*
> *Deer Foot, 60, mother of White Thunder*
> *Crow Woman, Whirlwind's "other mother"*
> *Rains-on-Her, 22, Brulé wife of White Thunder*

Chapter 13

When Whirlwind was twenty-five, the family in her husband's lodge should have been very prosperous. There were five hunters—White Thunder, those inseparable half brothers and friends Sun Goes Down and Runs-in-Timber, Covers Up, and White Thunder's brother Crazy Bear—all strong and active. To provide trade goods there were Whirlwind herself, her half sister Pemmican Girl, and two strong

116

grandmothers, all skilled at tanning and embroidery and sewing.

All the five hunters had guns now—very costly, from the trader at Fort Laramie—but those were for war. Arrows brought down running buffalo silently and more accurately than bullets, and a man could shoot a dozen arrows from his bow in the time it took to measure gunpowder and reload a gun.

But the family was not, in fact, prosperous, because the young men spent much time on the war trail or harassing the pale-faced people, the Wasichus, who traveled along the Overland Trail. The Lakotas called it the Medicine Road because there seemed to be no end to the stream of enemy strangers who traveled on it. These people were driving the buffalo herds away; they killed them for sport and wasted the meat, and hunters had to ride farther now to find game.

Whirlwind's father, Eagle Walks, had been dead for two years. By custom, Whirlwind's mother could not live in the home of her son-in-law, so she moved in with other relatives but visited her daughter often when White Thunder was away.

There had been some discussion of the propriety of Crow Woman's moving in with Whirlwind. But she was not Whirlwind's real mother, therefore not the mother-in-law of White Thunder, and anyway she was not a Lakota by birth but a Crow—although she didn't like to be reminded of it. She got along very well with Deer Foot, mother of White Thunder. Deer Foot was sixty years old. Nobody knew how old Crow Woman was. She had never said anything about that except, "I was born again when I became a Lakota."

Whirlwind did much quiet worrying. Where were all her menfolk at any one time? Were they all right or wounded or captured or even dead? Pemmican Girl had never become a

Buffalo Woman because the year she should have had that honor was the year her father died. Would those filthy Wasichus never stop coming, with their deadly diseases?

Those travelers died like flies along the Medicine Road. Worse than that, Lakotas died of their diseases—measles, smallpox, cholera. Eagle Walks himself, that good, honorable man, had died of the smallpox, along with several others who had been with him on an expedition to scare off a wagon train. Nobody could even mourn at his burial platform, because nobody was sure where his body had been left. Only two men had returned from that journey, with deep pits of smallpox scars disfiguring their faces and bodies. They had been too sick to take proper care of the dead.

Every summer more of the Wasichus came to Fort Laramie and then moved westward. Whirlwind had been startled to find that, unlike the French traders she had seen as a child, these men did have women of their own race, and even children. They were a surly lot, suspicious and afraid. They stopped their wagons at Fort Laramie and traded worn-out oxen (the Lakotas called them whoa-haws, because that was what the drivers yelled all the time) for coffee and sugar and scrawny horses. Coffee and sugar were good; Whirlwind liked to give these things to her menfolk for special treats. But the scared emigrants on the Medicine Road were so spoiled that they couldn't live without these foods! They also traded for flour—tasteless stuff and not good for anything, in the opinion of the Lakotas. The white-faces simply didn't know how to live.

Whirlwind worried quietly, but the two grandmothers talked constantly about things that were all wrong now.

"Everything is mixed up since we moved down to be nearer the trading post," Deer Foot sighed. "There didn't used to be fighting all the time."

"Everything is upside down," Crow Woman agreed. "The young men are always excited, they have their reputations to make and never mind hunting! There are more young widows these days, more children without fathers."

"We used to have good strong chiefs," Deer Foot remembered. "Now they are weak. They can't persuade the young men to hunt. There's more glory to be had in a battle. We need chiefs who can control the young men."

They had said it all so many times that Whirlwind could have recited it from memory.

Whirlwind had mourned often. She had a fine son, Morning Rider, five years old, but another boy baby had lived only a few days. Her hair was still ragged from mourning for him and for her father; it was not easy to braid when she dressed up, but she covered the braids by winding long strips of otter fur around them.

In the early spring of 1845, White Thunder took another wife, a Brulé girl named Rains-on-Her. Young as she was, twenty-two, she had been widowed already. He felt sorry for her—her family, living near the fort, had been wiped out by one of the Wasichus' diseases.

So many young men were dead! There was fighting against the Pawnees, those contemptible people who sacrificed human beings in religious worship, and against the Snakes, and the pale-faced strangers were likely to shoot any Indian even if he came in friendship or because he was simply curious.

Rains-on-Her was White Thunder's third wife. His second, a good, industrious girl, was dead—wiped out, with a small party of her relatives, on the way to visit another camp. Some Snake Indians had killed them.

Rains-on-Her was a good girl, a quiet friend, a willing worker. So was Pemmican Girl, Whirlwind's half sister, now

119

fifteen. They were doing the heavy work of fleshing a buffalo hide out in the April sunshine, and Whirlwind was mending moccasins, with a blanket around her, when Whirlwind announced, "I think the baby wants to see what the world is like. No, I do not want to go into the lodge yet."

Rains-on-Her said, "It will be good to have a baby in our home. Now who should go and who should stay while he makes his short journey into the world?"

"You and Pemmican can stay," Whirlwind decided. "Pemmican, first find Morning Rider, take along a blanket for him, and tell him to go visit somebody overnight." She counted her menfolk on her fingers: "My husband and his brother Crazy Bear are hunting. Sun Goes Down and Runs-in-Timber are fighting somebody somewhere. Only my brother Covers Up is in camp. Tell him to sleep in his society's lodge."

Just then the two grandmothers came around the lodge. Crow Woman remarked, "We heard you talking. Deer Foot will be your midwife. I will help her and keep people out."

Whirlwind smiled and said, "When White Thunder comes home, you can let him in. But he was going to hunt at some distance. I will go in now. Rains-on-Her, you can come in when you want to, and sometime I will be with you when you have a baby."

The baby was a fine girl. When her father came home, she had been looking at the world for three days (whenever she was awake) and protesting loudly about it.

He greeted her with tender affection as he sat beside Whirlwind's bed of robes. "I would like to name her Brings Horses Girl," he suggested.

Whirlwind agreed. "A pretty name, and lucky. Your grandmother's name; you have told me about her."

"Shall we have Grey Bull announce the name? Then I will have a reason for giving him something. He will give honor to our daughter. A great warrior and a holy man with much spirit power."

Grandmother Deer Foot, sitting at the entrance, said, "Someone is coming. Grey Bull, I think that's who it is." Her sight was not good for distant things, although she could see close things. She revered Grey Bull, the sad *heyoka*, the holy clown, so much that she stood up when she spoke to him: "Come in, come in."

Grey Bull immediately turned away. Deer Foot had forgotten that a Thunder Dreamer had to do things in a contrary way. She corrected her invitation; she said politely, "Please go away." He came to the entrance again but entered backward. Deer Foot, remembering how a *heyoka* must act, not sitting in comfort but on the ground, hastily pulled up one end of the robe that formed the floor of the lodge and moved it out of the way.

White Thunder invited him to stand up, and he sat down with a sigh. Whirlwind held up the baby, smiling. "You don't want to see our little one," she suggested, and the *heyoka* looked at the child with love. "You can't touch her," said Whirlwind, and he cradled her in his arms.

Now that the formalities were concluded, the holy clown spoke straight instead of backward. "I was sleeping," he told them, "and something told me to come here because you wanted me. You want me to name her Brings Horses, after a great-grandmother. I will do it."

Whirlwind whispered, "*Wakan!* That is true," and White Thunder echoed, "*Wakan!*"

"I am nothing, nobody, less than the smallest ant," the *heyoka* reminded them. "I do not deserve the honor. But I will do it. And I will pray for her often, because this child's life will not be like our lives. The world is changing."

He looked at the baby with deep pity. Whirlwind shiv-

121

ered, thinking, *He even sees her death—someday*. But she did not dare ask him. He looked straight into Whirlwind's face and prophesied again: "You will be a heroine."

Whirlwind smiled. "I am no warrior. Only a woman."

"But a woman of the Lakotas. Sometime you will remember what I have said."

And so the baby was named Brings Horses Girl, but her proud father said with a broad smile, "She cries loud enough to scare away horses!" Within a few weeks they cured her of that by putting water in her nose when she howled. The Lakotas never punished their children (as the wagon-train people did, to their disgust), but a crying baby could put a whole camp in danger when enemies were around, so they trained babies not to cry loudly by using the water-in-the-nose treatment.

The baby was two weeks old when the brother-friends came back quietly with five other warriors—quietly because they brought bad news. Nine of them had ridden out, but only seven returned. So although they had all counted coup and some brought Pawnee scalps, they also brought grief, and there was the wailing of heartbroken women in the lodges.

By this time the Lakotas and their allies the Cheyennes had much to avenge. A few years before, Pawnees had attacked a small party of Oglalas, some of them sick, killed a chief and some warriors, and captured some women and girls. The Pawnees caught the smallpox from the captured girls and many Pawnees died. But so did the sick Oglalas.

Another year, a captive Lakota girl named Haxti was sacrificed to Morning Star. The Lakotas attacked and killed a lot of Pawnees but almost starved on the way home and had to eat the ponies they had captured. There was no end to the bitterness and hatred and death.

The warriors who returned now to the lodge of White Thunder had traveled for several days. The Lakotas at the trading post were not a proud people any more, they said. The women and children lived poorly; they stayed by the fort for protection because the warriors were away so much on the warpath.

"The traders at the fort have plenty of good things from the East," the travelers reported, "but we could not buy anything, having nothing with us to trade. Maybe we should all go down there."

The elders of the camp thought so too. The trading post was an exciting place, and winter was over now. So the village moved down toward the North Platte River and arrived at Fort Laramie early in June.

When the fort came in sight, Whirlwind remarked that changes had been made. The walls there had been of logs only a few years before. Now the logs had rotted, and white-washed adobe walls, shining in the spring sun, had replaced them.

A few inquisitive Indians rode out from the camp that huddled close to the walls. One was a Brulé whom Sun Goes Down had met before.

"You are here in time for some excitement," he told them. "We keep hearing from camps downriver about lots of wagon-train people coming. But even faster, soldiers are coming, lots of soldiers. Their chief is named Colonel Kearny. They have guns of a new kind and fine big horses." He smiled broadly. "We hear they are bringing us presents."

There was no decent place to camp close to the fort, because the grass was beaten into mud by hoofs and there was much clutter, so Whirlwind's people pitched their lodges two miles away. While the women worked, some of the young men rode over to the fort to talk to the Lakotas camped there. A Brulé, riding so hard from downriver that his horse was lathered, pulled up and told them a story.

"Lots and lots of Wasichus came, warriors, all dressed alike in blue clothes. Our village was on the other side of the river, and these men startled us. They sent a scout over and invited us to visit.

"Fifty of us—I was one—rode across, making a big show. The Wasichus' chief, Kearny, talked about peace and put on a show of his own. His men have new guns. These do not load at the front like ours, but through the side, with the bullet and powder in a little package. So they can reload very fast. Ah, I would like one of those guns! Some of the soldiers have long knives they call sabers, and two great big guns on wheels. These wagon guns shoot very far with a noise like thunder.

"So we put on a show, too. A young antelope sprang up from the grass, and a dozen of us chased him on horseback, no matter how he dodged and jumped. We tired him out, and one man leaped off his horse and picked up the antelope in his arms.

"The soldiers were impressed. They can't ride like that, steering the horse only with their knees, leaving their arms free!"

The Lakotas were pleased to hear of this display and curious to meet the soldiers. They gathered around a council shelter near the fort. When Kearny and his men came, the Lakotas listened carefully to his words.

Kearny made a solemn speech, using an interpreter: "Your grandfather has sent me with a few of his warriors to visit you. I am opening a road for your white brothers, who go to live west of here. Your grandfather says his red children must not try to close this road. There are many whites coming now, to live on the other side of the mountains. You must

124

not disturb them. If you do, your grandfather will be angry with you. He is the enemy of all bad Indians but the friend of all the good ones."

He mentioned the presents he had brought and warned them against drinking whiskey, firewater. Then Chief Bull Tail replied with dignity:

"What you have told my people is right. I know now that if they are good to their white brothers, they will be well treated and will get more presents. Now we have found a father and we will live."

The presents were spread out on the ground and distributed by selected warriors to all the Indians—cloth and beads, mirrors and knives and tobacco.

A woman somewhere began to chant a song of thanks, not just for the presents but also for relief from fear. Other women, after hearing it once, joined in and sang as they received their gifts and scurried away.

A little later, Kearny had one of the wagon guns loaded and fired three times into the air. The shells exploded as they fell to earth, so these howitzers became known as the guns that speak twice. After dark, he had a rocket fired into the night sky. It seemed to scatter the stars.

Whirlwind and her people rode back to the mountains, much impressed, considerably frightened, hoping the Grandfather's white children would not do any more damage along the Medicine Road.

125

Part VII

SUMMER, 1855
The Evil Medicine Road

Living in the Lodge:

White Thunder, 45, head of the family
Whirlwind, 35, his wife
Morning Rider, 15, their son
Brings Horses Girl, 10, their daughter
Rains-on-Her, 33, wife of White Thunder
Sun Goes Down, 31, brother of Whirlwind
Deer Foot Woman, aged mother of White Thunder

Chapter 14

Every summer more white men with their wagons and oxen and mules and horses traveled west along the trail that the Indians called the Medicine Road. There was nothing sacred about it, but there was a great mystery: where did all those people come from? Surely there could be nobody left back there—but every summer more of them came. They called it the California Trail or the Oregon Trail.

They brought smallpox and cholera with them, and suspicion and fear that became hatred. They all stopped at the trading post that was called Fort William and then Fort

Laramie. Their stock ate up the grass so there was none left for the Indians' horses or for buffalo.

In the year designated 1849 by the white men's reckoning, the emigrant trains left such devastation over so wide an area that the immense herds of buffalo no longer crossed the Medicine Road. Some grazed south of it and some grazed north of it, and the Indians found it harder to hunt for meat and robes. They tried to scare off the white men, because this was *their* country, but still the white men came.

The Medicine Road stank of death. Worn-out oxen died. The white men shot buffalo, often just for the excitement of it, and the dead buffalo stank. Broken, deserted wagons and furniture and boxes littered the Medicine Road.

The Oglalas and the Brulés hunted but usually came back to Fort Laramie to camp and trade. Fourteen winters had passed since they had moved down there from the beloved Black Hills to be near the traders, who were their friends. Then the Grandfather back East—who, the Indians were told by the few white men they trusted, was *their* grandfather, too—bought Fort Laramie and sent out blue-coated soldiers to protect the wagon trains. The soldiers were *not* the Indians' friends.

They were warriors of a hateful kind. There were not many of them, compared to the thousands of free Indians, but they brought greater trouble than the wagon-train people had. Some of the chiefs among them took pretty Indian girls for their wives, and the girls, visiting their relatives back in the lodges, strutted and showed off the fine things their soldier chiefs had given them.

Back East, the Grandfather listened to a few good white men who were friends of the Indians and agreed that the Medicine Road had upset their lives, made it harder for them to hunt and live. So he said that certain tribes should have

127

certain territories to hunt in and that they should be paid something for the damage that had been done. He sent men out to Fort Laramie in 1851 to explain this and to hand out presents and to get everything written down on paper.

Whirlwind's people were there at the Great Council with all the other Lakotas and their friends, the Cheyennes, and many other tribes, including some bitter enemies, the Snakes. Their older enemies, the Crows, came late. Whirlwind remembered that exciting time vividly—a huge gathering of Indians with a few white soldiers, many feasts, the young warriors dressed in their finest beaded buckskin and feathers, madly riding their best horses, showing off, everybody proud. There were fine speeches by distinguished chiefs, and enemies smoked the pipe together and made peace.

There was much talk, through interpreters, between the white chiefs in their language and the Indian leaders in their many languages. Everything was explained: for one thing, each tribe would hunt within a certain territory. The Lakotas could not agree to this, so it was decided that all tribes could hunt everywhere in the area covered. The Grandfather's two representatives promised that their government would protect the Indians from mistreatment by the white people, who had done so much damage already.

To pay for this damage, there were wagon loads of presents, and there would be more every year for fifty years. But before any presents were distributed, each Indian nation's head chief had to touch the pen to the treaty—make an X after his name, which an interpreter pointed out on the paper-that-talks.

For the Lakotas, this was impossible. Their separate tribes *were* separate, all one people but with no chief for the entire nation. There were more Lakotas than any other nation. So the white men chose a head chief for them, a good man named Brave Bear. He did not want the honor, because the Lakotas said they could not make one chief to speak for all of them. But finally he accepted, knowing it would mean his death sooner or later. Brave Bear for the puzzled Lakotas, along with the chiefs of other nations, one after another solemnly touched the pen. The Grandfather's representatives were satisfied, even quietly triumphant, refusing to understand that all the Lakotas could *not* be bound by the promise of only one chief. Their own government had never worked that way.

Then the presents were distributed. Some of them were useless—flour and soda (the Indians knew these were something to eat but not how to use them so they threw them away, keeping the useful cloth sacks) and big copper kettles too heavy to pack on horses or pony drags.

Whirlwind remembered the touch-the-pen ceremony. The warriors stood in a great circle, with the women and children behind them. And the presents, some of them very nice to have. She still had two good blankets in the lodge.

She remembered, too, how brutal the white soldier chiefs at Fort Laramie were. They hated living there and some of them hated Indians.

Whirlwind was thirty-five, but sometimes she was so discouraged that she felt like an old woman. Too many things were going wrong with her family and her people. Her husband's second wife, Rains-on-Her, had no living children after ten years of marriage. She had mourned two dead babies. She was a sad woman who worked hard, did not talk very much, and never laughed at all.

129

Whirlwind's own mother, Many Bones, had died two years earlier, and her other mother, Crow Woman, a year after that. When the village camped anywhere near the high platforms on which they lay under the sky, many days' travel apart, Whirlwind took time to visit and make sure the burial bundles were tight and tidy.

My dead ones are scattered over much country, she sometimes reflected. Grandmother Earth Medicine and my father and my two mothers—so far apart, and my baby boy who died.

This summer she had a chance to visit the cemetery platform of Crow Woman, her other mother. She planned to spend the whole day away from camp.

On the way, she watched closely for places where certain root vegetables ought to grow and for anything else useful in cooking. When she reached the platform, she picketed her horse where he could graze. Nothing had disturbed the bundle, and the platform was still solid. So she sat down and wailed for a little while. Then she talked to the spirit of Crow Woman:

"We miss you all the time. But you are with my mother, Many Bones, and with my father. My hair was ragged from mourning, and I hacked it off again when you went away from us, and gashed my arms. Look after the two babies of Rains-on-Her. Their mother grieves for them. Look after my baby. He would be six winters old now.

"We have only one grandmother in the lodge. My husband's mother, Deer Foot Woman, is the old-woman-who-sits-by-the-door. She is a good woman and works when she can, but she cannot see very well.

"Your son, Runs-in-Timber, we have not seen for a long time. He married a girl of the Brulé Sioux and lives with her people. My brother Covers Up still lives with our people. He married before you left us. Ah, Mother, I worry about these bold young men, because there are so many enemies to fight now and the chiefs cannot control the proud young warriors! The Pawnees, those abominable people, and their allies the Arikaras, and all these white-faced people traveling through or marching in, wearing blue coats, to fight us. Their chiefs speak to us with forked tongues."

Whirlwind mourned and wailed for a while and then walked away with her head bowed, unwilling to burden the spirit of her other mother with news of some family members who were causing much grief. Crow Woman's daughter, Pemmican, was suffering from bad treatment by her husband. He had been a sound young man until he lost his wits over the white men's firewater. Whirlwind's band had moved away from Fort Laramie, but he stayed there so he could get firewater, and Pemmican was with him. He had become dangerous and cruel.

Whirlwind's full brother, Sun Goes Down, was a widower and lived in White Thunder's lodge, but Whirlwind wished he would go somewhere else. His wife had died of cholera, that hideous disease that the pale-faced people with wagons had brought with them. Sun Goes Down was not even looking for a wife. He secretly courted married women. It was disgraceful. When a man seduced a single girl, that was bad enough. She could never make a good marriage, but the man was not blamed very much. Seducing a married woman was much worse. That was adultery. The man lost the respect of other people, and the woman was likely to be punished in horrible ways.

Crazy Bear, White Thunder's younger brother, was tormented by a lazy, jealous, bad-tempered wife who wanted to go back and live near Fort Laramie. Whirlwind didn't think his patience would last much longer.

She wondered whether her two mothers in the Land of Many Lodges knew about these sad, bad, shameful things back in the world. If not, she was not going to make them unhappy by telling them.

Especially she was not going to tell them that those life-long friends, the half-brothers Sun Goes Down and Runs-in-Timber, were friends no more. They had grown up together, they had fought side by side in battle, each had saved the other's life, they had been the finest examples of the *kola* relationship. But there was a deeper meaning when two men were best friends, long-time friends, who shared danger and good fortune, would risk anything for each other. Sun Goes Down and Runs-in-Timber had been *kolas* in that sense, more than brothers.

Nobody knew what had angered them with each other. Nobody would ever ask. Runs-in-Timber had ridden away and the family heard from chance travelers that he had joined the Brulé people and married. Sun Goes Down was bitter and hateful.

She took her time riding back to camp, dismounting often to use her digging stick in harvesting roots that would be good in stew, or her knife to cut leafy vegetables for greens and salad. She had two bags filled when she finished. By that time she was hungry; she had not eaten since early morning. The sun had gone down when she rode over a hill and saw the camp.

Ah, she said to herself, we must be moving tomorrow! There were horses picketed near some lodges, and she could see people bringing out bundles and parfleches, doing the familiar chores that would make packing easier in the morning. The big council lodge had already been struck. She gave her horse a gentle tap with the quirt.

Something was wrong at her own lodge. She could hear

excited talk and a small child crying. No small child lived in that lodge any more. She called to a boy, a neighbor's son, "Please picket my horse," and ran for the lodge. Another woman was running beside her in the dusk—Pine Top, who lived near.

"I want to help," Pine Top said. "There is trouble."

Whirlwind recognized the voice of her half sister, Pemmican, sounding frantic, but could not catch the words at first. Something about running away—"But I think he is following us!"

She heard her young son, Morning Rider, reply stoutly, "I won't let him touch you!" and almost collided with the boy as he emerged from the lodge. He was carrying his bow over his shoulder and wearing his arrow quiver, with a knife at his belt and a pistol in his hand.

Without waiting to see what the trouble was, she told Morning Rider quietly, "You are a good protector and brave, but don't do it alone. Get your father and Sun Goes Down and shout for Covers Up when you pass his lodge." The boy sped off.

She stepped into the lodge. Pemmican was lying against the backrest, sobbing, while half-blind old Deer Foot tenderly washed her bloody feet. Pemmican's face was dark with bruises and there was some dried blood on it that warm water had not removed. Her dress was in tatters.

Rains-on-Her was cradling a crying baby in one arm and trying to make it suck from an animal bladder with warm broth in it. She was crooning with love in her voice.

A three-year-old boy was whimpering with exhaustion and hunger as Whirlwind's daughter, Brings Horses, ten, held a horn cup of broth to his mouth. His feet were wrapped up strangely—in his mother's moccasins, far too big for him.

Whirlwind took charge of the cooking fire and the soup

kettle and put more water on to heat. "Tell me the story later," she said. "The baby is hungry because Pemmican has no milk?"

Pine Top said at once, "I have plenty, and my baby is asleep."

Rains-on-Her immediately handed over the crying infant, and Pine Top opened her dress and began to nurse him.

Pemmican's baby was nursing hungrily in the woman's arms when the men ran in, with Morning Rider behind them. They seized their weapons. White Thunder ordered, "Sun Goes Down and Covers Up, you had better watch the trail into camp. Hide in the brush. Don't kill him. Morning Rider, you are my *akícita*. Leave the gun here. Get five or six more men. That fellow is out of his mind by this time if he still has firewater."

He sat down beside Pemmican and said gently, "Now you had better tell us what happened."

His mother remarked, "You are in my way, so *you* can put this soft grease on her face to soften the dried blood and heal the cuts." He did so obediently while Pemmican talked:

"He beat me and I was afraid for the children. He was crazy drunk all the time. He went out of the lodge, yelling, and I grabbed the children and a blanket and one package of jerky and we ran. We traveled four days—lost once, before I found your trail, my own people. We had no fire, and somewhere I lost my knife, after everything began to go around and around." She wept quietly. "Strikes Two had no moccasins, and he had to walk, so I tied mine on his feet. He was such a brave little boy! Where is he?"

"Asleep," Rains-on-Her answered.

Old Deer Foot said, "Now give me that grease and I will put some on her poor sore feet."

134

Whirlwind was busy making up another bed and searching for some decent clothes for the refugee family. "You will not go back to him," she announced, and Pemmican answered, "Never. I have come home. I throw him away. Please, some more to eat."

Pine Top suggested, "Brings Horses, you go to my lodge and tell my little girl to find the new moccasins I just finished. They will be about the right size for Pemmican's boy. There must be a buckskin shirt he can wear, too—good thing I didn't throw it away when my boy outgrew it."

Whirlwind said, "You are a good woman. We have no little ones any more, so we have no clothes for them."

Other women, attracted by the excitement, looked in to see what was going on and offered to help. They had their own work to do, packing up, but their hearts were full of pity for Pemmican and her children.

Nobody slept very much that night, for who could tell what that drunken fool might do if he came? There were guards all night, and scouts along the trail, with their horses.

Morning Rider traveled farthest along the trail, lightly running. He could go more quietly that way than on horseback. There was a bright moon, so he could see well. And after a long time he heard the noise of a horse's hoofs as the animal changed position in the brush. The boy moved as silently as a fox. Under a tree he saw a man asleep—or unconscious; he was sprawled out on a ragged blanket. Morning Rider saw his face and drew in a sharp breath.

He put an arrow to his bow and called, "Sit up and look at me! I am Morning Rider, and you deserve to die!"

The man grunted. Startled, he sat up. Morning Rider released his arrow and shot him in the throat. Shivering, he heard the man choke and saw him die. Then he went over and removed the arrow. It was marked with his mark, and nobody should know who had avenged Pemmican Woman.

He didn't forget the horse. He cut the picket rope that was around its neck and struck it a blow with a rock. The horse went galloping back along the trail by which it had come. The rider it had carried would never ride again.

Halfway back to camp, Morning Rider broke that arrow and hid the pieces under logs in the woods. He could never tell anybody what he had done this night. And he would never know whether he was right or wrong, because he could not ask advice of old, wise men. But he thought he was right, or he wouldn't have done it.

To kill an enemy was to gain glory. To kill another Lakota was murder. The relatives of the dead man had a right, by common tribal law, to punish the killer in any way they wished.

But it was not fear of punishment that worried him—the dead man's relatives would be too much ashamed to want vengeance. What sickened Morning Rider was that the first man he had ever killed was not an enemy but one of his own people.

Morning Rider whispered, "It was my duty. I saw Pemmican's bruised face and bloody feet, and I heard her children crying."

Nobody found the dead man, but the wolves did. Later, when some hunters found the scattered bones, they wondered but not for very long. There were plenty of scattered bones in the woods.

Everyone in the camp was tired in the morning but they moved, as had been planned.

The head men held a short consultation: Should they ride farther to make sure of getting away from the madman?

They asked advice from Grey Bull, the *heyoka*, who was well known for his ability to see things that happened at a distance. He had suffered much, had become a holy man, a priest with great powers.

Grey Bull was very thin now from fasting, and his body bore many scars from the vows he had made and paid to the Powers, as well as from wounds received in battle. He was a noteworthy warrior, protected from death although he was so brave in fights that he seemed to be courting it. Long ago he had earned the right to wear a full war bonnet of eagle feathers, but he was too humble ever to do so. He seldom wore even a single feather in his hair.

When the head men asked him, he answered, "The Thunderbird sent me a dream. I saw that man following Pemmican. He rode a horse while she trudged on foot with her children, but he could not catch up. He was too angry. He stopped too often and drank firewater from a jug and went to sleep. That made him slow. He will never come now. He is dead."

And so the people and their horses went farther from Fort Laramie, as the head men had decided, deep into the mountains. Pemmican thought she could ride a horse, but Whirlwind would not let her try it—she was still exhausted. She rode on a pony drag, resting.

Morning Rider worked as an *akícita*, with other members of his society, riding out from the main stream of the people, watching for enemies and looking for game.

When the people made their first stop for rest and a little food, Whirlwind and other women saw to it that Pemmican had plenty to eat, and Pine Top nursed Pemmican's baby as well as her own.

Pemmican said, "Thanks. Thanks." She added, "He wanted

137

to sell me to the soldiers at the fort, and I would not let him. That was why he was angry."

She never mentioned him again.

The ideal woman among the Lakotas did not gossip, but no woman achieved this ideal. During everyday work, especially monotonous work like tanning hides, what else was there to do but talk? And what subject was more interesting than other people? Gossip wasn't always bad, anyway. Often, it was praise for the courage or industry or kindness of this or that man or woman. Only those nonentities who never amounted to anything weren't talked about, those who just walked along through life without doing any more or any less than was expected of them.

But gossip could be vicious. The wife of Whirlwind's young brother-in-law, Crazy Bear, was a vicious gossip. Many Winds Woman was always wanting to be back at Fort Laramie, which she remembered as a marvelously exciting place. Her husband scolded her for her laziness, which embarrassed him, and her bad temper, which irritated him. Once in a while he hit her, when she had it coming and he was exasperated and tired after a hard, unsuccessful hunt. He kept telling her—unwisely—that she should be more like Whirlwind.

Many Winds Woman was even more unwise when, without considering the possible consequences, she began to drop hints that Whirlwind wasn't such a paragon. "I could tell some things if I wanted to," she remarked to a friend, and then to another friend, "And so could two or three of the men. I know what I know!"

Whirlwind noticed that some of the younger women, of the age of Many Winds Woman, began to look at her in a peculiar way, out of the corners of their eyes. There came a day when one of Whirlwind's friends, on a visit while they both sewed moccasins, told her quietly, "That wife of Crazy Bear is saying bad things about you. I think you had better give a feast for good women and challenge her."

Whirlwind was shocked and angry. She began to plan immediately. "It must be soon, but not until most of the men are home from hunting. I want my man here and Crazy Bear and many other men. Oh, yes, I'll challenge her! Let me see, what totally respectable old woman shall I ask to announce this?"

Old Deer Foot was eligible—her reputation was spotless and she had not married again after she was widowed. But she agreed that the herald for the feast should be someone outside the family. They decided on her friend, the aged and virtuous Red Pony Woman. Then they made preparations and spread the news quietly and informally while waiting for all or most of the men to return to camp from hunting expeditions or whatever they were doing.

When that time came, Red Pony Woman, who had to use a staff in walking, went around the camp circle shouting, "Whirlwind Woman has had only one man! Let all other women who can make this claim come and eat! Let all who challenge her virtue come to bite the knife!"

Whirlwind and Rains-on-Her carried kettles of food to the center of the camp circle. Widows who had married again and women of bad reputation did not come forward, but all others with a claim to respectability did—including the gossip, Many Winds Woman, who acted sulky. What woman, only once married, would dare stay away? Men gathered around the outside, some of them grinning, nudging one another with their elbows.

Red Pony Woman, happy to be the center of attention, shouted, "All these women say they are virtuous. If any man knows one who is not, let him point her out and bite the knife!"

There was a scuffle among the younger warriors, someone among them yelled, "Whirlwind!" and they pushed a sheepish young fellow forward, all laughing. Whirlwind turned to glare at him, but he yelled, "No, no!" and turned to hide behind the others. They were simply being boisterous and having fun.

Old Red Pony Woman shouted, "Come forward and accuse! If you bite the knife on a lie, a knife will kill you pretty soon."

The knife lay on the ground beside the pots of food. A tall, good-looking man named Stops Them stepped forward. "Many Winds should not take part in this feast for good women," he accused—and picked up the knife and bit it for everyone to see.

That was about what Whirlwind and her supporters had expected. Many Winds screamed in anger, but the other women did not stop to argue. They picked up pieces of filth they had brought along, including buffalo dung, and threw them at her as she ran to hide. She had just been convicted of adultery.

That was a satisfaction to Whirlwind, whom she had unjustly accused in gossip. Then, to the surprise and horror of Whirlwind and her family, her brother Sun Goes Down stepped forward.

"That woman over there, Willow, I had her before she married Frost, and after that, too," he boasted. The young woman screamed and ran away as Sun Goes Down bit the knife.

The other women threw dirt at her, but she was fleet of foot and got away from them.

No other man came forward. Red Pony Woman shouted,

"Good women, married women who have had only one man, sit down and eat. Everybody else go away now."

Whirlwind was vindicated, but she was sick at heart as she served her guests. Sun Goes Down had done a cruel thing. He had a perfect right to accuse Willow, of course. But adultery was a bad thing for a man, although not so bad as for a woman, and he could have kept still instead of boasting about seducing that young woman who was not on trial.

The punishment for the two accused women differed. Crazy Bear simply divorced Many Winds. He ordered her to dismantle their lodge and go back to her parents, taking the things that belonged to her.

But from Willow's lodge came screams of pain and sobbing after the sounds of a struggle. Her husband kept her, but he cut off the end of her nose with a knife, as he had a right to do, so that she was hideous and ashamed to be seen all the rest of her life. That was not very long. The wound still had scabs on it when she went out into the woods one night with a horse's picket rope and hanged herself from a tree.

Part VIII

1866

War in the Mountains

Living in the Lodge:

> *White Thunder, 56, head of the family*
> *Whirlwind, 46, his wife*
> *Morning Rider, 26, their son*
> *Rains-on-Her, 43, wife of White Thunder*
> *Shoots, 3, motherless son of Morning Rider*
> *Plenty Feathers Woman, 27, widow of Sun Goes*
> *Down*
> *Little Bull, 6, her son*
> *White Cow Sees, 3, her daughter*
> *Deer Foot Woman, aged mother of White Thunder*

Chapter 15

By the year the white men numbered 1866, the Lakotas were constantly harassed by invading Wasichus. The pale-skinned people with their wagons still pushed westward along the Medicine Road in increasing numbers. The Wasichus had been fighting a war among themselves far to the eastward, but now that was over, so more blue-coated soldiers were free to fight the Indians and try to take away the country where they lived and hunted.

142

Life was harder now; it had never been easy. Whirlwind's husband, White Thunder, was head man of their village, which numbered only fifteen lodges. A few years ago it had been twice as big and much more prosperous.

White Thunder, at fifty-six, was old for hunting and for the violence of war. In bygone years he would have been a respected leader who advised and planned but did not have to hunt or fight. Now, in these bitter times, he did all these things, because young men were few.

His brother Crazy Bear had died in some fighting on the Medicine Road. There had been no news for a long time of Covers Up or Runs-in-Timber or Swims Under.

Sun Goes Down, the scapegrace brother of Whirlwind, had reformed, married a Miniconjou girl, Plenty Feathers Woman, and fathered two children. So when he died fighting the Wasichu soldiers in 1864 he left a young widow, a small son, and an infant daughter. White Thunder took them in because they needed a home—Plenty Feathers was far from her own people—but he did not take her for his wife.

The only young hunter in the lodge was Morning Rider, son of White Thunder and Whirlwind. Morning Rider's young wife had been killed by a grizzly bear while picking berries. He had a son, Shoots, three years old.

There were many to feed in the lodge—old Grandmother Deer Foot, blind and ailing, two wives, the young widow, and three small children—and many helpless ones in the camp who had to depend for meat on the generosity and hunting skill of a few strong young men.

Whirlwind worried, but she was comforted by the presence of her daughter, Brings Horses, whose lodge was nearby. Brings Horses had married a Hunkpapa, Elk Rising, a year before. Because of the great respect that existed between a man and his mother-in-law, Whirlwind did not speak to him, but she thought well of him.

Brings Horses confided to her mother, when they were working together at butchering a buffalo, "He talks of going back to his own people. If that is what he decides to do, I will have to go away from you."

Both cried a little, but there was no use to argue about it.

"I suppose he misses his family?" Whirlwind suggested.

"Yes, and there is a bigger reason. The Hunkpapa chief who is talked about all the time is Sitting Bull. When others surrender, he vows that he never will. That is how my man feels too. He says to surrender is to die. The Blue Coats never keep their promises—except when they say they will kill all the Indians."

Very early in the spring two young men came to visit and bring news, an Oglala named Black Lodge, from another camp, and a French trader's half-Oglala son. This one looked like a Lakota, tall and handsone, but his skin was lighter and his long hair was startling. It was black but curly. People always stared at him. Whatever his name was supposed to be, he had long ago stopped using it, because everyone called him Pretty Hair. He did not braid it but wore it loose, liking to show off how different he was.

The two men were welcome because they brought news and because they helped bring in meat.

When they had been there for several days, Whirlwind spoke quietly to White Thunder: "I do not trust them. They have no homes, they move around all the time. I don't think Pretty Hair knows who he really is, Lakota or Wasichu."

Her husband agreed gravely. "He lives in two worlds and does not belong in either of them. He has not decided yet."

"He is plenty old enough to decide whether he is on our side or the Wasichus'. Is he a spy, telling them about us as he tells us about them?"

White Thunder said, "He hates most of them. I think he lies to them when it pleases him."

Pretty Hair was a great talker and boasted that he could speak several languages: "Lakota from my mother, French from my father, English because I learned at my father's trading post, and some Shoshone and Pawnee, and the hand-sign talk, of course. Sometimes the Wasichu chiefs at the Fort pay me to interpret for them—when they can't find someone they like better. They do not like me very much." He laughed loudly, and Whirlwind's people understood that sometimes he interpreted carelessly or wrong on purpose.

The young men, like Morning Rider, envied him and Black Lodge their freedom to go anywhere and be welcome without having responsibilities. The older men, like White Thunder, did not completely trust them, because they could be troublemakers. But everybody listened when they sat by the fire and talked. Pretty Hair never waited until his advice was asked, as a young man should. He acted like the equal of the wise old men. He took credit for everything the Lakotas had done to harass the Wasichus.

"The time we chased back that bunch of Wasichus who tried to pass through the Powder River country three years ago—ah, that was fine!" he boasted.

White Thunder replied dryly, "Yes. I was there."

That was the first time the Wasichus tried to go through there with wagons. Led by two men named Bozeman and Jacobs, they tried to get up to the gold camps to the north-west. There were more than one hundred Wasichus, including ten women and several children.

145

Pretty Hair laughed. "We told them, 'Go back or we kill you. Go back or we wipe you out.' "

White Thunder answered, "One of our head men explained it to them. 'This is our hunting country, and we will not let our women and children starve,' he said. 'You go back or stay here dead.' So they went back."

Whirlwind and some of the other women who had been there made the women's sound of triumph and praise, a high trilling.

"But the next summer," one of the older men reminded them, "more wagons came and we fought them. I used some of the Wasichus' hair to trim my shirt." A great "Ah" of approval went up from the audience.

"Then last summer there was lots of fighting with the Wasichu soldiers," Pretty Hair reminded them. "The soldier chief named Connor gave orders to kill every Indian man over twelve years, to hunt us down like wolves. But we hunted them down like wolves—no, like rabbits! And we hunted their Pawnee scouts, too."

"They built a little fort on the trail," White Thunder said. "A few soldiers are there. We don't care about them. But we will keep them out of Powder River. Lakotas, Cheyennes, Arapahoes—we are all together in this. We must keep them out."

His people roared, "Ah!"

"The two Oglala chiefs that the blue-coat soldiers hung up last year at Fort Laramie," one of the older men remarked. "Do their bodies still hang there on the bluff? Two Face and Black Foot—I remember them."

Pretty Hair made his mouth into a snarl. "They are still hanging, what's left of them. Dry and rotten now, hanging in chains. Two Face brought in a white woman captive to trade her for supplies. He thought he was doing a good thing! She had been sold among the Cheyennes and the Oglalas, she and her baby boy, and she wanted to go back to the Wasichus. So the thanks Two Face got was that the Wasichus stood him and Black Foot on a wagon with chains around their necks from a scaffold and then lashed the horses so the men hung there and strangled. It was horrible. Then the soldiers shot their bodies full of holes."

A low roar of anger went up from the listeners.

"The name of the soldier chief who ordered that is Moonlight. He hates all Indians. When he first came to Fort Laramie, he talked big about how all Indians should be killed. Women and babies too. After the hanging of the chiefs, he made all the Oglalas move away from the fort—but I think it was a higher chief than Moonlight who gave the order. Our people have lived there for years. I was born in the camp there. The Lakotas there were friendly, not hostile. But they had to go east to Fort Kearney, Moonlight said. They are meek people, they don't fight the Wasichus, so they got ready to go.

"But the Brulé Lakotas, under Chief Spotted Tail, were with them, wanting to make a peace treaty with the Wasichus—and those Brulés were not willing to go east where the Pawnees could wipe them out."

Pretty Hair chuckled, remembering. The other men nodded; they had heard all this before, but it was right to be reminded of how this story came out. They would have to fight the Wasichus some more, they knew very well.

"So fifteen hundred of our people moved—friendly Oglalas and all the Brulés with Spotted Tail. The soldier chiefs were fools, fools. Ah, how we tricked them! One morning our people just left their lodges standing and everybody rode across the Platte River. An Oglala named Black Wolf found a crossing place, and while they struggled across he vowed to suffer in the Sun-gazing Dance if they all made it. Later he kept his vow, of course. The Lakotas went up toward White River, all safe—but they left some dead soldiers behind, all cut up."

An exultant roar went up from Pretty Hair's listeners.

One of the warriors took up the story: "The man Moonlight took a bunch of his pony soldiers to chase the Lakotas and kill them, but he had to walk back. I was with the men who got those horses. I have two of them yet, good American horses, bigger than ours but not so durable."

After a few more days, Pretty Hair and Black Lodge rode back southward toward the Medicine Road. The adventuresome young men sighed to see them go, free and irresponsible. But there would be fighting enough when the Wasichus and their wagons came up the road again, and meanwhile they hunted and made much meat.

That was the spring old Deer Foot went away. She told nobody except Little Bull, six years old. When nobody else was in the lodge, she put on her blanket and groped for the staff she used in walking, and called to him in her reedy voice, "Little Bull, where are you?"

"Right here," he answered. "I am going out to practice shooting with my bow."

"Can you wait a little while?" she coaxed. "I want to take a walk in the woods, and you will help me not to fall."

Little Bull was being properly brought up to be generous and compassionate to the old and helpless. He answered, without enthusiasm, "All right. You can hold the staff in one hand and put the other on my shoulder. But you may stumble in the woods. There is snow on the ground."

"That is where I want to go," she insisted. "It smells different there. It smells good."

So they walked for a long time, and the boy was vigilant about warning her when she might stumble over something.

She kept telling him what a good boy he was, and he thought so, too.

"Now we are in the woods," she said, "and I like the smell. I will rest here. You can go back now. I will follow after I rest myself."

He was heartily tired of the expedition by that time, but he was loyal. "I can't leave you here! You can't see."

"I can see more than anyone thinks," she told him, chuckling. "I like to fool everybody. When I get ready, I will go back to camp."

She convinced him, because he wanted to be convinced. He had been a good boy all afternoon.

"Before you go," she told him, when he was eager to be off, "tell me what is in the direction of this log I am sitting on."

"The downhill end points toward our village. The uphill end goes into deeper woods. But don't go that way. There is a stream with steep banks, and you might fall down into the water."

"I can hear the water," she said. "It talks. You are a good boy. Now go home while I rest."

Nobody missed her until almost dark, because sometimes she visited her old friend Red Pony Woman and they talked about times long past and people long dead. Little Bull had supper with a friend of his age group. Whirlwind went finally to the tattered lodge of Deer Foot's old friend to bring her home—but she had not been there. Whirlwind ran to find White Thunder.

"I cannot find your mother!" she told him.

No one could find her, but they did find Little Bull, who told them he had taken Deer Foot for a walk in the woods. He was thoroughly scared. "She wanted me to! She told me to come home. Did I do wrong?"

White Thunder picked him up and held him in strong

arms. "You did what she wanted. That was not wrong. But now we will get torches and you will lead us to the place where you left her."

A dozen men and women went out carrying blazing torches, following the lead of the small boy, until he said, "This is the log. I warned her there is a stream ahead with steep banks, and she said she could hear the water talking."

The child was crying, so White Thunder patted his shoulder and repeated, "You did not do wrong. Now you stay with your mother."

On the log they found Deer Foot's moccasins, set neatly side by side, and her blanket neatly folded.

The men who went up through the dark woods with him did not shout Deer Foot's name, because they knew she would not hear them. White Thunder slid down the steep bank of the stream while the others held torches above to light his way.

He found her lying in the water, face down. He picked her up in his arms—so old a lady, so light a burden—and the other men helped him up the bank.

"Ah, see," one of the men said quietly. "She put on her spirit moccasins with the beaded soles."

White Thunder knelt beside the gaunt old body and stroked the wet forehead and the thin grey braids.

"She can see well now," he murmured, "to find her way to the Land of Many Lodges. And the women can make her platform up here in the woods where she wanted to go."

Six-year-old Little Bull sobbed all the way back down to camp and could not be comforted by his mother or Whirlwind. They took turns carrying him and assuring him that he had not done wrong. He had obeyed old Deer Foot's last command, carried out her last wish.

150

"She trusted you to do it," his mother told him. "She could not trust anybody else."

He had courage, that little boy. Without wincing, he could let a seed burn on the back of his hand until it seared the skin, in the bravery games that older boys played. But now he wept like a helpless baby.

"She was always good to me," he sobbed. "But I killed her."

That night he had bad dreams and cried aloud, "No! No!" When that happened, White Thunder took him into his own bed and held him snugly and talked in a low voice:

"She was tired of living and being old and blind. She wanted to go away. She needed someone to help her. She is not the only one you know who ever looked for the Spirit Road on purpose. Two winters ago an old man wandered out into the snow and lay down to sleep. But maybe you don't remember."

"I don't remember," Little Bull said thoughtfully.

"I will tell you something I did," White Thunder murmured. "It hurt me to do it, but I am not sorry. Long ago, when I was young, I had a good friend. We grew up together. He was a brave warrior. He saved my life once in a fight with the Crows. But in another fight, he was badly wounded, so he could not hunt or fight any more. It hurt him to ride a horse, even after his wounds healed. He was still young, and he did not want to go on living that way, crippled.

"So after two more winters, he asked me to help him, and I did."

Little Bull caught his breath. "What did you do?"

"With some other friends, I helped him go into battle for the last time. We took him partway on a pony drag, because riding hurt him. But he rode into battle, and I helped him

151

dismount. We fought on foot, side by side, and he killed two enemies before the others killed him. That was what he wanted, to die in battle. Do you understand?"

"Yes. I understand. It was a good way for him to go. Like a warrior."

"I did that on purpose, remember. I will never forget it. You did not do anything on purpose. You only helped Grandmother Deer Foot go for a walk in the woods because she asked you to."

"Yes. That was how it was," the little boy agreed. After a while he went to sleep with his head on White Thunder's strong arm. White Thunder lay awake a long time, thinking.

She was a wise woman, my mother, he thought. She must have known how it would be—what way I would find to comfort this little boy. Nobody is to blame. She knew that I still grieve for my best friend, who died fighting beside me long ago. I must pay more attention to this little boy from now on, because of the burden he has to carry. I will call him Little Warrior whenever he does something good. That will lift him up. I must be more thoughtful of his mother, too, because she is much stricken.

I must find her a good man for her husband, a father for her fine children.

Chapter 16

They had moved camp when the half-Lakota, Pretty Hair, came again and found them. This time he had with him a northern Cheyenne warrior, very bitter and full of hatred for the Wasichus. His name was Sky Above. They brought important news. Pretty Hair did most of the talking, while Sky Above seemed tense and taut as a bowstring. They did not stay long, because they were going on to visit other camps.

"News has come from all over," Pretty Hair reported. "It was a terrible winter, and many people starved because the Wasichus did not send the annuities they promised when the Fort Laramie treaty was signed fifteen winters ago. There was much suffering among the people, and the sick and the weak ones died of hunger and cold.

"One who died was the daughter of the Brulé, Spotted Tail. She had lived too long around the fort and could not endure the hard life of her father's people. He grieved greatly and brought her to the fort for burial. There is a pretty good soldier chief there now; they call him Many Deer. He saw to it that Spotted Tail's daughter had a fine funeral, and the band played. That girl, poor thing, liked the Wasichus. She thought she would marry a chief among the soldiers at the fort. But she died. Many Deer is a pretty good man—Colonel Maynadier—for a Wasichu soldier chief.

"A few days after the funeral, the great Red Cloud visited the fort. He wanted to talk about a peace treaty because his people had suffered so much and needed so many things. So they have set a time to meet there. The Cheyennes are coming, too, and some Arapahoes and Miniconjous came in just before we left there. This is what we have come to tell you."

White Thunder answered, "We will talk about this. Maybe we should go. Red Cloud is a wise leader. Let our Cheyenne guest speak. Sky Above, how is it with the Cut Arm people?"

The Cheyenne stood in the council circle and said in the swift, graceful hand talk, "I do not speak your tongue well, only a little. I will talk with my hands."

White Thunder waited until the audience had moved so they could watch the Cheyenne's hands and arms. As he used

153

them, he also spoke his own language, so that the tones of his voice carried meaning, too. He was an impressive orator, because he was full of sorrow and despair and anger. He said:

"I do not care whether you make peace or not. I only want to fight, and I will fight on your side if you want me. I want to fight and die. There is nobody left to me among my own people. My mother and father were killed, my two wives and three children were killed, my brothers died in battle, and my one sister died fighting. All this was at Sand Creek. I have nobody left and I do not want to live. I will do everything I can to kill Wasichus before they kill me."

There was a gasp and a great murmur, a groan, among his audience. Now they knew why he was so tense. He was a man vowed to die. They noted the fringes of hair that decorated his shirt—no black Indian hair, but yellow or brown or red, short from the scalps of men, long from the scalps of women and children, many colors of hair. Sand Creek had been more than a year before, and this distracted man had dedicated himself to vengeance.

Sky Above added: "If you fight the Wasichus I am your brother. If you decide not to fight them, I will find some other tribe that will. Pretty Hair comes to tell you about a big meeting to talk peace. I am not going to talk peace. I have no voice in the councils of the Oglalas. I am a Cheyenne, with no relatives because the Wasichus killed them all at Sand Creek. I was not there. So I am doomed to live for a while until I find death in battle."

He threw his head back and gave the screaming war cry.

There was a great stirring among his audience, and some men shouted agreement. But White Thunder, thinking first of his duty to protect the helpless ones of his people, was silent until Sky Above had sat down with his head bowed, his

154

shoulders shaking in anguish, and a corner of his blanket hiding his face.

White Thunder said sadly, "Our hearts are on the ground. We grieve with you. We will talk about this and decide what to do." At a gesture from him, two of the *akícitas* helped Sky Above to his feet and took him away to a lodge where he could not hear the discussion. They stayed with him there, giving sympathy.

To Pretty Hair, who remained, White Thunder said, "We heard of Sand Creek. Tell us what you know. *Akícitas*, prepare the oath."

The young men brought dried buffalo dung and built it into a pile, and a boy brought a horse for Pretty Hair to ride in this ceremony that pledged he would tell the truth as far as he knew it. He rode off, out of the camp circle, and then rode back with the horse at a run. Leaping from the horse's back, he kicked over the pile of buffalo chips. That was the oath.

He stood in the council circle and told them the story: A big bunch of Cheyennes wanted to surrender, make peace— six hundred of them. Their chiefs were Black Kettle and White Antelope. They went to Fort Lyon and told the commanding officer there. He sent them to camp at Sand Creek, because he did not have authority to make a peace treaty but would send word to his superiors, who did. Meanwhile he would protect them.

But there was a soldier chief named Chivington who said, "The only good Indian is a dead Indian," and he rode out from Denver with almost a thousand Wasichu soldiers and attacked the Cheyennes and some Arapahoes who were waiting hopefully and peaceably at Sand Creek.

"What I am going to tell you I did not see, but people who

155

were there told me, and I speak the truth of what they said," Pretty Hair explained. "The Wasichus attacked the Cheyenne village at dawn. A woman saw them and raised the alarm. Chief Black Kettle ran out and put up a big American flag and also a white flag, for peace. But the Wasichus fired with cannons and rifles. The Cheyenne warriors had few guns, and some of them could not seize any weapons when they ran to try to get the helpless ones away to safe places.

"Chief White Antelope would not fight. He folded his arms and stood singing his death song:

> " 'Nothing lives long
> Except the earth and the mountains.'

"A bullet killed him. He was an old man. Black Kettle wanted to die, too, but the warriors made him go away—they dragged him. He had his wife by the arm, but he lost her. She was shot and fell down. Later he found her, still living. She said soldiers fired seven more bullets into her body while she was lying there.

"Women and their children hid in holes under the creek bank and begged to live, showing the soldiers they were women. The Wasichus shot them down. One woman lay with a broken leg. A soldier swung his saber and broke her arm as she reached, begging for mercy. Then he broke her other arm—and left her there, alive but dying.

"Cheyennes I talked to told me they saw two soldiers kill a little girl who carried a white flag on a stick. They saw a woman cut open and her unborn child lying bloody beside her. Soldiers scalped the people and cut them up in horrible ways. One woman wandered around, screaming—she could not see because a soldier had scalped her, and the skin of her forehead hung down over her eyes. Some of the soldiers

156

raped women who had been wounded with bullets or sabers and then killed them. Then the soldiers went back to Denver with some Cheyenne children as captives and showed them off and showed the scalps they had taken.

"All these things the survivors told me. I speak the truth. They told me even more than I have told you."

The fighting men in the lodge discussed these things. All of them had heard of some of the horrors of Sand Creek. None of them knew of any detail that disagreed with this story. They could believe Pretty Hair this time, although perhaps not always. Now he was all Indian.

White Thunder arose to sum up the decision. "So we will go to the fort and hear what Chief Red Cloud has to say about making a peace treaty when the Wasichus come to speak for the Grandfather. Then we will decide whether we agree with Red Cloud or not."

The men hunted and made meat, and the women tanned some robes and dried some meat, but there wasn't time to do things properly. They had to start moving toward Fort Laramie to find out what their head chiefs, their wisest men, were going to decide.

Some of the women were sulky about having to waste good meat that spoiled because they had to pack it up before it was dried enough in the sun. They grumbled about hides that stiffened for lack of time to finish the long, painstaking process of tanning. Someone was always leaving behind some small valued tool or work implement in the hurry of preparing to move camp.

Whirlwind was not sulky. She was exasperated and angry, and she often spoke her mind—even, sometimes, to her husband, although he had big troubles enough and she usually tried to protect him from small ones.

157

"We can't plan any more," she said bitterly. "When I was a girl, the people had time to do things right. Our daughter, Brings Horses, never went through the Buffalo Woman ceremony, as I did—we women didn't have time to prepare the gifts for that. This year we don't even know when or where the Sun-gazing Dance will be, because we have to go to the fort. There are boys who should be out lamenting for a medicine dream now—but if they did that, they would be left behind. How long is it since anyone could keep the spirit of a dead person? We hurry too much!"

White Thunder replied without words, with only a look of deep sadness, so that she threw the corner of her blanket across her face and ran out of the lodge, ashamed.

Their village moved. Other villages moved, all converging on Fort Laramie to see what the wise leaders would do and say. But in the end, each head of family would decide for himself what was best. No man was bound by allegiance to any leader. Each made his own judgments based on the reputation of a leader—for bravery, success, medicine power as proved by past events. Persuasiveness through oratory would count, too. The leader who was most trusted would attract the most followers.

As they traveled and joined with other villages they heard many rumors: the great Red Cloud wanted a peace treaty, indeed, he had asked for one. No, he had changed his mind. Well, they would find out.

Red Cloud was not at Fort Laramie when they arrived— he had gone to bring in more of the wild Oglalas. So they waited, vast numbers of people.

A man named Taylor, sent out by the Grandfather in Washington, made a long speech, saying that he did not come to buy their good hunting country but only to arrange that white men going to the gold camps up north should pass through the Powder River country without harm. These white men would not disturb the game, he promised. They only wanted to pass through that country. For this privilege, the Grandfather would give his Indian people presents.

This sounded much like the promises that had been made fifteen winters earlier at Fort Laramie—let the Wasichus go through, and every year you will receive food and clothing. But the prairie had been soaked with blood since then, the buffalo herds had been driven off or slaughtered, and Indians had starved or frozen to death because the presents had not always come. (The agents sent by the Grandfather stole most of them and grew rich.)

The Grandfather spoke with a forked tongue. At the same time he spoke through Taylor, making fine promises, he sent a great army—almost a thousand men—under a soldier chief named Colonel Henry Carrington to build permanent forts along the Powder River, in the heart of the Oglalas' hunting country!

A Brulé chief named Standing Elk brought news of that back to the tribes waiting at the fort. He met Carrington before the Blue Coats reached the fort and talked to him. Carrington said plainly what he was going to do. Standing Elk warned him clearly: "The Lakotas in the Powder River country will fight you. They will not give you the road unless you kill them."

Carrington had a lot of men—some of the white chiefs even had their women and children with them—and a lot of guns, but Standing Elk, estimating their numbers, realized that compared to the numbers of fighting Indians who would defend Powder River, these Wasichus constituted a small island in a very big and angry lake.

Carrington met with the chiefs at Fort Laramie. One of them said truly and with bitter anger, "The Grandfather sends us presents and wants a new road, but the white chief goes to steal the road before we say yes or no!"

While the parleying went on among the chiefs and head men, the women in the camps were like ants in an anthill that a horse has disturbed by stepping on it. They scurried, and sent their older children scurrying, to find friends and relatives among other camps.

They found Whirlwind's brother, Covers Up, and her half brother, Runs-in-Timber, and their wives and children, and distant cousins once close and still beloved. There was rejoicing and much talk—"What a big boy he is! . . . Ah, such a pretty little girl you have! . . . And tell us about So and So—ah, he is dead? No, no! . . . My husband wants to know about his sister. . . ."

There was laughter and there were tears.

Always, Whirlwind dutifully kept sending spoken messages: "Did any Hunkpapas come yet? My daughter's husband is a Hunkpapa, and he wants to see his people."

There was no official delegation of Hunkpapas. Sitting Bull preached the gospel of "Avoid the Blue Coats! Avoid all the Wasichus! I will make no treaty. I will accept no presents. I will listen to no lies." When he said "I" he meant "we," and he was very convincing. His Hunkpapas were satisfied that what he decided was good for all of them.

But there were always some footloose young men out looking for adventure, riding from one distant Lakota village to another, responsible to nobody, and some of these circulated among the tribal circles camped at Fort Laramie for the peace talks that came to nothing. Two of them rode up to White Thunder's lodge one afternoon and inquired politely whether Elk Rising lived there.

Whirlwind and Brings Horses were just unloading firewood from a pony drag—they had ridden far to find it, because the camps there over the years had used it up for many miles.

Brings Horses replied, "Not here, but I am his woman." She looked at them and said, "You are Hunkpapas?"

They were. "He will welcome you because you have news of his people," she said sadly. "His lodge is over there. Will you wait?"

When they had ridden away, she began to cry. "We will have to go to his people," she told Whirlwind.

Whirlwind cried, too, and hugged her. Then she wiped her arm across her eyes and announced, "Now you will not cry any more. Do you hear me? Your husband would be ashamed of a woman whose eyes leak water because she is going with him. Remember that!"

Brings Horses began to look sulky. Her mother said, "After you get to his people, sometimes you can be homesick. But now you must be willing to go. And you aren't sure, anyway."

But in another day they were sure. Elk Rising had decided. "There are eight Hunkpapa warriors here. One of them has his young wife with him, because they are not a war party, just traveling around and visiting. We will have a strong enough party to go back safely to the Hunkpapas. Sitting Bull wants to know what happened here. He is not going to sign any peace treaty, but he wants to know what the other chiefs are doing. Especially Red Cloud, because the Oglalas are many."

The Indians found out through the interpreters that the Wasichus sent out by the Grandfather put them into two categories, friendlies and hostiles. Friendlies were those who touched the pen to the new treaty and said they would do what the Grandfather wanted. Hostiles were those who wanted to be free, to make no promises.

161

All the wild, free-living Oglalas were hostiles because they would not sign. Red Cloud did not sign, after all. The only chiefs who did were a few who did not hunt along the Powder River anyway, or the Yellowstone or the Big Horn. Many of their young men, disgusted, rode away and joined the hostile Oglalas who were hurrying back to defend the Powder River from Carrington and his soldiers.

When Carrington and his army reached the Powder River country, Red Cloud and his Oglalas were waiting—their camps hidden in the mountains, their scouting parties concealed in canyons and behind rocks. They ran off herds of horses and mules, killed soldiers and men who went out to cut timber for the building of the forts. The men who did the building were under fire most of the time.

Chapter 17

The Wasichus with their wagons kept trying to travel up the Bozeman Trail to the new gold camps. The Oglalas ran off their horse herds, killed or captured their herders, wiped out one whole small wagon train on the trail that the soldiers were supposed to guard but could not guard. There were graves or bloody bones all along that trail.

Meat was not plentiful in the Oglala camps, because the hunters were occupied with trying to discourage the fort-builders and the travelers. The people tightened their belts and cheered their fighting men. More and more Indians, finding the hunting poor in other places, joined Red Cloud's people.

Red Cloud and Chief Crazy Horse planned a great attack

on Fort Phil Kearney—planned it carefully in December, when there was snow and cold and soldiers expected Indians to be holed up in their warm lodges for the winter.

Red Cloud gathered the head men of the various camps and they decided what to do: "We will set a trap. The Wasichus go out every day to cut down trees and haul them to the fort. Some of our warriors will attack them, and that will draw out more soldiers from the fort. Our men will ride away, pretending to retreat, and the soldiers will follow. They will come from two or three directions to try to cut us off. We will lead them farther from the fort—and there will be a great many of our brave men waiting to wipe them out."

The warriors, listening to the decision, roared their approval and the rocks around them roared an echo.

Red Cloud directed that trap, signaling from a hill with flashes of a mirror. But the trap did not work perfectly that time. Colonel Carrington, the Little White Chief (he was a small man), was too smart. There was pursuit, there was fighting, there was blood on the snow. Some soldiers died, a few warriors died, but the trap was not a success.

More hostiles joined Red Cloud in spite of the winter weather. The Miniconjous came, and some Hunkpapas came and some No Bows, Brulés, and Arapahoes, and many bitter Cheyennes. Once more a trap was set, two weeks after the first one. High Back Bone, a Miniconjou chief, planned this one with Red Cloud. Crazy Horse, the fierce young fighter, smart as a fox, led the decoy group.

They knew they would succeed this time, because a *berdache*, a half-man, half-woman, made medicine. Such persons did not usually fight—they dressed like women because they were afraid to be men, but some of them had strange powers. This one put a black cloth over his head and, the day before the battle, rode over the hills, zigzagging his horse while the warriors and the women watched. He fell off his horse and grasped dirt, shouting that he had a few soldiers.

The chiefs told him that was not enough; they made him do the same thing three more times. Then he shouted that he had both hands full—over a hundred enemies. The hostiles shouted in triumph. They knew they were going to win.

And they did. At Fort Phil Kearney there was an officer named Fetterman who sneered at all Indians. He had boasted, "Give me eighty men and I will ride through the whole Sioux nation!"

This time when the hostiles attacked the woodcutters, Fetterman rode out with eighty men—and he rode too far, enticed into the trap by Crazy Horse. He disobeyed the command of Carrington, the Little White Chief.

Waiting at the end of the trap were almost two thousand warriors. They rode screaming, they shot fast and straight, and they wiped out Fetterman and his eighty men. They used their knives on the bodies and shot them full of arrows.

There were howling victory dances in some of the villages that night, but in some there was grief. In Fort Phil Kearney there was great grief and horror and fear because so many men had been wiped out and everyone there might be dead before long. In Whirlwind's village there was sorrow for the death of Grey Bull, the *heyoka*, an old man who had wanted for a long time to die and had fought like a demon in dozens of battles because he did not care to live. Now at last he was free of his burdens as a Thunder Dreamer.

Sometime during the night the melancholy Rains-on-Her, wife of White Thunder, went outside the lodge into the blowing snow and simply never returned. They searched for her—she was so quiet a person that it was a long time before anyone misssed her—but no trace was ever found, not even in another year when they canped in that place and searched for her bones.

That big victorious fight at Fort Phil Kearney was called by the Indians "The Battle of the Hundred Killed." The blue-coated soldiers called it the Fetterman Massacre, for the officer who led his men into the trap set by Red Cloud and High Back Bone and triggered by the wily Crazy Horse.

When Little White Chief Carrington's men went out fearfully to bring back their mutilated dead, they found no Indian bodies. The Indans had removed them so there could be no count. Among them was the Cheyenne warrior Sky Above, who hated the Wasichus so bitterly because of what had happened to his people at Sand Creek. He had four fresh bloody scalps fastened to his belt.

White Thunder said with pity, "Now he does not have to taste the bitter bile of hatred any more."

In those days Red Cloud was a great leader against the Wasichus. He kept his warriors harrying the Bozeman Road that the forts were supposed to guard. After the summer those forts were built, the road was useless. No wagon trains dared use it, only the soldiers and their messengers, bringing supplies and mail.

Finally the Grandfather gave up. Red Cloud kept saying, "Keep your people out of here. This country belongs to me for my people!" until the Grandfather agreed.

He said, "I will take my soldiers off that road and nobody will use the forts any more if you will touch the pen to a treaty. I will command my white children to stay off that road. I will give you presents, lots of presents. You can hunt in the Powder River country, and I will give you much other land where you may live."

And so in 1868 Red Cloud signed—that is, he touched the

165

pen and made an **X** before his name, which he could not read. But the Grandfather had spoken with a forked tongue again. What he meant was, "I am giving you a reservation on the Missouri River and you must live there and learn to be farmers." His representatives did not make this at all clear to either the hostiles or the friendlies.

Red Cloud did not learn the bitter truth of this until much later. But when he touched the pen, many of his people stopped believing in his wisdom as their leader.

Among the minor leaders were White Thunder and other hostiles. Red Cloud did not speak for *them*. They rode back to Powder River and went on living as they had always lived, but with no Blue Coats to fight. Sometimes they rode, yelling, past the burned ruins of the empty forts.

Among the prominent leaders who refused to sign were Crazy Horse, that young Oglala who would be heard from in the future, and Gall and Black Moon, Hunkpapas. Of course, Sitting Bull the Hunkpapa was so completely hostile that he did not even go near the treaty-signing.

Part IX

WINTER AND SPRING, 1876

How Whirlwind Saved Her Cub

Living in the Lodge:

> *Morning Rider, 36, head of the family*
> *Young Bird, 32, wife of Morning Rider*
> *Reaches Far Girl, 8, daughter of Young Bird and*
>   *Morning Rider*
> *Angry, 12, son of Young Bird, stepson of Morning*
>   *Rider*
> *Round Cloud Woman, 21, wife of Morning Rider*
>   *and sister of Young Bird*
> *Jumps, infant son of Morning Rider and Round*
>   *Cloud*
> *Shoots, 13, motherless son of Morning Rider*
> *Strikes Two, 24, son of Pemmican Woman, nephew*
>   *of Whirlwind*
> *Grandmother Whirlwind, 56, the old-woman-who-*
>   *sits-by-the-door*

Chapter 18

Whirlwind was a widow now. Her hair, hacked off in mourning for White Thunder, had grown out long enough to make short, ragged braids, but she no longer cared very much how she looked. The cuts made when she had gashed her arms and her legs had healed to scars. She no longer had a lodge of her own. When White Thunder died of a wasting sickness—not in battle, as he had wished—she abandoned the lodge as was proper and let other people take away everything in it.

But she had a good home with her son, Morning Rider. She was Grandmother Whirlwind, the old-woman-who-sits-by-the-door. She worked hard and took pride in her work. She was the one who told small children the old stories about the White Buffalo Maiden and the other sacred spirits just as those stories had been told to her by Grandmother Earth Medicine when she was very small.

Her people lived in the still rich hunting country along the Tongue River, where the Wasichus did not come any more (or did not last very long if they tried it), which had been promised to them forever in the treaty Red Cloud finally signed in 1868. But their great leader now was Crazy Horse, who had never signed any treaty. Her people were a powerful and prosperous people, called hostiles by the Wasichus, while Red Cloud and his followers lived on the dry reservation and the Wasichus ordered them around. Red Cloud's people lived badly, and he grieved because the promises he made when he had touched the pen were not what he had been told at that time.

Twice in the years since White Thunder died, the camp stopped near enough to his last resting place so that Whirlwind could visit his body and talk to him and remember the days when they had been young and she had been afraid he would not ask for her.

She wailed her grief there, but mostly she sat huddled on the ground—covered with snow this time—and looked up at the platform where he lay wrapped in elk skins, and she told him what had been happening to his family and his people.

Rains-on-Her was in the Land of Many Lodges looking after him. "When I come," she told him, "I will be the sits-beside-you wife again as I always was, and I will tell her what to do to make you happy. But I have a good place meanwhile in our son's lodge. I keep the bed robes tidy and care for the fire and carry in wood. I can put up the lodge faster by myself than his two wives can do it together. I am strong and useful! They are good girls, but a little afraid of me."

If White Thunder could hear that, she thought he would smile. She was determined of mind as well as strong of body. Sometimes she bullied her daughters-in-law.

"Sometimes I see Plenty Feathers Woman and her children by Sun Goes Down. The man you found for her long ago is good to her, and they have a fine little boy. Her older boy, Little Bull, is brave and strong. You were so kind to that child. He never forgets you. His sister is very pretty.

"Three times I have seen our daughter, Brings Horses, when the Oglalas met the Hunkpapas. We camped together for a while. Her first baby was a boy. He is seven winters old now and his name is Stormy. She has a little girl, five, Red Pipe Girl. Fine children.

"Her man, Elk Rising, took another wife, Blue Rock Woman, and they have a son three years old. A fine family, but I wish we all lived in the same camp."

Whirlwind remembered, smiling now, how she had fretted for news of her daughter and her daughter's first baby. Hunkpapa messengers visited their camp, and Oglalas visited Hunkpapa camps, but none of them had contact with the village where Elk Rising and Brings Horses lived. Whirlwind was embarrassed to inquire of important strangers about the birth of a baby—babies were born all the time! But she inquired anyway, and that embarrassed her

169

son, Morning Rider. Finally she found a visiting Hunkpapa and talked to him, acting like a pitiful old grandmother. He condescended (and that made her angry, but she hid her wrath); he said, "Yes, I know Elk Rising. A good fighting man."

"Has he any children?" she asked pathetically. "I want to know whether I am a grandmother."

The solemn visitor almost smiled. "He has a son whose ears were pierced at the last Sun-gazing Dance," he replied, and Whirlwind ran back to her lodge, shrieking with joy, not even thanking him.

Now she told the spirit of White Thunder about his grandson, Shoots, who worried the family. "Shoots is a fine boy, a good rider, a successful hunter even at only thirteen. But he has not yet spoken of going out on a hill to lament to the spirits and pray for a medicine dream. He has not asked to go with a war party. Surely he can't be afraid, not the grandson of White Thunder and the son of Morning Rider! Why, his father ran away with a war party as water boy when he was only twelve, remember? How surprised you were to find him with you when it was too late to send him back! And how I worried."

She wailed a little for old griefs and newer ones. "If you can, please ask the spirits to inspire our grandson and make him brave so we can be proud of him."

What age will my man and I be when we are together again? she wondered. There was no knowing. But it would be all right. Everything would be all right in the Land of Many Lodges.

"This was a bitter winter," she told him, "but we are Crazy Horse's people and we live well. We stay away from the Wasichus. We do not depend on the things they want to sell us. We have plenty of warm robes, we made new lodges before winter came, we have enough to eat but we do not waste anything. Here on Tongue River is a good camp. I used to think maybe we would have been safer with Red Cloud, but you were right when you advised us to follow Crazy Horse, although he is young."

She wept a little while, wrapped in her blanket. Then, shivering, she trudged back toward the camp of the people. Maybe she should have told him of the threat from the Wasichus earlier in the winter, but why worry him? Messengers had come riding, bent against the wind and snow, and ordered all the hostiles—Lakotas and Cheyennes and all of them—to go at once to the agency where Red Cloud was. A date was given by the Wasichus: if the hostiles did not come in by that date, there would be bad trouble.

But on the reservation, people were starving. That was why so many Lakotas were with Crazy Horse, hunting, because at the agency there was no food. (So much for the promises of the Grandfather in Washington!) Some did not even get the message until the date was already past. If the Wasichus' messengers could not travel through that winter weather, how could men with their families and helpless ones? And they had heard often that Indians who went to the reservation had their guns and their ponies taken away from them. No wonder they starved!

Crazy Horse refused to go. Instead, his followers—a hundred lodges or more—moved from the Tongue River to the Powder to talk to another great leader, Sitting Bull of the Hunkpapa Lakotas, about getting guns and ammunition. Because when the grass was green the soldiers would come.

There was a great deal to worry about. The Wasichus had found gold in the Black Hills, Paha Sapa, the sacred hills where the spirits were so powerful that, although the Lakotas hunted there and cut trees for their lodgepoles, they did not live there. That country was holy—and the Wasichus wanted to buy it! The Wasichu chiefs could not keep adventurers out of it, but most of those who sneaked in found death along with gold.

Some of the Lakota chiefs who had been great were weaklings now. Red Cloud wanted to sell Paha Sapa. They spit on his name. Spotted Tail of the Brulés wanted to sell. But Crazy Horse, the greatest leader of the Oglalas now, would not sell. He had nothing to do with Wasichus. And Sitting Bull and Gall, leaders of the Hunkpapas, with many lodges, would not sell. Paha Sapa had been promised to the Indians forever—but that was before the men with a Wasichu soldier chief called Custer, known as Long Hair, found gold there.

Besides the hostiles who never went near the reservation, and the hungry, puzzled friendlies who lived there in poverty, there were hundreds of warriors who endured winter on the reservation but in the spring rode out with their families to be free again. These joined the hostiles and brought news and guns and ammunition.

The hostiles would not sell Paha Sapa, and they had refused to come to the reservation during the bitter weather. Late in winter the Wasichu soldiers marched through the snow up the old Bozeman Trail—where the ruins of the forts stood like blackened, broken stubs of teeth against the snow.

They marched and they searched, and on March 17 they attacked and destroyed a big Cheyenne village of more than one hundred lodges.

It was cold outside but warm inside the lodge. Grandmother Whirlwind sat by the door, keeping her granddaughter Reaches Far interested with the true story of the way Grey Bull had dreamed a Thunder Dream and had become *heyoka*. He was long dead now, but he had been a great man, both humble and full of strange powers, and should not be forgotten.

Round Cloud Woman was drowsily nursing her infant son. Young Bird mended a moccasin, although the light from the fire was not good for pushing threads of tendon through holes punched with an awl. Strikes Two was out somewhere —young men became restless, and who was going to insult them by asking, "Where are you going?"

At the back of the lodge, in the place of honor, Morning Rider, his son Shoots, and his stepson, Angry, were involved in a game that was also a lesson. They were practicing hand-sign talk, in which it was necessary to be skilled because among many tribes there were many languages, but this one was common to all of them, and to some Wasichus as well.

Morning Rider leaned against his backrest, amused, while his boys pretended to be pipe-bearers of opposing war parties and insulted each other in total silence. Now and then Morning Rider corrected one of them—"Not so with the left hand, but this way. Not jerky, but smooth and steady."

Angry suddenly complained, "Too fast! I can't read that!" Shoots repeated what he had said, but faster.

Morning Rider teased: "Angry, great warrior, where is your dignity? You must not admit ignorance. The enemy will laugh and then turn you over to their women."

Angry calmed his rage and answered Shoots with his chin at a haughty angle. He was tense and alert. He did not complain again. He learned. Then Morning Rider began to tell a story so ridiculous that both boys burst out laughing.

From her place by the door, Whirlwind spoke suddenly: "Hush! There is trouble!"

They could all hear a disturbance then—someone wailing, many persons shouting.

Morning Rider, who wore a buckskin shirt, high leggings,

and moccasins, seized his weapons and threw a warm soft robe around his shoulders. His two wives jumped out of his way and Whirlwind held the door open for him. As he leaped out, he ordered the boys, "Angry, come with me—Shoots is guard."

Grandmother Whirlwind tossed Shoots a small blanket and snapped, "Put that on. It's cold outside."

He gave her a glare as he picked up the blanket. She would not have dared to order him that way, like a small child, if he had ever showed any sign of wanting to grow up and be a warrior.

Angry, a year younger, had made one effort to follow a small war party as their servant. He had been caught and scolded and sent back, but the attempt gave him some prestige. Now he collected his things and ran to follow Morning Rider.

Shoots took his bow, slung his quiver of arrows over his shoulder, and belted on his good knife. Then he said quietly, "Women, get away from the door so I can watch." They obeyed him, smiling with pride.

They could hear yelling: "Cheyennes are coming into camp! Lakotas are coming! They are starved and wounded and freezing!"

They recognized the powerful voice of the camp herald: "The Wasichus burned their camp. Help them, all people! Feed the hungry ones, help the cold and bleeding ones!"

The women gasped. Young Bird ran out past Shoots to bring more firewood. Round Cloud Woman hung her baby in his cradleboard out of the way and built up the cooking fire. Whirlwind began to open parfleche boxes of *wasna*, the good, rich pemmican. She unrolled extra robes, large and small.

They could hear people in nearby lodges asking questions

174

that nobody could answer, hurriedly making preparations for the sufferers from disaster.

Shoots spoke from the doorway: "A woman is helping someone this way—a woman and some children."

There was shouting among the lodges as men circled out with their weapons and boys ran through the snow to make sure the pony herd was safe in the big pole corral and to bring back some horses in case they might be needed.

All over camp there were shouts: "Come in, friends. Here is food and fire. Here are plenty of warm robes. Come in!"

They could hear the wailing of the refugees, partly in misery and partly expressing their immense relief at reaching friends and shelter. Whirlwind put her head out and cried, as others were doing, "Come in, friends! Come and eat! Come and warm yourselves. You are welcome!"

Whirlwind ran out with a blanket to throw around a woman who was stumbling along, crying. Round Cloud, right behind her, lifted the woman's baby off her shoulders and carried it, murmuring. There was also a boy of about six, stumbling, holding to his sister's hand; she was slightly older. They were all crying. Young Bird picked up one under each arm and ran toward the lodge.

There was much movement in the lodge as the strangers were wrapped in warm, soft robes and the women rubbed their cold hands and feet. "Not too near the fire if you are frozen," Whirlwind warned. "You will be warm soon. You are hungry and you will be fed." The children clung to her as if she might get away.

Round Cloud began to undo the wrappings of the baby's cradleboard. "Oh, he is so wet and cold, the little one," she crooned. "But we will warm him and feed him."

Shoots stayed outside to be free of the turmoil and to guard the lodge as he had been ordered. Besides, he could hear and see more of the excitement in camp that way. People were still coming in at the other side of the camp circle. Some of the men were leading horses, but nobody was riding. The horses were too worn out. Boys were running to bring them tender cottonwood bark and what dry grass they could scrabble out from under the snow in sheltered places.

About this time the women in Morning Rider's lodge discovered that their exhausted guests did not understand the Lakota language. It was obvious from their clothing and the style of their moccasins that they were Cheyennes. Women did not usually learn much of the hand-sign talk, but just now they did not need it. The Cheyenne woman made a hopeless sign, easily understood, that she could not nurse her baby. She had not had enough to eat in the past terrible days to make milk.

But Round Cloud had a young child and milk; she nursed the newcomer while Young Bird gave good rich soup to the older children and Whirlwind helped the mother to eat. Reaches Far, sent to bring more firewood, ran willingly and brought plenty, although she was only eight.

Shoots, on guard, saw something across the camp circle that lifted his heart. There stood the great leader Crazy Horse—not so tall as most Lakotas, lighter of skin, with brown hair instead of black, a silent man, young for so trusted a leader, a strange man in many ways, but trustworthy and wise. He was surrounded by other men, Lakotas and the exhausted warriors of the refugee Cheyenne people. They were talking. He was listening. But when he did say something, it was worthwhile. He spoke little, but he said that little in both Lakota and sign. Now everything would probably be all right.

The group of men separated, and the boys who had been listening hard behind them in their council sped in all directions. Shoots waited for Angry to arrive breathless with the news.

"I will tell the women," Angry said, "and you can hear from outside."

"The strangers in there are Cheyennes," Shoots informed him. "They can't speak our language—or sign talk either."

Angry nodded and slipped into the lodge. Shoots listened. He was very cold, but he was going to stand guard if he froze to death.

Angry told the women: "The Cheyenne men do not know where their families are, so as fast as possible their men will come around and find out. A few of them speak some Lakota, but they can all talk sign to our men. A few families of them are Lakotas with He Dog as their leader; they were camping with the Cheyennes.

"When the suffering people are fed and warmed and their wounds attended to, then He Dog and the Cheyenne chief, Two Moons, will tell what happened, and then the chiefs will decide what to do."

Shoots heard Whirlwind answer, "Our women had better set up the very large council lodge for this meeting. Tomorrow some of us will be free to do that."

The village was full of activity and noise. Young girls were carrying firewood to many of the lodges, small boys and girls were running errands, big boys were moving the pony herd close to camp, and warriors were riding out, grim faced and fully armed, to guard all the people and search for stragglers. There was wailing in most lodges as the refugee women cried out for news of relatives and children cried because of pain and fear.

Shoots stayed where he was, walking around because his feet were cold. When he saw a strange man plodding toward him, Shoots set an arrow to his bow and challenged him. But the man was Cheyenne and what he said meant nothing to Shoots. The boy could not talk sign while holding his bow ready, so he called, "Angry, come out with your knife in your hand and help me talk to this stranger!"

The Cheyenne had been wounded; there was dried blood on his face, and one arm had a wrapping of buckskin. He spoke in a desperate way, but his speech was incomprehensible. Shoots advised Angry, "Now put your knife in your belt and ask him in sign what he wants."

The stranger, much relieved, answered with swift hand movements. Both boys understood: Someone had told him his wife and children were in this lodge. Angry asked, *What is your name?* and the hand-sign reply was *Bear Walking.* . . . *What is your wife's name?* The answer was *Pine Cone.*

Shoots said, "He may be all right, but I'm not going to let him in where the women and children are until we're sure."

"His wife should recognize his voice," Angry suggested, and said in sign, *Say your wife's name loud.*

The Cheyenne shouted it in his own language, and there was a scream of joy from inside the lodge.

Both boys stood aside and let the man enter to reassure his frantic wife that he was safe and to assure himself that she and the children were in good hands.

Such reunions took place all over the village, which was very crowded after all the refugees had come in. The population was almost doubled now, and the stir and noise went on until late at night. Robes had to be carried from those who had many of those who needed them for making up extra beds. Clothing, especially warm moccasins, was unpacked and given freely to the needy ones, who wept their gratitude. Lakota mothers nursed Cheyenne babies. Lakota boys, with Cheyenne boys helping in spite of frostbite, brought in armloads of green cottonwood bark and dried grass for the gaunt

Cheyenne horses. There were few of them—the Wasichus had captured most of them in the sudden attack, so the fleeing Cheyennes had walked all the way, because the remaining ponies were staggering, too weak from hunger to carry riders. Only a few fighting men had been able to ride, ranging out as scouts, looking for soldiers.

The following day the head men, the warriors, and as many Lakota women as were free and could squeeze into the crowded council lodge met there to hear the real story of what had happened. The rumors throughout the camp had been wild, but the truth was not very different.

Chapter 19

The chiefs smoked the sacred pipe with courteous deliberation. Four Lakota men and four Cheyennes—the sacred four —helped to interpret. Crazy Horse spoke briefly, in the Lakota language and in sign talk, welcoming the refugees and asking them to tell what had happened. But the movements of his hands and arms could not be followed by all the refugees in the light of the council fire, so the four Cheyennes took turns interpreting into their language.

He Dog, a minor Lakota chief who with some of his people had been with the Cheyennes during the attack, spoke next, in the Lakota tongue and hand sign. The four Cheyennes interpreted his signs into their own spoken language.

He Dog said: "My people were with Crazy Horse's people before—you know us. But before that we lived at Red Cloud's agency. We were hungry there. The Wasichus promised us food. We did not get it. That was why we came to Crazy Horse's camp last fall, so we could hunt and make

179

meat. The Wasichus took away our guns and ammunition, but we are good hunters with the bow. We made meat and robes.

"A messenger came to Crazy Horse from the reservation, telling us to go back. We did not want to fight the Wasichus any more, so we started back, four lodges of Lakotas. Crazy Horse lent me a good spotted horse for buffalo hunting because we needed robes for lodge coverings back at the agency. For a while we camped with Two Moons' Cheyennes in a canyon near the mouth of the Little Powder and hunted with them and they were good to us. Plenty of game not far away. The wise old men warned that the Wasichus wanted all Indians on the reservation so they could sell us whiskey and kill us.

"We heard rumors that the soldiers would come to fight us, but we were not in a hurry to go back to Red Cloud's agency and starve. The Cheyennes lived well, they were rich and contented, they were not bothering anybody. Then five days ago the Wasichu soldiers came at dawn. Most warriors were still asleep. We fought the soldiers and helped our women and children up into the rocks to hide. But the soldiers drove off the pony herd and killed many ponies and burned the lodges with everything in them.

"And so we came to you, to the people of Crazy Horse, and you took us in. How great and good and kind are the people of Crazy Horse!"

There was a roar of agreement from the Cheyennes and a satisfied "Ahhh!" from the Lakotas. He Dog wrapped his blanket around him and sat down with great dignity.

Then the Cheyenne chief, Two Moons, stood up to tell his story. The Lakota interpreters translated his signs into their own spoken language, making sure the meaning was accurate.

180

"We have lost everything, but the people of Crazy Horse make us want to live again. We had about a hundred lodges, counting the wickiups of single warriors, ceremonial lodges, and shelters for pregnant mares and bitches. We were comfortable, with many robes and furs to trade, great numbers of horses, plenty of meat.

"The day before the Wasichus attacked us, some of our hunters saw them, so we had ten young men on guard that night. But the soldiers sneaked around them so we had no warning. Our fighting men ran out without enough clothing, without all their weapons. The women screamed and snatched up their children to save them. Our old people hobbled through the snow to get away. Our warriors divided up any old way—some helped the helpless ones to hide and others fought the soldiers.

"Two of our men were killed and one woman. An old woman, blind, we could not find when it was over. The soldiers drove off our pony herd and slaughtered most of them. They burned our lodges with the furs and robes and meat and clothing. Some lodges exploded, because we had plenty of powder in there for the guns. When we got away, we had a few horses but could not ride them because they are too weak. The cottonwood bark burned with our lodges. We had a little raw buffalo meat to divide among many hungry, frozen, suffering people. We traveled for three sleeps, walking in ice water by day, and every night the water froze.

"The Lakotas of Crazy Horse are kind to us. How good, how generous are the Lakotas! Now we want to talk to your leaders and decide what we should do to protect our people from the Wasichus."

He sat down, and there was much excited conversation in the audience—a low roar of discussion and shock.

The head men continued in council, with leading warriors

crowded around them, but now it did not matter whether all the people knew what was being said. The leaders would decide what should be done next. People left the council lodge on errands, returned and listened again when they felt like it, retelling what they had heard, both angry and afraid.

When the council was over, Crazy Horse announced, "We are going to join Sitting Bull and his Hunkpapa people. He has a very large camp. He is a wise chief. We will send *akícitas* to find out where he is. We will leave here tomorrow when the sun is high. We have plenty of horses so that the weary ones can ride."

He added earnestly: "Sitting Bull has much medicine power from the Great Mystery. He has danced the Sun-gazing Dance several times. You will see the scars on his back and chest. Last fall he made a sacred vow that if the Powers saved his people during the winter, he would dance and sacrifice again this spring in the Moon of Fatness when the grass is green."

A roar of admiration and relief went up from the audience. With the intercession and sacrifice of so great a leader as Sitting Bull, everything was going to be all right.

Every day was exciting during the move to the camp of the Hunkpapas, the camp of Sitting Bull. Whirlwind kept saying, "Now we will see Brings Horses and her family! Hurry, hurry!"

Even her dignified son laughed at her and said, "Mother, your joy has made you lose your wits. You would sit your horse backward if my wives didn't look after you."

She paid no attention. "Stormy must be a big boy now, seven winters old, and little Red Pipe Girl is five. And Elk Rising has another wife and a baby boy we have never seen. Oh, hurry, hurry!"

The Cheyennes and the Oglalas traveled together for three

sleeps. When they camped, there was much running of errands from one lodge to another, because things had become mixed up and mislaid with the doubling of the population and the need for outfitting the refugee Cheyennes. Mothers would say, "Take these moccasins over to see if they will fit the little Cheyenne girl, and see if you can borrow a blanket from your aunt."

Because the lodges were so crowded, the young men built wickiups for themselves, of the kind they used on journeys when they did not have women along. These were oval huts of brush, with hides over the top to keep the rain off. If hides were scarce, the men slept wet and did not complain about it.

Strikes Two, Whirlwind's nephew, slept in one of these with two of his friends and two young Cheyenne warriors. They were welcome to eat at any lodge fire. The two boys, Angry and Shoots, clamored to move into a wickiup with the men, but Whirlwind put her moccasined foot down:

"You are not yet warriors. They have their own things to talk about. So you stay here to sleep. It wouldn't hurt you to go out and cut some firewood. When you are warriors, you will have to do that on the trail."

Her daughters-in-law were as firm as she was on this matter, and so was Morning Rider when he came in from a meeting. "Stay out of the way," he advised sternly.

To the surprise of everyone in the lodge, the boys really did bring in a heap of firewood, looking very virtuous and not complaining at all that they were doing women's work. Then they ran off to talk to Cheyenne boys and help feed the pony herd.

Whirlwind laughed. "They are buzzing bees—they are everywhere. And they bring home honey—much information."

Round Cloud Woman suggested, "They could teach us some sign language, and a Cheyenne boy could teach our guest. Then we could talk."

This worked very well. The boys put on airs because they were so smart. There were new people to get acquainted with and language problems all the time because few women in either tribe had known the hand-sign talk.

Morning Rider, the lodge master, kept busy at meetings of leading warriors, who had a great many problems to solve and decisions to make for the good of the people. When he was at home he tended to scowl and think seriously about problems, so he didn't talk very much.

But Strikes Two, Whirlwind's nephew, was the very best source of information for the women. He associated with young warriors, learned things that the younger boys didn't, and was amused when the women in the lodge begged him to tell them what he knew.

"Our friends the Cheyennes," he reported, "don't know about the White Buffalo Cow Maiden, who brought so much good to our ancestors. Instead, they have a hero named Sweet Medicine. He brought the buffalo and horses to his people, and the Sacred Arrows, and their most important ceremonies. He founded three of their *akícita* societies."

Whirlwind and her daughters-in-law murmured to show their great interest, but Strikes Two could tell them no more on that subject. Smiling indulgently, he reminded them, "Warriors have other things to talk about than religion."

"Of course," Whirlwind agreed. "Men also talk about girls."

"I have noticed that the Cheyennes have some very pretty girls," Strikes Two admitted, grinning. "But they are as well guarded as ours, so Lakotas talk to their brothers. They think we have some very pretty girls, too."

The women in the lodge laughed with him.

"But we don't always talk about girls," Strikes Two pointed out. "I learned that the Cheyennes have two kinds of contraries, neither of them just like our *heyokas*."

Whirlwind still grieved sometimes for Grey Bull the *heyoka*, dead in battle ten years ago. "Tell us more," she pleaded.

"Some contraries are clowns—there are many of them. But not because of a vision. They are people who especially fear the thunder. They belong to a society and there are women in it. Most of them are old. They have healing power. Sometimes these clown contraries can cure a sick person by jumping over him or by holding him upside down.

"The other contraries are very brave warriors, not clowns at all. Nobody laughs at them. There are very few of them. They live in a hard way, lonely and apart from other people, and they carry a sacred thunder-bow with a lance head on one end. They have to do and say things in a contrary way— yes when they mean no, for instance. They are the bravest of the brave in battle. Having one of them along in a war party makes the hearts of all the other men strong."

Akícitas riding ahead found Sitting Bull's camp—the biggest one they had ever seen—and told of the people who were coming. The generous women of the Hunkpapas had their pots boiling when the first of the Oglalas and Cheyennes came in sight. Two big lodges had been set up for the Cheyennes who had lost everything. One was for the men, the other for the women and their children. Now the Oglalas' homes were not so crowded. There was room to breathe.

To these big lodges, while the Oglala women were pitching their lodges and unpacking, came the big-hearted Hunkpapa women with cooked meat, and then more meat.

185

The Hunkpapa herald went riding around, calling, "The Cheyennes have lost everything. They are very poor. Everybody who can spare anything should give to them."

Hunkpapa women and girls came crowding in, asking, "Who wants this blanket? Who needs a lodge?" The men came driving horses, crying, "Who needs a horse?" Their horses, too, were gaunt after the hard winter, but now there were plenty so that none of them needed to be used hard.

The gifts were so numerous that the Cheyennes could now set up their own camp circle. There was room for everyone.

Whirlwind did her full duty in helping to pitch her family's lodge, but she kept urging crossly, "Hurry, hurry, why is everyone so clumsy today?" until Round Cloud Woman said, "Mother, go now and look for Brings Horses. We don't need you here!"

Whirlwind was gone in a flash, running toward the Hunkpapa camp circle—a very large one; how would she ever find her daughter among all those people? She kept running and asking, "Where is the lodge of Elk Rising?" but when any woman she asked had to stop to think about the answer, she said, "Never mind," and ran on.

And in the middle of the Hunkpapa camp circle, running toward her with arms outstretched, was Brings Horses Woman. They hugged each other, crying a little. Then, with their arms around each other's waists, they went to Brings Horses' lodge so that Grandmother Whirlwind could exclaim, "So this is Stormy—such a fine big boy! And here is Red Pipe Girl. Such a pretty child!"

Elk Rising, a kind and thoughtful man, not wanting to interrupt this touching reunion, went to his sister's lodge for supper, since custom forbade him to speak to his mother-in-law. His other wife, Blue Rock Woman, served a good meal

186

to Whirlwind and Brings Horses, and Whirlwind held Blue Rock's three-year-old son lovingly and said, "I will be your grandmother, too."

The next day Brings Horses took her children to visit her mother and other relatives in the Oglala camp. Both children rode their own ponies.

The three camp circles stayed in that place for six sleeps while the chiefs conferred and young men on the strongest horses scouted far, looking for Wasichu soldiers.

A fourth band came in. These were Miniconjou Lakotas. There was danger where they had been, so they joined Sitting Bull because he had so many Hunkpapas with him. Sitting Bull's policy was to stay far away from the Wasichus, even the traders, although they were not soldiers.

So big a camp could not stay long in that place—the game became scarce and better grazing was needed to strengthen the horses. So they moved again. The order of travel was agreed upon by the chiefs—the Cheyennes first, because their anger was greatest, then the Oglalas and the Miniconjous, with the Hunkpapas last. First and last were the most dangerous positions.

They kept traveling, looking for game and grass, traveling slowly because the horses were poor, camping one sleep here, three sleeps there. More people joined them—a bunch of Sans Arc Lakotas, or No Bows.

They found new grass growing green on a creek flowing into Powder River. The boys kept the herds separate and kept busy making sure the animals did not stray. Here another band of Lakotas joined them, the Blackfeet Sioux. A few others came—some Santee Sioux, called the Waist and Skirt people, from Canada, and some Burned Thighs, Brulé Lakotas. And then two more groups of Cheyennes.

Grass was plentiful now, hunting was good, everyone was busy. Early in June, when it was time, the Hunkpapas held their Sun-gazing Dance and Sitting Bull paid his vow to the Great Holy. Other bands watched reverently.

Chapter 20

Because Sitting Bull was a leader of the Hunkpapa tribe of the Lakotas, the Sun-gazing Dance that he had vowed was run entirely by the Hunkpapas, although all other Lakotas and their allies the Cheyennes were welcome to be present and share in its spiritual benefits.

When it was Sitting Bull's turn to suffer at the sacred pole, thousands of people were watching. He came limping—long ago he had been wounded in the sole of one foot and he had never walked quite right afterward—with his adopted brother, Jumping Bull.

Those who were close enough to see marveled at the knotted scars on his chest and back—he had suffered many times in the dance as an offering for his people. Jumping Bull shouted, "Sitting Bull has vowed to give one hundred pieces of his flesh!" and all the people moaned.

Sitting Bull sat, bare from the waist up, leaning against the sacred pole, and began to sing. His adopted brother used a sharp-pointed awl to lift a bit of skin from his right wrist, cut it off with a knife, and laid it aside. He began at the wrist and worked up to the shoulder, fifty times he did it, while the blood ran down, and Sitting Bull's voice never once faltered in the song he kept sending to the Great Holy, crying for mercy on his people.

Then it was half finished. Jumping Bull began with the awl on the left arm. All the people were counting on their fingers and suffering with him, praying with him. Then it was all finished, the paying of the vow of one hundred pieces of skin from his own body. And it was time for him to dance.

He danced around and around the pole, staring at the sun, continuing his cry for mercy for his people. Hour after hour he danced without resting. One of his wives ran forward and tried to force water into his mouth, but he did not even know she was there. He shook her off and she went away, weeping.

He had started shortly after dawn, and he kept on until darkness was drawing in. Then he fell to the ground. It was finished.

For a while nobody could waken him. He was in a trance, not in this world. He was having a vision of the future.

When he regained consciousness and drank water and let them wipe away some of his sweat and blood, he told what the vision was:

"I heard a voice saying, 'I give you these because they have no ears,' and I saw soldiers and Indians on horseback falling upside down into our camp."

The whole vast camp was buzzing with the news within a few minutes, and with the meaning of the vision. It was agreed that those who had no ears were their enemies, who would not listen, and that enemies falling into camp meant there would be an attack on the camp but the Lakotas and their allies would be victorious.

The Great Holy had spoken through Sitting Bull, and the people were uplifted. Their hearts were full of gratitude.

The day after Sitting Bull's Sun Dance ended was sunny and beautiful. The people were triumphant, uplifted by the religious rites that had renewed the life of the tribe for one more year. Their hearts were filled with new hope because of the great vision that brave chief had experienced. Now there would be triumph and they would be safe; they would live again. All over the huge encampment there was singing and drumming, and all over people were busy.

There was much to be done, because they would move again very soon. The pony herds needed new grazing.

There was plenty of work to be done in the lodge of Morning Rider, but there were plenty of women there to do it, so Whirlwind left on a project of her own.

"I'm going to dig roots," she explained to Round Cloud Woman. "Shall I take the baby for company?"

"He has just been fed, so take him if you like," her daughter-in-law agreed. His ears had not yet been pierced, so he did not have a boy name yet; his baby name was Jumps.

Whirlwind slung her baby grandson's cradleboard onto her back with the ease of long practice and went walking at a brisk pace, answering the baby when he made small sounds. She had two things hidden under her dress: her digging stick and a soft leather bag for carrying roots. She thought she knew where biscuit root would be growing—desert parsley. The roots were good to eat raw, or she might dry and grind them to make big flat cakes. The biscuit root made good mush with a wild onion cooked in it.

As a rule she liked company when she worked, but there was no point in inviting some other busy woman to come along to dig something that might not be there.

She did tell her destination to one person, her grandson Shoots, thirteen years old. She met him when he was returning on foot from his turn at guarding part of the vast pony herd.

"Your little brother is going to help me dig biscuit root over there," she said. "Don't tell anybody where we are. Let the other women be sharp-eyed and find their own roots."

Shoots smiled and promised. He patted his baby brother's cheek and said, "Ho, warrior, old man chief. Take care of Grandmother." The baby jumped in his buckskin wrappings and cooed.

The biscuit root was plentiful on flat ground under a cutbank, just out of sight of the lodges. Whirlwind carefully propped the baby's cradleboard against a rock so the sun wouldn't shine in the child's face. Then, talking to him quietly, she began to dig skillfully, filling her buckskin bag, stooping and kneeling and rising again like a young woman. She was not young, she had lived through fifty-six winters, but she was strong and happy and healthy.

Her back was toward the baby when she heard him shriek with glee. She turned instantly—and saw a dreadful thing. Between her and the baby was another kind of baby, an awkward little bear cub, the cub of the frightfully dangerous grizzly bear. The cub itself was harmless, but the old-woman bear, its mother, must be near, and she would protect her child.

Whirlwind did not even think of danger to herself. She ran to save *her* cub. She snatched up the baby on his cradleboard and threw him, with all her strength, above her head toward the level top of the cutbank.

At that moment the old-woman bear appeared. She snarled and came running, a shambling, awkward-looking run but very fast.

Whirlwind saw with horror the cradleboard with its precious burden sliding back down the cutbank. She had been too close when she threw the baby upward. The baby was screaming. Grandmother Whirlwind ran, picked up the cradleboard, ran back a few steps, and then threw hard again. This time the bundle stayed up there.

Whirlwind ran again toward the cutbank and climbed as

fast as she could, digging into the dirt frantically with clutching fingers and digging toes.

The upper part of her body was on the flat ground and she was gripping a small tree as she tried to pull up her legs. Just then the old-woman grizzly reached up and tore at the legs with curved claws as long as a big man's middle finger.

Whirlwind thought, I am dead—but my cub is safe if the sow bear does not come up here. No, I am not dead yet. I have something more to do. She screamed as hard as she could.

And her scream was heard.

Shoots was an untried boy. He had never even asked to go along with a war party to do errands for men of proved courage, to watch how a man should act. He had only thought of going on the hill to starve and thirst and lament to the Powers, praying for a powerful spirit helper. He had not yet done this thing. He believed his heart was strong. That day he found out.

He was only playing when he heard the she-bear snarl. He was practicing a stealthy approach, intending to startle Grandmother Whirlwind. He was creeping quietly through thin brush, pretending that she was an enemy. He did not really expect to surprise her; she was usually very alert. She would scold when she discovered what he was up to, and then she would laugh at him because she had caught him.

He saw a bundle fly through the air and slide down the cutbank. It happened too fast for him to see that it was the cradleboard with his baby brother. He heard fast movement in the weeds as Whirlwind ran back and threw the cradleboard again. He stood up, mouth open, just as she scrambled up the bank. With horror he saw the old-woman bear's claws rake her struggling legs.

With his heart in his mouth he did the best thing he could

think of. He dropped his bow and grabbed the cub with both hands, so that it squalled with fear and pain. Then he threw it hard—past its mother.

Hearing her child cry, the woman bear whirled away from the cutbank to protect her cub. Shoots snatched up his bow; it was a good one, as strong as he could pull, and in a quiver on his shoulder he had six hunting arrows tipped with sharpened iron. At his waist he had a good steel knife.

But his enemy was better armed, with twenty immensely long, curved, sharp, death-dealing claws and a mouthful of long, sharp teeth, and she weighed more than five times as much as he did. She was protected by thick fur. Shoots was almost naked.

He stood his ground and fired his arrows at her, fast but very carefully. Few grizzlies had ever been killed by one man alone; there were true tales of some bears killing men even after they should have been dead themselves. The woman bear yelled in pain and fury. She batted at the arrows deep in her flesh. She bit at them. But she kept coming.

Then Shoots did the last thing he could do, because it was too late to run. While the grizzly fought at the arrows, especially one that had gone into her left eye, he leaped on her back. With all his strength he sank his good steel knife into her throat, through the heavy fur and hide.

Then, as Grandmother Whirlwind had done, he clambered up the cutbank while the bear groped and swiped at him. He wondered why he could not see very well. He wondered who was screaming. He wondered if this was the day he was going to die.

Whirlwind, lying helpless with the calf of one leg torn away, screamed louder when she saw him with blood running down his face, but he did not even know blood was there.

She cried, "Take the baby and run!" in so commanding a voice that he never thought of doing otherwise. With the cradled baby under one arm, he ran toward camp, howling for help, but stumbling.

His yells were heard. Two men on horseback lashed their ponies and met him. One seized the squalling baby. The other pulled Shoots up behind him on the pony. They rode fast toward where Whirlwind lay.

They leaped off—the one with the baby hung the cradleboard on a tree branch—and Shoots tumbled off. He had just realized that there was something he ought to do to prove his valor. He did something that his people talked about for many years afterward. While the men knelt by Whirlwind, he slid down the cutbank, picked up his bow, and struck the bear with it. She was coughing and dying. He shouted, as warriors do, "I, Shoots, have killed her! I count the first coup!"

Whirlwind and the men above heard him say it. They shouted in wonder and admiration. For a man to kill a grizzly without help was a very great thing indeed, and he had actually gone back into danger to count coup and claim the credit that was due him. He had counted coup against an armed enemy, after he was wounded, although he had never gone to war before that day. Now he was entitled to wear an eagle feather upright in his hair for first coup, a feather tipped with red paint because he had been wounded in battle.

He was the one who rode toward camp for more help while the two men stayed with Whirlwind and did what they could to make her comfortable. A crowd of people came hurrying after he delivered his message. There were women on horseback with poles and hides to make a pony drag for

Whirlwind, because a great chunk of the muscles in the calf of one leg had been torn out by the she-bear's claws. There were men riding and boys riding, leading horses. More women brought supplies to help the wounded, and a medicine woman came with them, carrying her bundle of magic things. Round Cloud Woman came riding, crying, and Morning Rider came at a hard gallop to see about his mother and his infant son.

Whirlwind fought them off, so keyed up and triumphant that she did not yet feel much pain. "Let me carry my grandchild!" she ordered when Round Cloud tried to take him away.

"I saved your cub," Whirlwind kept boasting, laughing and proud. "And Shoots saved us both. He is not a cub any more. He is a warrior!" She tried to make a victory trill in his honor, but as they lifted her gently onto the pony drag she fainted.

Morning Rider himself attended to the wound of his son Shoots, who did not even remember when the old-woman bear had slashed his forehead. The boy was able to laugh as he said, "She tried to scalp me!"

Morning Rider covered the wound with clotted blood from the bear and tied the flap of skin down with a strip of buckskin around the boy's head. He remarked fondly, "You will have a big scar there. The girls will keep asking you to tell how you got it. I am very proud of you."

Now maybe Grandmother Whirlwind would stop treating him like a little boy, to be ordered around.

He heard her shouting, laughing: "Behold Shoots—he is a warrior. He fought a grizzly bear and killed her."

Shoots shouted back, "Behold Whirlwind! She is a warrior. She was wounded in battle."

195

He began to sing a praise song for her, although he was feeling weak all of a sudden.

She laughed hysterically. "I am a warrior who was wounded while running away! Take the hide of the enemy—it belongs to Shoots."

Women were skinning out the dead, bloody bear and fighting with a horse that reared, not wanting to carry the hide on its back. The medicine woman filled a big dish with bear blood. She washed the great wound on Whirlwind's leg with water, chanting prayers. She covered the wound with the bear's thickening blood and then cut a big piece of the bear's hide, covering the wound and the blood with the raw side of the fresh hide.

She said with pity, "My friend, I think you will have trouble walking—always, as long as you live. But nobody will ever forget how you saved your son's cub today."

They killed the great bear's cub and cut off its claws to make a necklace for the baby when he grew older. They cut off the immense claws of the woman bear; these were for Shoots. Not long afterward, when he went out to lament for a vision, his dream was a powerful one and when he made up his protective medicine bag, one of the claws was in it. The others he wore for a necklace when he dressed up.

That night the people had a victorious kill dance over the bloody hides of the great bear and the little one. Morning Rider rode around the camp circle leading a fine horse to give away, with Shoots riding beside him. Morning Rider sang:

> "A bear killed a woman long ago.
> A bear killed a mother long ago.
> Now the woman's son has avenged her.
> The warrior son has avenged his mother!"

Morning Rider gave the fine horse to a very brave old warrior, who gave Shoots a new name. The warrior shouted, "The boy Shoots counted first coup on a grizzly bear and killed her to save two people. So I give him an honorable name. Kills Grizzly is his name!"

Grandmother Whirlwind lay on her bed, smiling as she listened to the singing and the triumphant drumming of the kill dance in honor of Shoots—no, now she must remember to call him Kills Grizzly. Her daughter was with her, and the medicine woman, who used all her spells and prayers and medicines to try to ease the pain. No matter how Whirlwind lay, with her foot propped up, the pain was very great, but her pride was greater.

"It does not hurt," she said. "It is nothing." She pretended to sleep.

Brings Horses stayed, and Morning Rider's wives came back with their sleepy children. They spoke softly but were full of talk that Whirlwind wanted to hear: about how everyone was honoring Shoots for his courage and talking about how brave Whirlwind herself was.

"Everybody wants to see you," one of them remarked, smiling, "but we refused them all—all except one, who will come soon."

They were hurrying around, Whirlwind noticed, to tidy up the lodge—her work, but she could not do it now. It must be an important visitor or the women would not be so careful to have everything neat and nice this late at night, with the baby and the little girl, Reaches Far, asleep.

Men's voices came nearer, two men. One was Morning Rider; his mother did not recognize the other one. Morning Rider entered and ushered in his companion. He said, "This is Whirlwind Woman, my mother. She saved my baby son."

197

The other man stood looking down at her. He smiled a little and said, "I am Crazy Horse."

Whirlwind gasped. For once in her life, she had nothing to say. This was the great man, the quiet one, whose very presence made the hearts of his people big.

Morning Rider told her, "I have asked Crazy Horse to name the baby, and he agrees. When the boy is old enough, we will have the ear-piercing ceremony. But today Crazy Horse will give my youngest son a name."

Round Cloud Woman brought the sleeping infant. She was shaking with excitement.

Crazy Horse looked long at the sleeping little face. Then he touched the child's forehead and said, "I give you a name that you can make great in honor of your grandmother, who saved you, and your brother, who counted first coup on the bear. I name the child She Throws Him."

A murmur of delight went up among Morning Rider's family: "Thank you, friend, thank you!"

Round Cloud Woman said to her child, "Wake up, She Throws Him, so that sometime you can say you looked on the face of Crazy Horse the day he gave you your name." The baby opened his eyes, yawned, and went to sleep again.

Now Whirlwind thought of something to say: "My son has forgotten his manners. I did not raise him right. He has not asked our visitor to sit down in the place of honor beside him."

The two men chuckled, and Morning Rider explained, "I asked him before we came, but he thought he would not stay long enough. Will the visitor sit down and smoke?"

Crazy Horse would. Morning Rider filled and lighted the sacred pipe and smoked it to the Powers of the six directions. Then he passed it to Crazy Horse, who did the same and gave back the sacred pipe.

"I wish also to speak to the warrior woman," he said. "Grandmother, how is it with you in your pain?" He used the term "grandmother" in the sense of great respect.

"Not so bad," she replied stoutly, as a warrior should.

Crazy Horse stood up, then knelt beside her and looked into her face. "I give you a name, too, Grandmother. Your name is Saved Her Cub."

Then he nodded and left the lodge, leaving Whirlwind speechless for the second time that day.

When she got her wits back, she complained happily, "But I am too old to remember another name for myself!"

Morning Rider replied, "Others will remember."

Chapter 21

The next day the whole big camp moved. Whirlwind could not do her proper work. It was as if the woman bear had robbed her of her place in the family. She had to lie there in pain and watch others do the packing and dismantle the lodge. In addition, they made provisions for moving her on a pony drag. Everyone was kind and thoughtful, nobody complained, but being helpless made her angry. She thought resentfully, This is not the way I have lived, being in the way, being waited on! I am the one who looks after others!

But there was nothing for her to do except to endure, and when the horses and the people began their march, enduring was enough burden. The women did their best to keep the great raw wound on her leg from being pressed by anything. They laid her on the travois a little on her side and tied her that way; they tried to elevate the foot of her wounded leg on a block attached to the lower end of one of the poles.

"Are you comfortable, Mother Whirlwind, Saves Her Cub?" they kept asking—her daughter, Brings Horses; two daughters-in-law; all her pitying people.

"Oh, yes," she lied, gritting her teeth. But there was no comfort. There was only pain. She could hold it off sometimes by telling herself, I am a wounded warrior. I am a Lakota. I can endure.

On rocky ground or steep slopes they did not let the ends of the limber travois poles drag on the ground, but various people, both men and women, took turns carrying them so they would not bump.

She wondered why so many people did this during the moving. She asked a young man—who surely should not be bothering with women's work, and she could not even remember his name.

He replied, smiling, "It is an honor to help a wounded person who is as brave as you are, Grandmother."

That was the only time she cried during the whole terrible ordeal of the camp moving.

In other years, every time camp moved she had noticed hills and valleys and streams and rocks and trees and good places to pitch a lodge or pick berries or dig wild roots. She had always been part of the world, riding a horse, watching, learning. But on the pony drag she was isolated in a small world of her own, and it was filled with pain. She did not even care where the camp was going. She cared only that it should stop sometime.

All the people were going back to the Little Big Horn Valley. They had been there a few days before the Sun-gazing Dance, but there were no buffalo. Now the *akícitas* reported that buffalo were there and hunting would be good.

Other reports kept coming in, too, from far-ranging scouts

and hunters: Wasichu soldiers were around. Some were seen coming from the south the day the Sun-gazing Dance began, but plans were easily made to protect the people from them. If they came within half a day's journey from the camp, warriors of the big combined camp would ride to meet them.

It was an immense relief to Whirlwind when the great camp settled down for a few days at the forks of a creek in the Little Big Horn Valley. She did not require so much care from other people. She even tried walking a few steps, with her son grasping one arm and Brings Horses supporting her on the other side. But so much of the muscle was gone from the calf of her leg that her foot did not work right. It flopped, and she had to shuffle.

"But I will walk," she proclaimed. "When the skin grows again."

"Of course you will, Mother," her family agreed.

They had been in this place for five sleeps when something happened. There were always young men riding out as scouts, to watch for enemies, and many hunting parties brought in meat. At daylight one morning, people in the Cheyenne camp circle heard wolves howling and coming closer. A young man named Half Moon leaped on his horse and rode toward the howling, knowing that it was a signal. Five Cheyennes were coming. They had been near the head of the Rosebud, roasting meat, when they saw soldiers, and some Indians with them. The upper valley of the Rosebud was black with troops!

Men leaped onto their horses and rode to summon leaders of the many tribes to a meeting. The old-man chief of the entire enormous camp was the Hunkpapa, Sitting Bull. He had to be present at the war council, although he was still recovering from the torture of paying his vow at the Sun

Dance only a few days earlier. All the wise leaders assembled in a big council lodge to decide how to protect the people.

There was excitement and much chatter in the lodges, but nobody was afraid. Here were many bands and many fighting men, the Cheyennes and five tribes of Lakotas. And among the chiefs was that quiet man Crazy Horse, whose very presence had a kind of power.

The chiefs talked a long time. Then the word went out to the whole camp: Tonight more than a thousand warriors will ride to fight off the Wasichus. We won't wait for the soldiers to come here. We will attack them—when they do not expect us. We will attack when the sun comes up! And we will have a chance to wipe out some of our enemies, who are their scouts—the Crows and the Shoshones.

Boys ran to bring the best war horses of their big brothers and their fathers and their uncles. Fighting men hurried to pick up their weapons and ammunition, to make sure they had their medicine bags and to pack up their finest ornaments and grandest feather headdresses and war paint.

They rode out in a long column, singing and shouting, while the women and children and old people cheered and waved. And even with so many warriors going away, there were still plenty left in camp to fight off enemies if they came from some other direction. Some of those left behind were sulky, even angry, at losing this chance to gain glory. Even Sitting Bull, suffering as he was, rode with the huge war party.

All night in the big camp the drums beat as chanted prayers went up to the Powers. All night the great war party rode. At dawn they stopped at the Rosebud River and got ready for battle.

A man wanted to look his very best when he fought, because he might die, and he would not want an enemy, seeing his body, to think, "This man was poor—he was nobody." They fought naked except for breech clout and moccasins, not wanting any garments to hamper their arms or legs, but they combed their hair carefully, some wrapping their braids with fur. They wore their best ornaments, and every warrior who had counted coup wore a feather in his hair. A few of the leaders wore full warbonnets so they would be recognized by their followers. All the men painted their faces carefully and some painted medicine symbols on their war ponies. Then they rode.

The fight took place on both sides of the Rosebud, in rough, broken country. The Wasichu soldier chief, whose name was Crook, had thought he was going to attack a village. But there was no village. The Lakotas and Cheyennes had ridden far to surprise him. He buried his dead and retreated the next day, glad to be out of there.

The victorious Indians rode back jubilantly to their homes. The defeated army, waiting for reinforcements and supplies, spent the summer hunting and fishing.

That was the Battle of the Rosebud, June 17, 1876.

The Cheyennes called it "Where the Girl Saved Her Brother." In the fight a Cheyenne chief had his horse killed and was surrounded by enemies when his sister, Buffalo Calf Road, who had come along, galloped in so he could jump onto her horse.

A very few Indians had been killed, in spite of all the shooting the Wasichus did. Not many Wasichus had died, either, but there were some wounded. For the Cheyennes and the Lakotas, it was a victory. For General Crook it was an embarrassing defeat.

But was this victory what Sitting Bull's vision had promised? He had seen dead soldiers and Indians falling into camp. The battle had taken place a full night's ride from camp. There must be something more to come.

They moved the camp, as was the custom after a fight. The new location was on the east side of the Little Big Horn. They were there when his vision came true, eight sleeps after the Rosebud Battle.

Part X

SUMMER, 1876

Battle on the Little Big Horn

Living in the Lodge:

Morning Rider, 36, head of the family
Young Bird, 32, wife of Morning Rider
Reaches Far Girl, 8, daughter of Young Bird and Morning Rider
Angry, 12, son of Young Bird, stepson of Morning Rider
Round Cloud Woman, 21, wife of Morning Rider and sister of Young Bird
She Throws Him (formerly Jumps), infant son of Morning Rider and Round Cloud
Kills Grizzly (formerly Shoots), 13, motherless son of Morning Rider
Strikes Two, 24, son of Pemmican Woman, nephew of Whirlwind
Saved Her Cub, 56, who still uses the name Whirlwind

Chapter 22

After the fine victory over Three Stars, General Crook, at the Battle of the Rosebud, there were victory dances in the camp circles along the winding Little Big Horn. The flames of bonfires leaped, everybody was triumphant. There was fine singing to the stirring beat of the drums, and between dances the warriors paraded around on their best horses, dressed up and painted, shouting about the coups they had counted, while the rest of the people cheered.

Whirlwind's family offered to carry her out to watch, but she said crossly, "Leave me alone." Even when her nephew, Strikes Two, brought her a Wasichu's bloody scalp on a stick, she did not care.

"How can I dance the scalp with the other women?" she demanded. "My foot flops."

They knew from her bad temper that she was sick indeed. She was burning up. Someone ran to find her friend the medicine woman. She came with her little bags of herbs and drummed and sang a magic song. Whirlwind was quiet for a moment. Then she tried to call out, "Grey Bull! *Heyoka!*" but nobody could understand.

"I must look at the wound on the calf of her leg," the medicine woman said, but Whirlwind struck her as hard as she could and yelled, "Go away, Death!" Whirlwind was having a vision; a cruel old woman with great teeth like a bear's hurt her and passed by, grinning. She understood that Death was very near.

The lodge cover was rolled up at the bottom to let in cool air, but Whirlwind was burning. Nobody was helping her. Everyone was fighting her, trying to hold her down. Her own family was fighting her! Morning Rider said, "Lie still, Mother. You will hurt yourself. Lie still."

The wound was raw and nasty; the leg was swollen tight. The medicine woman said, "Bad spirits have entered in. I am doing what I can." She applied some ointment to the wound, gently, and sang again.

But Whirlwind had to fight, she had to follow the cruel old

woman who was Death, she had to kill Death to protect the people. Nobody could understand this. Everything whirled —the whole earth, the big bonfire where the victory dancers were, the lodge she lay in.

Her son knelt beside her, holding her so she could not do her duty and follow Death to kill her and save the people. Her own son, Morning Rider, who should have been out there dancing, because he had counted coup at the Rosebud.

She was struggling against his strong hands when she heard a strange man speak. Morning Rider answered, "My mother is very sick. I cannot talk to you now."

The medicine woman said, "Why, he is a *heyoka*, but not Oglala. I do not know him."

Later they told Whirlwind what happened. The stranger said, "I am not a *heyoka*, not a Hunkpapa. My name is not Another Horse."

So they knew he was a *heyoka*, a contrary. Morning Rider, holding his struggling mother, said politely, "Stay away, Another Horse," so the stranger came in, backing through the doorway.

(Whirlwind was climbing the cutbank again and the woman bear was clawing her leg and she was screaming because she could not find the baby.)

The *heyoka* had a dried-up little dead bird tied in his tangled hair, and he carried a bunch of white sage in one hand. He was tall and thin and his clothes were ragged, made of worn-out lodge-cover leather.

One of the women courteously spread a small robe for him to sit on, but he kicked it away. Morning Rider asked, "Why have you come?"

"I did not have a vision that sent me here," the contrary explained. "I have no power and am no use to anyone. Cheyenne contraries have no power, either." He backed out through the doorway and went away.

Brings Horses began to cry. "Maybe he has gone for a Cheyenne who has curing power. Mother, lie still. It will be all right."

Whirlwind shouted at her, still trying to find the baby at the top of the cutbank.

After a long time, the *heyoka* came back with another man. The Cheyenne camp circle was at one end of the huge camp, the Hunkpapa Lakotas were at the other end.

The Hunkpapa contrary spoke swiftly in sign, and the Cheyenne disagreed, meaning "Yes." He carried a bunch of white sage, too. He knelt beside Whirlwind and touched her sweating forehead with the sage and sang in his own language.

In sign talk he asked, "Do not move her toward me," so Morning Rider picked her up and moved her, while two of the women moved her bed of robes. Whirlwind tried to fight them all.

The Cheyenne kept singing, kept waving the white sage to purify the lodge. Then he bent over and put the sage in her hand. She grasped it.

He bent his knees and jumped clear over her, chanting. He jumped back and jumped again, weak and tired now. Then he backed out of the lodge, and so did the Hunkpapa *heyoka*.

The earth did not whirl any more. Whirlwind was no longer burning. The baby was safe. The woman bear was dead. The pain was endurable. Whirlwind slept.

Those in the lodge murmured in awe, "*Wakan*! Holy!"

The next day her head was clear and the evil spirit was going away from her wound. The whole camp was talking about the *wakan* thing that had happened. How did the Hunkpapa *heyoka* know he was needed? Because that was part of his power—to see what was going on far away. How did he know where to find the Cheyenne contrary who had healing power? Nobody understood that. It was *wakan* and it was good.

"I want to give each of them a horse," Whirlwind said weakly. "And send some meat to their lodges."

Strikes Two took the gifts to the Cheyenne, while Morning Rider took them to the Hunkpapa. The Cheyenne accepted, saying he was not grateful. The Hunkpapa accepted, too, but gave his horse away at once to a man who was not nearly so poor as he himself was.

Morning Rider kept shaking his head in amazement. "The Thunder Dreamer saw you sick, Mother—from so far, with so many lodges between, that no ordinary man could possibly have done it. And he knew somehow that the Cheyenne contrary had healing power."

That was an immense camp by the Little Big Horn, each tribe with its own camp circle opening to the east and each lodge facing the east. The people felt the thrill of victory and the conviction that more triumph was to come. The ponies were fat now. The hunters were successful. There was plenty to eat. Women worked contentedly together, staking out fresh hides and scraping them clean in the sunshine.

Young warriors visited around in other camps and did some careful courting by taking gifts to the brothers and fathers of girls they admired. Girls worked hard with their mothers, making sure they looked nice while they proved their skill and industry—and pretending not to see the young men smiling down from their fine painted horses. Old men drummed and sang of the brave deeds of their youth.

Boys looked after the pony herds; rode like the wind, showing off; made friends with boys from other camp circles.

209

Except a few, like Kills Grizzly, thirteen years old, who undertook the harsh and frightening ordeal of lamenting on a hill to beg for a vision and gain medicine power for protection in war.

As Kills Grizzly rode off with his attendants after the ceremonial sweat-bath cleansing, Grandmother Whirlwind weakly sang a brave-heart song for him. She would never again treat him like a little boy.

Angry, a year younger, stood in the shade of the lodge and looked sullen as he watched Kills Grizzly go, his best friend, his almost-brother. Morning Rider had refused Angry's urgent plea to be allowed to go out lamenting. So had the wise old priest who accepted Kills Grizzly as a pupil in this sacred undertaking.

"But I have already gone twice as water boy with scouting parties!" Angry argued with his almost-father, Morning Rider. "Shoots never did. He never even talked about doing anything until he killed the woman bear."

Morning Rider was going to a meeting of his warrior society, but he delayed. He put his hand on the boy's shoulder and said, "Come, let us talk."

They sat down where nobody could hear them, and he explained, "What Shoots did was very brave, but it was foolish, too. He had no medicine protector. All the wise old men agree that he must not be foolish again. He must not put too much faith in himself. He must have spirit power to help him or the spirits may destroy him for insolence. He must learn to be humble—and that is just what he is going to do in the next few days. When he comes back he will have a medicine protector, if all goes well. He will be different."

Angry was despondent. "He will not be my friend any more. He will be above me, far from me. He will be a man."

"Before long you will be friends and equals again," Mornng Rider assured him. "Because you will go out to lament nd pray for a vision. But not right away. Friendships don't end so easily, with one friend riding off while another stays. In the time to come, before you seek your vision, Shoots will act with more dignity and he will be learning new things from older warriors, but do you think he will forget you? You have always been friends. Your beds are still together in the lodge. I think Kills Grizzly, who was Shoots, will miss being a boy without responsibility. He may envy you. Yes, you will be good friends again, and fight side by side in battles to come. Now why don't you go swimming? I see young warriors over there in the river who have counted coup many times."

There was much gaiety in the big camp. The various circles had big social dances at night. Strikes Two dressed in his finest clothes and painted his face most carefully, looking into a small mirror that Angry held for him. Whirlwind, leaning against her backrest, smiled with pride at him and remembered the long-ago time when almost nobody among the people had a mirror.

"You look good," she assured him, as he left the lodge to mount his horse. "All the girls will ask you to dance. Come back to us sometime." Strikes Two smiled and waved.

Later, between sleeping and waking, she could hear the music, the fast drumming, the songs by the best singers. She imagined the big bonfire and all the pretty girls and the stalwart young men. She thought, I will never dance any more. But I did when I was young.

The dance didn't stop until dawn tinged the eastern sky. Whirlwind was not quite asleep when she saw a hand reach in under the rolled-up lodge cover to take a blanket from Strike Two's bed. He slept for a while outside, came yawning in for breakfast, then went down to the river for a swim and

211

conversation with other young men. After that he came back and went to sleep again in the shade of the lodge.

Morning Rider went to a sweat lodge with some men of his age group to purify themselves and pray. All of them had boys who had gone out to lament to the Powers, and Shoot —Kills Grizzly—should be back today.

Morning Rider's wives were busy fleshing hides out in the sun. With the help of Brings Horses, who came to visit her mother, they put Whirlwind's bed and backrest outside and assisted her in shuffling out there where she could sit with her back to the sun and watch what was going on.

Angry was out with the pony herd. Reaches Far, eight years old, played house with some other little girls and kept an eye on the baby, She Throws Him.

The sun was good, the earth was kind, the people were happy. Until something happened. They were always alert even when no trouble was expected. Suddenly the quiet busy Oglala camp came to life. A man somewhere yelled, "Dust to the eastward! Horses over there, running!"

The pony herd was not in that direction. There were distant shouts from the great Hunkpapa camp, which was There was gunfire from over there.

The old herald began to ride fast through the Oglala camp, roaring, "There is fighting over there! Young men, get ready to fight!"

They came boiling out from everywhere, the young warriors. The men in the sweat lodge came running out. Boys jumped onto picketed horses and galloped toward the pony herd to bring in the other animals. Women screamed for their children and went running. Children screamed for their mothers and ran home.

Strikes Two rolled into the lodge from his napping place

212

and began hurriedly to comb his hair and paint for war. Whirlwind yelled, "I will hold the mirror for you!" It was important that a fighting man should look good.

Round Cloud and Young Bird seized the young children to keep them out of the way. "Make up small packs," Whirlwind advised. "In case we have to travel fast."

Morning Rider plunged toward the doorway with the sweat still shining on his body and began to paint and collect his weapons—stout bow, many fine war arrows, his lance, his sacred medicine shield, and a revolver he had got in trade. But he had very little ammunition for it. He painted hurriedly, with firm strokes.

Everyone was moving now, doing something, even Whirlwind, although all she could do was hold a little mirror for her men. The camp was in an uproar, and the gunfire from the Hunkpapa camp was louder.

Akicitas galloped by with information and advice from Crazy Horse, the Oglala chief. He had had word by courier from Sitting Bull of the Hunkpapas, who sent messengers also through the Sans Arcs and Miniconjou camps, then on to the Brulés and the Cheyennes. Soldiers had attacked the Hunkpapas, but they had been driven back across the river. Get ready to fight!

The word from Crazy Horse to the fighting men of the Oglalas was: There are two bunches of soldiers. The Hunkpapas drove back one bunch and are keeping them on the run up the bluffs. The others are riding northwest. We go that way to attack them.

Warriors who were ready and mounted were running their horses hard, back and forth, so the animals would get their second wind. The men yelled, *"Hoka hey!* Let's go! It is a good day to die!"

Whirlwind, watching her son and her nephew leap onto their best war horses, sang a brave-heart song as loud as she could.

Then she said to her daughters-in-law, "Give me my knife from my sleeping place. If you have to run, take the children and small packs, but leave me." She shouted, as the men did, "It is a good day to die!"

The attack by the soldiers was not startling. Scouts had kept reporting soldiers in one place or another. The only questions were where and when the attack would occur. Crazy Horse led the main body of the Oglalas and Cheyennes downstream and forded the river near the Cheyenne camp circle. Crazy Horse put heart into his galloping followers by yelling, "It is a good day to die! Cowards to the rear—brave hearts follow me!"

Chapter 23

Women and children and old people scurried like disturbed ants, mothers found their children, old women packed up things in a hurry, old men shouted encouragement to the young proud warriors galloping out to battle. Boys dashed around taking messages, arguing to go along, helping with the horses, all yelling.

The battle had started at the end of camp where the Hunkpapas were, and there the excitement was the worst. Some lodges were burning. Women ran for the hills behind the camp, carrying babies, dragging small children, helped by the older men. Others stayed at first, hastily dismantling their lodges. Then they gave up and fled, leaving everything.

From all the camp circles the warriors swarmed out, gal-

214

loping and yelling, to protect the people, to kill or drive off the enemy Blue Coats and their Indian scouts, who were long-time enemies, especially the Crows.

Not all the warriors rode to the attack, much as they longed to do so. Some stayed close to the camp circles, riding back and forth, armed and ready to fight if the battle came closer, all brandishing their weapons, all yelling, their feathers flying in the wind they made.

Boys too young to fight were self-appointed messengers, riding out close to the battle and returning to tell what they had seen. They told accurately, not describing the overall picture but only what they knew because they had seen it. Scouts—and they would be scouts in two or three years—had to tell the truth.

There were two battles, the faraway one where the Blue Coats had attacked the Hunkpapa camp and retreated, and a closer one where another bunch of Blue Coats had suddenly appeared on the far side of the river. Crazy Horse was the leader in this one—that fearless Oglala who kept yelling, "*Hoka hey*! Brave hearts follow me! It is a good day to die!"

That closer battle did not last very long. A few of the younger Lakota and Cheyenne women mounted their horses, forded the stream, and went over to watch the end of it, singing brave-heart songs for their men. In that battle, all the Blue Coats died. All of them. The Cheyennes said a few killed themselves with their revolvers to their heads rather than risk capture.

When the dust died across the river and the shooting stopped because the Blue Coats were all dead, Whirlwind was tired out from being so excited. Her daughter had not left her, in spite of her urging, and neither had her daughters-in-law. Suddenly from behind another lodge appeared a rider wearing the hated blue uniform. He pulled up his horse so it stood on its hind legs as the women screamed. He said, "How do you like my new clothes?" and they saw it was Strikes Two, grinning at them.

His aunt, Whirlwind, shrieked scoldings at him and brandished her knife. The other women, still trembling, laughed a little at this joke. He wore the blue pants and shirt of a Wasichu soldier—with a big dark patch of blood on the shirt—and his long black hair hung down from under the hat. He carried a carbine and an ammunition belt heavy with cartridges.

He said, grinning, "Morning Rider is all right. You might as well come over. There may be some things you want."

The women's horses were ready, in case they needed to flee. "I'll look after the small children," Whirlwind said. "Hurry up."

"No, Mother," said Brings Horses firmly. "You were very, very sick and you are not yet well and strong. I'm going to stay and look after the children—and you too."

In all this confusion, two people rode to the lodge and dismounted wearily—a tired old man with grey braids, and a big-eyed, solemn boy. Kills Grizzly was back from his vision quest, with the old holy man who had helped him.

The women screamed welcome. Young Bird ran for food. Round Cloud ran to bring out a backrest for Kills Grizzly, who looked exhausted, and one for the priest. Brings Horses gave horn cups of cold water to both of them. They thanked her gravely and drank, but not as if they were thirsty, not fast.

Grandmother Whirlwind yearned toward the youth, holding out her arms, but let them drop again. He was not a little boy any more, to be cuddled and comforted. He had lamented and debased himself to the Powers. He had had experiences that he would tell, at the proper time, to a council

216

of the elders. He had passed through fear and suffering, and he had learned humility. Now he was a man, to be treated with respect.

While Kills Grizzly and the old priest ate, Angry returned from across the river carrying a fine gun and some clothing. Instead of boasting, he quietly laid them down and sat staring with awe at his almost-brother.

There was no use asking Kills Grizzly about his dream—he could not tell that until the elders assembled. So his family told him and the priest about the fighting. They could still hear occasional firing from across the river from the Hunkpapa camp, where some of the Wasichus were besieged behind their dead horses on the hot, bare hill.

Kills Grizzly's eyes kept going shut; he had slept very little during his vision quest. But he opened them wide when Angry picked up the fine carbine he had brought from the nearer battle and laid it across his lap. That was the grandest thing Angry had ever owned.

"A gift for a warrior," Angry said softly. "For the man who killed the bear." Then he ran out of sight beyond the lodge as Kills Grizzly spoke for the first time: "My brother, thanks."

Now there was wailing in the Oglala camp. A few warriors had died in the fighting, and some were wounded. Widows and sisters of the dead men cut gashes in their legs as signs of mourning. Medicine men and women worked over the wounded.

The grieving relatives of the dead rode across the river, with blood dripping from the knife cuts on their legs, carrying knives and axes. The victorious warriors had already scalped most of the dead Wasichu soldiers, stripped their clothing off, and hacked some of the bodies. The mourning women hacked and cut some more, screaming and keening their grief. Boys picked up small items scattered around—

217

pocket watches, a compass, paper money, pictures—and tossed them away, not knowing what they were.

But there was much good, useful loot in their camp when they finished—saddles and pieces of uniform and cartridges and guns—in addition to flags and pennants and those good American horses.

There was no victory dance that night because of the mourning for the Indian dead. But there was great triumph.

"Now," said the Hunkpapa old-man chief, Sitting Bull, "the Wasichus will not come any more. When these dead are found, they will learn their lesson and leave us alone."

But Crazy Horse was not so sure.

All over the great camp there were true stories and rumors. Sometimes it was hard to tell them apart, except when the *akícitas* took an oath in reporting to the chiefs. One rumor that came to the lodge where Whirlwind lay was about Rain-in-the-Face, a Hunkpapa warrior who had been in the fighting right across the river where all the Blue Coats died.

Strikes Two told the story in the lodge, not as something seen but as something everybody was talking about.

"There was a blue-coat chief called Little Hair that Rain-in-the-Face hated. Once Rain-in-the-Face was a prisoner at the Standing Rock agency, and Little Hair was in charge of the soldiers who guarded him. He locked up Rain-in-the-Face with only one blanket in cold winter where snow blew through the cracks of the jail. Rain-in-the-Face got away and joined Sitting Bull and Gall, and he sent Little Hair a message—a piece of buffalo hide with a picture of a bloody heart painted on it.

"Little Hair was in this battle today, and of course he was killed. Rain-in-the-Face had not forgotten him. He cut out Little Hair's heart as he had promised—and he ate it."

218

When Grandmother Whirlwind heard that, she pursed her mouth and said, "How nasty! Did he do that to get the courage that was in the heart?"

"No, no, just for revenge. Rain-in-the-Face was treated very badly in that jail when he was a captive."

Whirlwind announced, "I still think it's nasty."

Strikes Two asked, grinning, "Would you dare to tell that to Rain-in-the-Face?"

Whirlwind was feeling spunky, like her old self.

"If he wants my opinion, bring him here," she challenged. "I am somebody, too!"

There was no doubt of that.

Akícitas who had been watching on the far-off hills rode in to report to the chiefs:

"More Wasichu soldiers are coming. They are moving up the river. Maybe they were to meet the others, who came downstream. These new ones are very many, and they have some wagon guns."

The chiefs conferred briefly and announced, "We will all move on tomorrow, away from this place, and go to where the hunting is good and we can hunt in peace and plenty. The women can get ready to move."

But some warriors asked to be left behind. They argued that up on the bare hill across the river from the Hunkpapa camp there were still Blue Coats and they were in bad shape. They had got there with terrible effort and heavy losses. Those who had not been killed among the trees or in crossing the river had shot their horses up on that hill and forted up behind them for protection against bullets and arrows. How they must be suffering from thirst, especially the wounded! A few brave ones had crawled down the bluffs to fill canteens with river water. Some of them actually succeeded. Others died.

"Let us stay and finish them off, wipe them out like the others," the hot-blooded warriors urged.

But the high chiefs decided this was not wise. "It is not worth while," they said. "We would lose some more men. We have already taught the Wasichus what they needed to know. Let the new army rescue that handful. We will leave a few of our men on the higher hills to keep the enemy there for a while by shooting sometimes. Then our men will follow us later."

So on the afternoon of the second day after the battle the great gathering moved out in proper order, Cheyennes leading, Hunkpapas at the end. They set fire to what remained of the dry prairie grass as they left, so the valley was blue with smoke. A few lodges were left standing with everything in them, including the bodies of the warriors who had been killed. Altogether, in all the camps, thirty men had died.

The Indians did not know exactly how many of the enemy were dead—why bother to count? But almost three hundred Blue Coats had died, according to the bitter tally of the army that came upon that stinking, bloody battlefield when it was too late to help.

Sitting Bull's vision had been true: enemy soldiers *had* fallen right into the Hunkpapa camp. They had charged in and met death there or among the sagebrush and prickly pear on the slopes and in the coulees, some of them in the trees by the river as they tried to cross and scramble desperately up to that barren hill on the other side. And the hundred small wounds on the muscular arms of Sitting Bull still had scabs on them, would leave scars as long as he lived.

The great camp kept moving for sixteen sleeps, staying only one sleep in each place. Every day small groups of hunters ranged out to bring in meat, but with so many people traveling together, game was frightened off. The people kept moving to get far away from the Blue Coats who were searching for them.

Then for five sleeps they camped while the chiefs conferred about what was best for all the people.

Quite a long time later the Indians found out that the chief of the soldiers they had wiped out was a man they hated, especially the Cheyennes, who had suffered from his attacks, but also the Lakotas, because he had reported that the sacred Black Hills were rich in the yellow metal, gold, that had brought greedy white men swarming there. The Lakotas called him Pa-huska, Long Hair, but they did not recognize him when they were killing him because then his hair had been cut short. His Wasichu name was George Armstrong Custer. The subchief whose heart Rain-in-the-Face had eaten was his brother Tom.

When the second army arrived at the Little Big Horn they found no living creature on the battlefield except a few badly wounded horses. They did rescue the frantic soldiers who were forted up behind their dead, stinking horses on that bare hill.

Part XI

WINTER OF 1876-1877
Whirlwind's Last Journey

Living in the Lodge:

Morning Rider, 36, head of the family
Young Bird, 32, wife of Morning Rider
Reaches Far Girl, 8, daughter of Young Bird and
    Morning Rider
Angry, 12, son of Young Bird, stepson of Morning
    Rider
Round Cloud Woman, 21, wife of Morning Rider
    and sister of Young Bird
She Throws Him (formerly Jumps), infant son of
    Morning Rider and Round Cloud
Kills Grizzly (formerly Shoots), 13, motherless son
    of Morning Rider
Strikes Two, 24, son of Pemmican Woman, nephew
    of Whirlwind
Grandmother Whirlwind, 56

Chapter 24

The natural thing for the people to do after the big battle
and the many movings of camp and the long, solemn con-
ferences of the chiefs was to divide into small bands and

222

scatter so they could hunt and prepare for winter. This was how they had always done it.

But those times were not like these times. The chiefs were now sure that they would have to fight again to discourage the Wasichu soldiers from bothering them. Every day before dawn young men rode out, rode far, to report everything that moved on the visible earth. Sometimes they saw buffalo and rejoiced and the hunters went out. Sometimes they greeted families fleeing from the reservation agencies to join them. The Grandfather's agents, they said (as hundreds of others had reported before them), did not give them enough provisions. The agents did not want them to get away from the agencies—but if they did not hunt, they would starve. They had despaired until the big victory at the Little Big Horn brought hope. The news of it had sped faster to the agencies by "moccasin telegraph"—riders on fast horses—than it did to the Wasichus by their methods of communication.

Some of the people from the agencies, Red Cloud's people, said their ponies were going to be taken from them; so were their guns. Then they would indeed starve. They were afraid to go back. They did not want to fight. They only wanted to live. Some of them spoke about going north to a country where the Grandfather did not rule and his Blue Coats could not go. There might be hope there. On the reservation there was slow death from hunger and disease.

There were divisions and worrying conflicts of opinion among the people. Move northward where the Blue Coats dare not follow? Break up into hunting camps and try to avoid them? Stay with one of the great leaders, Sitting Bull or Crazy Horse, and be strong enough to wipe out the Wasichu soldiers?

The three warriors in Whirlwind's lodge discussed these

223

matters among themselves, where the women could not hear them, and also in council.

They did not yet know very much about life in that northern country. A dozen lodges of the more desperate people from the agencies, along with a bunch of adventuresome young warriors without families, headed north, promising to send back a messenger when they had something useful to report. Strikes Two wanted to go, but that would leave the lodge without much fighting protection.

Morning Rider admitted that he had not decided. "We are stronger for fighting if we stay together, but we cannot make meat for winter unless we separate into camps and hunt," he said. He scowled at Kills Grizzly, who had not said anything. "You do not have an opinion," he warned. "You have courage and good medicine protection, but you are not as big and strong as you will be two or three winters from now."

Kills Grizzly did not argue, because that was true.

During the days of discussion among the chiefs, the decision had to be made. Sitting Bull had long followed a policy of avoiding the Wasichus. He had never touched the pen to any treaty. He said, "The Great Holy gave me this country, and I will stay free in it." He would fight the Wasichus if he had to, but he would not pursue them, and he said he would never surrender. All he wanted was to be left alone so that his people could live the way they knew how to live.

Crazy Horse, the Oglala, never said very much, but there was talk among his people that he had a premonition of death not very far off. Maybe it was no use fighting any more.

Morning Rider and other Oglala warriors listened to small, private arguments on both sides. No oath of loyalty bound them to follow Crazy Horse. A leader was great only as long as he was successful. Red Cloud had been very great, but now that he lived on a reservation his people suffered.

Morning Rider's responsibility was to his family, and he was concerned about the way the Lakotas who surrendered with Red Cloud had been deprived and cheated and lied to and starved. But it was hard to decide to tear up his family by the roots and take them away from relatives who might not want to join Sitting Bull's people.

The men would decide what to do. The women would have no voice in their councils. But Sioux women tended to speak their minds at home, very firmly, and a disagreeable woman could make a whole lodge miserable. Before the men voted on an important issue that involved their families, they knew their women's opinions very well.

While the men talked in council about what to do, the women talked in the lodges among themselves and with their friends while they worked.

Some of them had heard by moccasin telegraph about the country up north.

"That is the Grandmother's Land. She lives far away across the big water but rules her children through men who wear red coats. They ride in pairs, not in armies. They are brave men. Their laws are strict, but they are just. They speak straight, not with forked tongues. The woman chief's name is Grandmother England."

A young bride said, "I don't see how a woman can be a great chief."

Whirlwind gave her a hard look and answered, "Why not?" Everyone respected Whirlwind, so there was no argument.

The woman who knew so much explained, "She is a hereditary chief. The Wasichus have strange customs."

"Does she lead her warriors in battle?"

225

"What's the difference? They rule that big country for her. And the Blue Coats dare not go there! There is a row of heaps of stones that they must not cross. That line is sacred to the Grandmother. It is the Medicine Line. Many Indians live up there. They are not hungry."

Whirlwind's daughter, Brings Horses, came to visit, looking sad. She was pregnant and was hoping the people would be settled down somewhere to hunt before her baby was born.

"My husband wants to leave soon," she explained. "I wish you would come with us. He is talking about going north."

Whirlwind considered. "We should leave the Oglalas and go with the Hunkpapas?"

"I did it," Brings Horses reminded her. "I missed my own relatives, but if you were with us, I would be altogether happy. My man has talked to many of the refugees from the agencies. They are desperate and angry. They are going north. Maybe it is the right thing to do."

Whirlwind had a great turmoil in her mind when she went to sleep that night, and she dreamed a frightful dream that brought her awake, moaning. One of her daughters-in-law was kneeling beside her, saying her name, asking, "What is the matter? What is wrong?"

For one thing, her leg was giving her much pain. For another, the dream was still upon her. The others in the lodge were awake now, listening and concerned.

"There was an old woman," she said. "I saw her face only once, because it was snowing so hard." She had seen that face before in delirium. It was the hideous face of Death. But she did not tell them that.

"There was a blizzard out of the north, and we were facing it, moving into it, with the old woman just ahead. She was saying, 'Come! Come!' Maybe it was the woman chief who rules the country up there, inviting us to come there. But we had to fight our way through a blizzard, blowing snow."

Whirlwind was no visionary. She did not have meaningful dreams. So this dreadful one was all the more impressive. Even Morning Rider was startled; he was sure the dream meant something.

"I think I will call in a holy man in the morning," he said. "Maybe he can explain the meaning of this."

His mother, still shivering from the cold in her dream, said, "Nonsense! Am I a boy looking for a medicine vision that has to be interpreted? It means that we are going to join the Hunkpapas and go north, and it will not be easy. But that is what we are going to do."

Morning Rider sighed deeply. "That is what I had decided to do," he told her. "We are going with the camp of my brother-in-law, Elk Rising."

He bowed his head and talked as if to himself, not asking advice of his mother, but just talking. She would give advice without asking.

"So many people are afraid to break up into hunting villages," he mused. "They want the protection of many fighting men and the wisdom of Sitting Bull. But men who are fighting cannot hunt, and everything we hear is that Sitting Bull is the man the Wasichus most want to catch, either to kill him or make him go on a reservation. Maybe they will not bother much with a smaller group."

Whirlwind asked, "What does Elk Rising think of the chief of his own village?"

"A good man, brave and smart. He wants to separate now, move north and hunt and stay out of fights until we reach the Grandmother's Land."

"So you decided right," his mother assured him. "And it would be right if your lodge's place in the circle were next to your brother-in-law's. I want my daughter for a neighbor."

A few days before they started, Whirlwind welcomed a new grandchild, a boy baby born to her daughter, Brings Horses. He was small and weak, and it would have been better for him if they could have stayed in camp for a while —better for his mother, too. But Brings Horses did her work and nursed her child and helped look after Whirlwind and rode wearily in the ragged procession heading north.

Those who were parting from relatives and lifelong friends did so with grief and courage. The parting and the joining with almost-strangers was especially hard for the old ones, Whirlwind realized, not complaining as she saw her oldest friends ride away for the last time. How hard it was for the old men who had known great honor for the brave deeds of their youth, who had been admired by little boys and respected by warriors for as long as they could remember! Now they were weak and dependent, among strangers.

Hard for her, too. She had always been somebody, ever since she became a Buffalo Woman when she was thirteen winters old. Now she was the useless grandmother in the lodge of Morning Rider.

His lodge was given a place in the camp circle of the Hunkpapa village, next to that of Elk Rising—and she found she was still somebody. Hunkpapa women were friendly; they came to visit Brings Horses with baby presents; she had been one of them for a long time. And they came to visit Whirlwind to hear the story of the grizzly bear.

The men hunted and the women got the meat ready for winter. There were many messengers riding in, usually with bad news. The riders told of hundreds of families who were giving up the quest for freedom and returning, without hope, to their agencies on the reservation.

They told of other hundreds who had ridden hard for the

228

Medicine Line, to find peace where the Grandfather's soldiers could not follow. The messengers brought word from the agencies that the Wasichus ordered all the Indians to come to the agencies or the soldiers would destroy their camps and their goods, run off their pony herds, and kill everyone, including babies.

An old priest in the camp, a very holy man whose dreams were much respected, had a strange vision one night. He spent the hours until daylight pounding on his small medicine drum and chanting prayers while he thought about what the dream must mean. In the morning he announced it:

"I saw the men chopping the poles of the lodges to make them shorter. I saw the women remaking the lodge covers so they were smaller. That meant that everyone would be crowded into smaller space to live, but it was necessary. Because they had to travel fast, and the ponies were thin and weak. They could not pull the weight of long, heavy poles and big, heavy lodge covers. There were not enough ponies for that.

"The warning is that bad times are coming. It is time right now to get ready. The women and girls must cut the lodge covers smaller and sew them in a hurry, without ceremony. Boys and old men can cut the heavy ends off the poles."

The idea was shocking. Every woman was proud of her lodge, cut and sewed to an age-old pattern, with a fitted lining for winter to help keep it warm. But the pattern was in their hearts; when this bad time was over, they would have tall lodges again and enough bed spaces so nobody would be crowded.

They began to do as he said, not all at once, but two or three at a time, helping one another, crowding in with other families temporarily.

The camp could indeed move faster now; there was less weight to lift and drag and carry. But the horses were still in good shape, so they knew there was more of the dream to come true—bad things were coming. A Hunkpapa village led by Chief Four Horns was about two days behind them; that made everyone feel a little better.

The cold came early that year. Hardly anyone, even the oldest, could remember when it had come so early and so viciously. And there was no peace. Sitting Bull, still with a great number of fighting men, had a confrontation with Bear Coat, a big chief of the Wasichus, and then a fight. In other years the blue-coat soldiers had spent the cold time in their forts, but not this year. Bear Coat, Colonel Miles, had no cavalry; he had Walk-a-Heaps, toughened by long campaigning. They were bundled in buffalo coats, they could endure hunger and deprivation and suffering, because he trained them that way.

The soldiers came from everywhere, attacked Lakotas and Cheyennes, destroyed their goods, drove off their ponies, killed their people. The soldiers had only themselves to protect—no women or children or helpless old ones.

Whirlwind's new people could not rest or relax. They kept moving north. The women pitched their smaller lodges in a circle, as always, with each lodge facing east, because that was right, but they pitched them close together, with ropes between and the pony herd inside the circle. Everybody worked to peel cottonwood bark for horse feed. Campsites were chosen with an escape route in mind—a rocky place to run and hide in, a river cutbank to hide under. Everybody had small bundles of *wasna* ready to grab and run. They slept with their weapons, and every night two or three people did not sleep but listened.

The attack came just before dawn, before anyone was stir-

:ing. Morning Rider's lodge was on the far side from where it
began. Whirlwind heard shots and screamed in warning as
she sat up in her bed place nearest the door opening. She
swung the leather door flap wide open and slashed the
leather hinges with her knife so it could not swing shut
again, in the way.

Her son, Morning Rider, slept farthest from the door. With
his knife he slashed through the lodge lining and the heavy
covering and rolled out into the snow, roaring, "*Hoka hey*!
Protect the helpless ones!" He had a good revolver (eleven
cartridges), a sharp short spear, and his knife. He ran
through the milling pony herd to fight on the side of the
circle that had been attacked first.

Right behind him went Strikes Two, that strong fighting
man. This was the way it had been planned if the attack
came as it had.

Young Kills Grizzly followed with his strung bow and
plenty of war arrows in his quiver, to stay inside the circle
and protect the pony herd.

Twelve-year-old Angry did as he had been ordered: he
stayed to help the women and little ones.

The attackers were not all on the far side of the camp
circle. Round Cloud Woman, just stepping over the high
threshold of the doorway with her baby in his cradle bag on
one arm, took a bullet in her body and screamed and fell in
the snow and died. Angry jumped over her body, fired his
revolver at a moving shadow, and dropped the soldier who
had killed her.

Everyone was screaming now. Angry could not help the
women get away; he had to protect them. He ranged out,
skulking, looking for more soldiers. The back of the lodge
began to burn—the Walk-a-Heaps had enemy Crow scouts
along, using fire arrows, and the leather of the lodge cover

231

was dry and old, not wet enough with snow to kill the flames.

Young Bird scrambled out, dragged the body of her sister out of the way, and picked up the screaming baby. Reaches Far Girl, only eight, tossed out the emergency packages of *wasna* as she had been told.

Whirlwind could not get over the high threshold. She slashed the leather with her knife and shouted, "Help me!" and Reaches Far gave her a shoulder to lean on. Then Whirlwind crawled to Young Bird, commanding, "Put the baby on my back and help get things out."

With the baby on her shoulders, Whirlwind began to crawl toward the rocks where they were supposed to take refuge. She could not hope to climb them, but she put the baby bundle up as high as she could reach. Then she dropped, exhausted and panting. She was out of the way. She could see people running, ponies running, lodges burning. To the women, who seemed dazed and frantic, she kept shouting, "This way! The rocks are this way! Climb the rocks!"

The circle was destroyed now, and the ponies were loose. She had a glimpse of Angry and yelled to him: "Save the ponies!"

Kills Grizzly rode by, bending low on a pony, driving others away from the burning camp, away from the soldiers. Angry leaped on one of the loose horses and rode back to get more.

Young Bird kept throwing things out of the lodge, and Reaches Far Girl carried whatever she could toward the rocks, then ran back for more. More people were at the rocks now. Whirlwind was overjoyed to see her daughter, Brings Horses, baby on her back, partway up, taking things that someone handed up to her.

Then she screamed. Her son's lodge had collapsed in a shower of sparks and a geyser of flame. Young Bird ran away from it with her hair burning. Someone knocked her down and smothered the fire with snow.

After a while it was over and the Walk-a-Heaps were gone, dragging their dead and wounded.

All around there was wailing. The air was full of it. The cries went up to the sky.

People began to build fires, and some came down from the rocks to find and carry firewood. Out of the wreckage the fighting men appeared, most of them on horseback now, and looked sadly at the cowering people, at the utter ruin of the camp.

Whirlwind cried, "Where is my son, Morning Rider? I do not see Strikes Two, either."

A young man she did not even know said gently, "Your son is coming, Mother—a little wound, nothing much. He is bringing Strikes Two. Mourn for him. He was a brave young man."

Whirlwind began to howl. She saw Morning Rider leading a horse with the limp body of Strikes Two slung across its back. She did not know Morning Rider at first; he wore a buffalo coat, knife slashed, that he had cut off a soldier he killed.

Strikes Two, that laughing, joking, brave and loyal man, was almost cut in two with bullets. Morning Rider lifted the body down gently and laid it on the bloody snow. Then, seeing the body of Round Cloud, he asked numbly, "My wife?"

"Dead at the very first," Whirlwind answered, choking. "Young Bird is alive, but she has bad burns. She was so brave! She saved so many things. Reaches Far is a little heroine. The boys saved many horses. The baby is safe."

"Some families suffered worse," Morning Rider said grimly. Two older men rode toward them, with the grey-braided

233

old-man crier. He kept shouting, "Warrior society members, young men, come here with the best horses you can find!"

Perched in the rocks or clustering around these three men, the people listened to the message:

"Two strong riders needed, men without wounds, on the strongest horses. They must ride back toward the village of Four Horns. They must warn him of the soldiers and ask him to hurry to us here before our weak ones die."

A dozen men came forward, eagerly volunteering for this hard mission, but if they were wounded the two leaders motioned them back. Boys brought horses, the fastest, most durable horses. Women came clambering down the rocks to offer packages of *wasna* and blankets.

Every man and boy wanted to undertake this dangerous mission. The two who were chosen were not young and hot-headed, they were thirty years old and had proved themselves wily and wise as well as strong and courageous.

The people sent them off with a cheer that was more like a wail of sorrow. If they were lucky, Four Horns' people might come to the rescue in three days or four.

Those who were left seemed lost and hopeless, dazed with grief. The boys tried to peel cottonwood bark, but axes were few. They wrangled over the axes with men who wanted to cut down small trees to make lean-to shelters against the rocks.

The little girl, Reaches Far, who had been so quick and worked so hard to save things, knelt in the bloody snow and screamed without ending, now that she had time to realize what had happened. Then she covered her face with her blanket and ran to lean against the rocks, crying.

And Whirlwind, not caring any more, gave up. Bowed over the bodies of Round Cloud and Strikes Two, she howled he agony of her grief and heard other howling like an echo everywhere.

Her son spoke sternly: "Mother, be still!" and grasped her shoulder hard and shook her.

"Be still when these of ours are dead?" she screamed.

He shook her again. "Be still. Be strong. Because the spirit of the people is broken, and they will all die if it is not mended with your strength. Be strong—*and be seen*, Mother. You are Saved Her Cub. They all know you. Do something for these sufferers. Let them see you grieve in silence, with strength that cannot be broken!"

Staring at him through her tears, with her hands cradling the dead face of Round Cloud Woman, her hands caked with the dried blood of Strikes Two, Whirlwind knew he was right.

Morning Rider said gently, "Let them see your courage. You can howl silently, inside yourself."

"Help me up," she commanded.

She looked around and saw that the spirit of the people was indeed broken. Each family was making some effort to take care of its own, but they were not united. They were not following the proud Lakota tradition of helping one another, of sharing what they had.

Whirlwind let herself be seen. She trudged through the snow leaning on her staff, slowly because her foot flopped. To a weeping woman nursing a baby, she said quietly, "Have you enough milk for another whose mother is dead?" To little girls crying, she suggested, "You can bring some firewood over here to warm these wounded." To bewildered young boys, she said, "Will you help with the wood? You are stronger."

To an old man scrabbling in the ruins of a burnt lodge, she

235

said, "You are still protecting the helpless, as you always did. Tell the women how to divide up the food they can find, and the bedding that is not quite destroyed."

The people stared and stirred, moving slowly, thinking what to do. The spirit was broken, but life remained.

Except for the smallest, they knew the way of famine. The warriors must eat something, because they needed strength to protect the people. The children must eat something, for they were the future. The mothers needed something if they were nursing babies. The old people needed little, because they had already lived. They would be the first to go without.

She watched them help one another. She said quietly and often, "Four Horns and his people should be here in three or four days."

Now the men and older boys were not squabbling about the few axes. They had built lean-to shelters with warming fires in front of them. Some people helped the wounded into them. Others carried the dead to the foot of the rock cliff, wailing. But nobody was hysterical any more. Not all the lodges had burned. Six were left. Some of the women began to dismantle them and move toward the rock cliffs.

Whirlwind sat down at last by a fire with her head bowed and howled her grief and despair silently, inside herself, remembering that her name was Saved Her Cub.

She began to cough in the sharp cold. Others were coughing too.

Morning Rider bent over her. "The spirit of the people was not quite broken," he said, and went on to help somebody.

Brings Horses Woman came to her and asked, "Mother, are you all right?" She looked dazed.

"I am all right. How is it with you and yours?"

"Two in our lodge wounded, none dead. The far side of the

camp suffered worst. That is where most of the men are now."

"Let me hold your baby," Whirlwind said. "I wish you would go and see whether anyone has found grease to soothe the burns on Young Bird and if some woman with milk has Round Cloud's baby."

"He can be weaned now with soup and chewed food. We found a good iron kettle." Brings Horses handed over her own infant and walked on, a little faster, less dazed.

Little Reaches Far came stumbling. "My mother says she feels better with bear grease on her burns." She gulped. "But my other mother is dead!"

"Come sit by me near the fire," Whirlwind urged, "and pull a corner of my blanket around you. Let me tell you where your other mother is going. She is going there now, to a fine place. She will miss you, but you will join her there sometime. I will tell you about the Land of Many Lodges."

Young Angry came up to them, horseback, looking sick. He slid off and said, "I went to the other side of the camp. I saw a child with its head crushed by a rifle blow. I saw a woman who had been ripped open with a bayonet. She had a baby in her."

He turned away and vomited over and over.

Whirlwind said gently, "I think you should go back there. Do not look at anything, but make sure children do not see anything. Someone has to look out for the children who are wandering around. And you are a man."

He vomited once more, swallowed snow to cleanse his mouth, leaped on his horse, and rode back to follow her advice.

Now old men were carrying bodies, old women were digging in the ruins for useful scraps, passing morsels of food to the exhausted, hungry ones. Whirlwind accepted a piece of

237

scorched *wasna*, took a bite, and gave the rest to Reaches Far. But every time anyone looked at Grandmother Whirlwind she was chewing contentedly.

Maybe Four Horns' people will have plenty, she thought. Anyway, I have lived. And it was good. I have always been somebody.

Chapter 25

While they waited for help from Four Horns, they did the best they could to put their dead in decent places, high up among the rocks, but there could be no ceremony except wailing. Men and women who still had strength enough lifted them up with ropes, wrapped in scraps of partly burned robes or blankets.

A few widows, in their grief, began to gash their arms with knives, as was the custom, but the camp leaders stopped them with firm, low-voiced warnings: "Mourn later when we are safe in the Grandmother's Land. All the people need your full strength now, or all the people will die." So the widows swallowed their grief and saved their strength for the hard days to come. They helped mend the broken spirit of the people.

Snow began to fall. The best of the hunters went grimly out to look for game and brought back one deer. So few people were left now that this made a little fresh meat for everyone. Even Whirlwind ate some.

Other people blundered through the snow, cutting cottonwood bark for the horses, bringing firewood.

Then the white wolf of the blizzard began to howl across

he plains, down from the north, and the people worried
ilently: Would the people with Four Horns be able to find
hem?

They did, late on the fourth day. They did not have much
neat and had lost some horses in a short fight with the
Vasichus several days before, but everything they had, they
hared.

They, too, had shortened their lodgepoles and made the
odge covers smaller and lighter. No longer were two horses
needed to pull the poles for one lodge. The big dogs carried
mall packs or pulled small drags carrying goods. Everyone
walked who could walk, but there were some wounded and
.ome aged who had to ride or go on pony drags, and there
were children too small to walk.

Changes had to be made when the two camps joined. The
nomeless ones were divided up among already crowded
odges. Family ties were still strong even when families no
onger lived together. Nobody said, *That is my horse, that is
my buffalo robe.* Everything belonged to the people during
these hard times, to be used where it was most needed. Even
the rigid, age-old customs of respectful avoidance could be
overlooked. Whirlwind talked briefly, when it was necessary,
with her daughter's husband, Elk Rising, although according
to the old ways they had not spoken since she became his
mother-in-law.

His lodge had not been destroyed in the battle, and none
of his family was killed. Those belonging to his lodge when
the fight was over were his two wives, Brings Horses and
Blue Rock Woman; their four small children; and White
Mountain, his brother, and Standing Tree, his adopted son,
both wounded. The family, then, had only one able-bodied
provider, Elk Rising himself, and one strong young wife,
Blue Rock; Brings Horses was sickly since the baby's birth.

239

Morning Rider's lodge was gone. His younger wife was dead, his other wife's burns were bad. Strikes Two, that fine hunter and strong fighter, would never hunt or fight again. Whirlwind was crippled. So there was no woman at all able to do the work of women; Reaches Far was only eight.

The baby, She Throws Him, was being cared for by a kindly woman. Angry and Kills Grizzly were not full-grown men, but they tried to hunt like men, and they carried wood uncomplainingly like women.

When Four Horns' people came, after the disaster, many decisions and changes had to be made, based on family needs.

Two young widows without children came to join Morning Rider's family, where women were much needed. No matter how willing the boys were to do women's work, they simply did not know how to dismantle a lodge or pitch it for another camp. Whirlwind moved away from her son's family and into her son-in-law's lodge, to sleep in the bed place his mother had had. She could work with her hands and crawl in the crowded lodge when her flopping foot made her too awkward to walk.

Morning Rider did not take the widows for wives; this was no time for marrying, it was a time to struggle to stay alive. One of the widows had lost her family but saved her lodge.

In the lodge of Elk Rising, Brings Horses and Blue Rock Woman cared for the two wounded men. White Mountain could not walk with a bullet wound in his hip, or ride either. He was pulled on a pony drag when camp moved. Standing Tree had some ribs broken and wore a tight binding of soft buckskin to keep them from moving. He could not ride because jolting hurt him so much. He walked, and that was agony, but he never said so. He could not sleep at all because of the pain if he lay down on his bed robe, so he spent the nights sitting up against a backrest and slept a little. Some-times, asleep, he cried out in pain and was ashamed. When he was awake he simply endured in silence.

As they moved northward, in the misery of cold and hun-ger and crowding, more and more of the people suffered from chest pains and dreadful coughing like Whirlwind her-self.

When a gaunt horse died of exertion, they butchered it for food, being careful to give some to the dogs. They needed the dogs. Whirlwind drank a little soup but said she was not hungry. By this time she really was not. She kept remember-ing, "I have lived, and it was good." When she was too weak to ride, someone tied her on a pony drag. The racking cough did not kill her, although two other old women died.

Once she was sick enough to whimper like a child. She said, "Everything is wrong. The world is upside down! When are we going to rest?"

The others in the lodge explained—she was not sure who explained, because everything was going around:

"We are going north to the Grandmother's country to be safe from the soldiers. We are with Four Horns now."

"Now I remember," Whirlwind said. "We are going to see Grandmother England." Nobody cared to argue with her.

Game was very scarce and hard to find in the white hell of winter. The hunters became weary and gaunt; they had to have food, because they were the protectors of the people. The children had to eat sometimes, because they were the people's future.

Travel was torment for the sick and wounded who could not ride horseback—and by the time they thought they were near the Medicine Line there were many sick, with frozen hands or feet or pains in the chest like knives twisting when they coughed. These traveled on pony drags, wrapped in fur

241

robes and blankets, trying to hide their faces from the swirling snow and sleet.

The good of all the 'people was more important than the survival of one person. Once after a coughing spell Whirlwind said to Brings Horses: "Leave me." But her daughter answered angrily, "No!"

When her head was clearer and she could think straight Whirlwind knew that she was not going all the way to the Grandmother's Land. She could not do her share any more, she who had been so proud of her skills and of her strength.

Maybe I have been too proud, she thought. But these things were mine, my skills and strength. Now I have lost them, and I am not a help to the people any more, only a burden.

And so she took thought about what she could give away to those she loved. Her share of the food she was already giving secretly, to the children. Could she give the people the strength they had to use in helping her? Weakened with hardship, they needed all the strength they had left. Yes, she thought, those are worthy gifts but I cannot speak of them. Material possessions she did not have any more—she did not own any fine robes or handwork or anything of value. But there was one thing, her name won in honor.

In camp one windy night she asked to see the baby grandson she had saved from the grizzly bear, he who was not living in the same lodge with her any more. There were so few lodges, families no longer lived the way they were supposed to, according to relationships. Everyone just crowded in wherever there was room to sleep sheltered from the snow and the wind. But someone brought the baby, well wrapped and warm, not fat but not starving to death either. She held him for a few minutes and sang him a little song. She knew she was telling him good-bye.

"It is well with him," she said. "She Throws Him will be a mighty warrior. Now let Brings Horses bring her baby son."

Brings Horses—gaunt from hunger and sickness—laid the puny child in her mother's arms. He was almost too weak to cry.

"He will be a warrior," Whirlwind said to encourage her.

"No," said Brings Horses. "He is going to die. I have not enough milk. No other nursing mothers have enough to spare."

"I want him to have a good name," his grandmother said stubbornly. "I want to give him my name. Maybe it will encourage him to live."

Those around them in the crowded lodge murmured, "Ah, it is good."

"So I give him my name," Whirlwind said. "The name Crazy Horse gave me. When the boy is older, you must tell him that. His name is Saved Her Cub."

Her son-in-law, Elk Rising, said, "It is a brave name, to be remembered with respect. He should have that name."

Whirlwind lay back, exhausted. She had publicly given away the one thing that belonged to her and to nobody else. This was her last will and testament. For she could not tell anyone that she was giving away her share of the food and her share of the people's strength. Somebody would try to stop her, and that must not be. She could not endure hearing the little children whimper with hunger.

I have lived a long time, she remembered. She tallied the years on her fingers. Most of them had been good years. Fifty-even winters she had lived. Just now she was almost comfortable. Outside there was winter, but in the lodge under a worn fur robe she was warm and her leg did not hurt very much. She had time to think now; when the camp was moving she sometimes could think of nothing but her misery.

She said suddenly in a strong voice, "I have had a good life." Her daughter said, "Yes, Mother. And when we reach the Grandmother's country, life will be good again. The hunters will bring home meat then. After we cross the Medicine Line, the soldiers will not chase us. They can't go there."

"Good," said Whirlwind, sighing comfortably. "Good."

But she would not be with them then. She would be in another country, from which there was no returning. Her father and mother would be with her there, and her husband and all the others she had loved and respected. With plenty of buffalo meat, plenty of hides to tan, fine new lodges, everybody happy. Everything would be good, as it had been when she was young.

"I have had many honors," she said. Her daughter agreed but was puzzled by the remark. What Whirlwind was thinking but did not say was *I was never the least among my people, and I need not be humble among my people in that other country either. I wonder how long it will take to get there.*

She could not, as some useless, hopeless, brave old people did, simply walk out into the snow and never come back. Walking was too difficult for her; someone would follow and bring her back and make a great fuss. The only thing she could do was what she was doing: refrain from eating, and wait. She was cunning about it. Remembering how clever she had been sometimes about deceiving those she loved, she laughed.

Her daughter wondered at that—there was nothing to laugh about these days—and Whirlwind explained, "I suddenly wondered—when we go across the Spirit Road to that other country, how old are we when we get there? Will I be older than my mother?"

"No need to wonder about that," her daughter said, smil-
ng wanly. "It will be a long time yet."

"Yes, it will be a long time," Whirlwind agreed.

She did not eat at all if she could hide her food and give it
ecretly to the children. Only if someone was watching, she
rank a little soup to avoid a fuss.

She was by no means the first or the last of her people to
o that way. It took a different kind of courage from that of
elling warriors, painted and armed, riding into battle, fac-
ig death. They came back with honors if they came back at
ll. Her battle was long and slow and quiet, she was not
oming back, and if she were clever she would not even be
reatly honored because nobody would be sure that she sac-
ificed her life for the people. But she had honors enough.
Now she simply said she did not want to eat because she was
ck.

She really was not hungry any more; she was no longer
empted.

Travel was no longer so hard for her, because sometimes
e seemed to float instead of bumping along through the
now on the travois. She slept a great deal. When she was
wake, and heard children crying weakly, when she looked
p and saw the suffering in the gaunt faces of people who
ame sometimes to bend over her and speak to her, she was
lled with love for them. Silently she gave them love, and
here was always more to give.

They knew at last what she was doing. She was a warrior
oman, giving them her food, giving her life because she did
ot need it any more. Nobody made a fuss. They honored her
ith their visits and their silence.

Whirlwind knew that what she was doing was right; she
as aware that the Powers were helping to make her time of

passing shorter with the racking cough and the chest pains. Some people died of that disease alone, even without purposely avoiding food. In moments when her mind was clear she gave thanks silently to the Powers, understanding that disease was not always bad. It only seemed that way when one had been well and wanted to live. The Powers did look out for human beings who needed to let go of life.

Her daughter's baby, not strong at birth, grew weaker. When her daughter bent over the child, weeping bitterly, Whirlwind said in a voice not much more than a whisper, "Put him inside my dress against my skin and I will keep him warm for a little while."

"But he is dead," Brings Horses answered.

"I know. But give him to me. He is very young to travel the Spirit Road alone. I can find it. I will carry him to the far country in my arms."

The blizzard stopped that night, and so did the loving heart of Whirlwind. Brings Horses Woman, wailing her grief, nestled the baby's thin body inside his grandmother's dress against her skin.

Next morning the sun was shining. Those who had loved Whirlwind lifted a blanket-wrapped bundle, not very heavy, onto the lower branches of a cottonwood tree and fastened it there.

There could be no proper mourning for Grandmother Whirlwind, no sacrifice of her horse, no destruction or giveaway of her possessions. The people could not afford the loss of a horse or robes or a lodge as a sign of decent grief. They could not spare such things now. They were too poor.

Just as the people finished tying the bundle in the tree they became aware of something strange: there was warmth in the air. The blizzard had stopped the night before. Now the sun shone, but not the cold, distant sun of winter, and

246

warm wind was blowing. This was the sudden miracle of the prairie known as the chinook. It did not come every year. It was the *wakan* wind, so warm and gracious that piled snow slid from branches and slanting rocks while one stared at it, and the sharp edges of wave-shaped drifts drooped and collapsed.

The horses noticed, too. They held up their heads, sniffing. Somewhere a man started singing softly, a praise song to all the spirits.

Then they rode on northward, no longer shuddering with cold. Morning Rider rode back through the melting snow from his proper position on the far margin of the moving camp and spoke to Brings Horses quietly:

"I have been thinking. I think our mother and your little one are happy on the Spirit Road. Maybe they interceded for us with the spirits."

"Yes, something *wakan* happened," Brings Horses said. "Our mother did great things. I can do only small things. I am not going to hack off my hair for her. The people have their own grief, without seeing mine."

"You are the true daughter of Whirlwind," he said, and rode back to his place.

About the Author

Dorothy M. Johnson was born in Iowa, grew up in Whitefish, Montana, and lives in Missoula, Montana. She is not quite comfortable unless there are some mountains around somewhere, preferably the Rocky Mountains. She is honorary police chief of Whitefish and an adopted member of the Blackfeet tribe with the name "Kills Both Places."

She lived in New York City for several years, writing western stories, working as a magazine editor, and missing the mountains. Then she returned to Montana where, she says, "We have all this wonderful space with practically nobody in it. All of Montana has fewer people than the city of Seattle."

Miss Johnson used to be an assistant professor of journalism at the University of Montana, of which she is a graduate. She is the author of many books and short stories about the West, and three motion pictures—*A Man Called Horse*, *The Hanging Tree*, and *The Man Who Shot Liberty Valance*—as well as several western television programs have been made from them.